Veridan

The second book in the Hleo series

By

Rebecca Weller

copyright © 2017 – ISBN 978-0-9950316-1-6

Paula
Hope ya like it.
Bobby
Webb

This book is dedicated to the lights of my life.
You make me laugh harder and love
stronger than I ever thought possible.
Abbey and Jesse, Mommy loves
you to the moon and back.

One

Life was good. My opinion was pretty biased though, built on the basis that I was in love with Ethan Flynn, and confidence that he was just as infatuated with me.

I pictured Ethan's perfect smile as I double-checked the arrival gate at Bradley International Airport to make sure I had the right one. My excitement grew as the seconds passed on the huge wall clock overhead. Twenty after eleven. Dad's plane was expected to touch down in about half an hour, so I settled into the end chair in a long row, positioning myself so I could see the passengers as they cleared customs and came out the security doors.

It had been three months since the night of the Masks gala, when I'd almost had the life choked out of me, literally. Three months since Ethan, a member of an ancient secret society of bodyguards, the Hleo, had saved me, and then admitted that he loved me. After that night the attempts on my life had stopped. Adam Chambers, Ethan's nemesis who had showed up in East Halton and fooled me into thinking he cared about me in order to lure me into a deadly trap, had disappeared.

Endless searching had proven fruitless. There hadn't been any sort of trail turn up that we could follow to his whereabouts. I knew his disappearance concerned Ethan, but the lack of threats had given us an opportunity to enjoy being together, and I was definitely enjoying it.

I started to pull *To Kill a Mockingbird*, assigned reading for my western civilization class, from my bag when an image flashed in front of my vision. A woman wearing a red 1940s swing dress, staring at a display of war-era clothing and hats in a shop window.

Her blonde hair was pinned back in big curls, a fitting style for that time period, and she had on bright red lipstick.

I groaned as I dropped the novel and grabbed my sketchbook instead. *Might as well get this over with.* In an attempt to figure out why I kept getting visions of protecteds—the chosen people the Hleo watched over—to draw, Ethan had come up with a new process for me. Every picture, once completed, was dissected to figure out its significance. As many details as possible were gleaned from it and written on the back of each sketch before a digital version was sent out to other Hleo. Once the *who* and *when* were determined, the picture was added to the timeline of drawings as well as the analysis grid on the computer in order to search for patterns.

I hadn't admitted this to Ethan but I dreaded getting flashes now because of the scrutiny that accompanied each one. Especially since no real patterns had emerged.

My pencil flew across the paper, filling in the shadowing of the girl's dress and the detail in the window. I frowned. Something struck me as odd about the image, but I couldn't quite put my finger on what it was.

I held my sketchbook out to stare at the drawing. *What is out of place here?* Then I noticed it, a car parked across the street showed in the reflection of the store window. My eyes narrowed. The car was a brand new Lexus. What was going on with my brain?

In all the analyzing of my drawings Ethan and I had done over the past few months we had discovered that I had seen protecteds from as far back as four centuries. And Hleo from around the globe had confirmed a large number of drawings as current protecteds in unfamiliar scenes. Images from the future? Perhaps. But a drawing of both the past and the present? That was something new.

I was so engrossed in trying to figure out what could be going on I didn't notice someone come up behind me, until I felt a tap on my shoulder. "Ah." I jumped and dropped my sketchbook on the floor.

I twisted in my seat. Dad stood behind me with a black bag slung over his shoulder and a large suitcase beside him. On the other side of him stood Ms. Woods, my art teacher.

"Dad." I allowed myself to be scooped up in an exuberant hug, giving Ms. Woods a friendly yet confused smile at the same time. It had been months since Dad had left for his trip to England to teach at Oxford. He had ended up extending his stay when his colleague Rupert had broken both his legs in a skiing accident. Dad had taken over Rupert's classes to help out, and now, almost four months later, the middle of February, he was finally returning to his normal teaching duties at Hartford University.

"Hannah. It's so good to see you. How are you?" He pulled away from the hug and took a step back to look me over.

"I'm okay, glad to see you." I clasped my hands together.

"That's very well done." Ms. Woods pointed to my drawing.

I quickly bent down and scooped up the sketchbook, flipping it closed and dumping it back into my bag. "Hi Ms. Woods. Thanks. Were you guys on the same flight? I didn't even realize you knew each other."

"Hello, Hannah, it's very nice to see you." She fiddled with the strap on her faded flower-print suitcase. Ms. Woods had gone on a trip to England over the Christmas break and ended up staying into the new year because of family issues. A slew of supply teachers had covered her class over the last month and I was glad to see she was back. I had missed her calm presence in the room.

I turned to Dad in time to catch the warm grin that crossed his face as he looked over at her. My skin prickled. They definitely knew each other. Did I want to know how? Or how well? I pressed my lips together tightly.

"Rose, er … Ms. Woods and I spent some time together sightseeing and getting to know each other while we were in England." Dad spoke carefully, as though putting extra effort into his choice of words.

I narrowed my eyes. "That's nice."

"Well, I should be off. I just wanted to say hello before I headed home for a nice hot bath and a sleep in my own bed." Ms. Woods' usually pale face was fully flushed as her gaze darted towards the exit.

"That sounds like a great idea. I'll call you later this week," Dad assured her. The two of them exchanged a knowing look while I waited patiently to be let in on whatever was going on.

Ms. Woods gave us another smile and waved as she headed off in the direction of the parking lot. I stood very still until she disappeared, then glanced over at Dad, who was also watching her go.

I raised an eyebrow. "So, how was your *trip*?" I crossed my arms and waited for him to respond.

Dad exhaled slowly. "Hannah, can we talk about this when we get home?" He suddenly sounded very tired.

"Talk about what?" I kept the innocent expression on my face.

"The visibly awkward run in that just happened and what it all means." Dad looked so sheepish that I relented and uncrossed my arms.

"Okay, we can talk about the fact that you and my art teacher have obviously hooked up in some sort of romantic way when we get home," I replied, partly joking and partly annoyed that I was finding out the way I was.

"Hannah, please." Dad rubbed his forehead.

"Let's just get you home." I rested a hand on his shoulder. He nodded, and we ambled down the airport terminal out to the parking lot in the same direction Ms. Woods had gone. *Please don't let us run into her*. It was too weird to think of my beloved art teacher dating my widowed father. If he had to date, a stranger would be better, not someone I saw every day at school.

Of course, like everything else that was going on in my life at the moment, no one had asked for my opinion.

Two

I scanned the rearview mirror for signs of the army-green Jeep that had come to be a sign of security for me. Ethan would be behind us, following like a shadow to make sure everything was all right. What would he think of my dad dating?'

Since Adam's attempt on my life, Ethan had become a constant presence. He slept in the guest room of my house most nights, drove me to and from school, and always made sure that I got home safely from work. Once we had admitted our feelings for each other, our relationship had taken off. I loved every minute we spent together, but we had to be very careful about how we acted towards each other in public. Ethan was always worried that it was going to get back to the leaders of the Hleo, The Three, that he had broken the most sacred rule the Hleo had by beginning a romantic relationship with a *protected*, so we kept it a secret from everyone. That meant our time at my house was the only time we were able to let our guards down. I sighed. Now that Dad was back, we would lose our private retreat.

Not only would we be forced to hide our relationship, but we had spread out all of my drawings in the dining room in order to try and figure out my ability and these had to be stored away as well. Ethan had taken them to the bungalow he shared with the new Hleo who had come as the replacement for Evelyn, his former partner.

Dad closed his eyes and rested his head against the window of the passenger door. Purposeful evasion or simple travel exhaustion? I couldn't be sure; either way I let it slide and kept my attention on the road.

I grinned, picturing Ethan in the Jeep behind us with his new partner. Simon Kemp was an amusing British guy who appeared to be in his early thirties although, as I had learned from Ethan, the age of an immortal was extremely difficult to determine. Simon was a bit of a technology geek. He kept his light brown hair short, he actually needed the thick-rimmed glasses he wore, and although he was thin he would joke about his squidgy stomach. The thing I liked the most about him was that he knew about my relationship with Ethan—thanks to a weak moment where Ethan and I forgot to make sure my house was empty before locking lips—and he was okay with it. Not only okay with it, but with keeping it a secret.

Simon would most definitely be sitting in the passenger seat talking Ethan's ear off about something or other, while Ethan quietly let him. That was a great aspect of Ethan's personality; he was an amazing listener, probably because he'd spent most of his long life observing rather than participating.

Thanks to the unseasonably warm weather over the last week the roads were snow free, and basically empty since it was after midnight. As I took the cutoff for East Halton, I could clearly make out the Jeep's headlights following right behind.

During our evenings of scrutinizing my drawings and trying, without success, different concentration exercises to see if my ability could be controlled, Ethan had told me about his past and the different lives he'd led. He'd been a personal bodyguard, a butler, a mechanic, and a college roommate. He'd spent time on an Arctic Circle expedition team, been a football coach, a piano teacher, and part of the sound crew for a rock band back in the sixties.

And that was only a handful of the identities he'd assumed through the years. I loved learning about them and yet something nagged at me. How much did I know about the real Ethan Flynn? He was more than willing to discuss all the different Hleo personalities he'd adopted and the different people he'd protected. He always seemed to hold back, though, when it came to revealing information about himself such as things he'd done when he wasn't protecting others, or what his life had been like before becoming a Hleo. Those parts of himself he continually kept guarded.

Once we were home, Dad carried his stuff upstairs to his bedroom, while I went to the kitchen and brewed us a cup of tea. It was late, but there was no way I was putting off the conversation we needed to have. I tugged my phone from the back pocket of my jeans. Should I text Ethan about what had happened at the airport? I should tell him about my latest puzzling vision anyway. My finger hovered above the keyboard, then I set the phone down on the counter. I would talk to him in depth later, once I knew more about what was going on and my father had gone to bed.

"Did you make tea?" Dad walked into the room and sank into a chair at the kitchen table.

I filled the mug in front of him and set down the teapot. "I did. I figured since you've been living in England for the last three and a half months you probably got very used to tea." I sat down and picked up my own mug, blowing on it before taking a sip.

"Thank you, that's very thoughtful. I did drink more tea than I ever have in my life, and I have gotten used to a nightly tea break, so this is nice." Dad picked up the cup but set it back on the table without drinking from it. He stared at it for a moment, as steam swirled and danced above the hot liquid, obviously trying to come up with a way to begin the conversation.

Help him out. I gripped my mug tightly, bracing myself. "So, you're dating Ms. Woods."

"Hannah." Dad's eyebrows shot up, as though my bluntness was offensive.

"What? Isn't that what you're having such a hard time telling me?" I asked, trying to sound completely at ease.

"I wouldn't refer to the situation as simply as that." Dad shifted in his seat.

I cocked my head to the side, wanting him to just get it out so I could come to terms with it. "Then explain it to me, because honestly I'm very interested." I spoke in as supportive a tone as I could muster.

Dad propped his elbows on the table, and rested his chin on his folded hands. "Rose, or Ms. Woods…" Dad stopped and frowned, clearly uncertain how he should refer to her.

"Rose is fine."

His shoulders relaxed. "Rose and I met at a New Year's Eve party that Rupert was hosting. Rose is an old family friend of Rupert's, and she had flown over for the Christmas holidays to be with her relatives. Rupert felt the need to introduce the two people he had invited to the party that, by coincidence, both lived in East Halton.

"She and I had only been talking a few minutes when we discovered we had something in common: you. Rose speaks very highly of you and your work. She told me that she hasn't seen anyone with your natural ability in years and feels honored to be your teacher. I think she believes you're going to make it big with your art one day, if that's what you want." Dad reached forward and rested a hand on my arm.

I smiled at the pride in his voice. It was nice to receive such positive feedback about my artistic skills, but now that I understood the flashes weren't coming from my own imagination it was hard to feel as though I could take the credit. I couldn't explain that to my dad, though.

Ethan and I had decided that, for now, until we figured out why I could do what I could, it would be safer not to say anything to Dad about me being a protected. I didn't like lying to him, but I wasn't sure how to explain my ability, and saying nothing was just easier.

"That's very nice of her. I'm not sure I'm as skilled as she thinks, but I'll take the compliment." I shrugged and took another sip of tea.

"In any case, Rose and I spent most of the evening chatting about East Halton, and Brown University, since Rose went there as well. She was a few years behind me in her studies, but a couple of professors I had were still there when she attended."

Definitely more than a few years. Dad would have graduated from Brown long before Ms. Woods ever went there. I wasn't completely positive, but I would put Ms. Woods in her mid-thirties. Even if she was older than she appeared, she couldn't be more than thirty-seven or thirty-eight. That would make her at least ten years younger than my dad, something that added to their dating being hard for me to accept. There were worse things than an age difference, though. I swallowed hard. Ten years was nothing compared to the 128 years between Ethan and me.

"The evening was very enjoyable. It was nice to talk to an American, especially one from home, after so much time away from the States." Dad had a distant look on his face, as though he had gone back to that night and was reliving it. "When we said our goodbyes, Rose offered to take me on a tour of the English countryside. She had relatives scattered all over England, so she knew the best and most scenic places to visit. We went the following Saturday. She drove me from Liverpool to Leeds, and stopped in all the small towns between there and Oxford, showing off different old buildings, gardens and other interesting historical sites. It was one of the most pleasant days I've had since… well for a very long time."

Had he been about to say, "since your mother died"? My chest squeezed.

"We went out a few more times, then her grandmother, who lives in England, suffered a stroke. Rose managed to get a small leave of absence from your school so she could stay and help take care of her. I would take her out when she needed a break from nursing duty. One day we went to The National Gallery in London, which you would have loved, and another time we took the ferry across to Ireland and spent a couple of days exploring there."

A twinge of something that felt like jealousy shot through me but I pushed it back. "That's a lot of sight-seeing." I got up from the table to put my mug in the sink, needing a bit of space. I decided to ignore his mention that they had gone away overnight together, and what that probably meant, and tried to focus on the happiness in his voice. The more he talked the more his eyes gleamed.

"I know this is a lot to take in, and very unexpected. I'm sorry I didn't tell you about it, but it wasn't news I wanted to try to explain over the phone, nor did I think it was necessary to share unless our relationship was going to continue after England." Dad watched me closely. "I enjoyed Rose's company a great deal while we were over there, and I would really like to continue getting to know her, but we do know this might be a bit awkward for you. I would like you to consider if you could accept me dating your teacher. I don't want an answer right now. Rose and I want to do what's best for everyone, so if you decide it's too strange, then we will part as friends," Dad said, his voice heavy with the concern of a parent trying to make a responsible decision, even if the outcome would be hard for him. He stood and crossed the room to set his mug down beside mine in the sink.

I leaned back against the counter. "I have to admit this is weird for me. I knew there was always a possibility you would start dating again, I just didn't think it would be someone I knew, especially not my teacher. I want to be okay with this Dad, and I really want you to be happy. I think I just need a little time to absorb it all."

"I respect your honesty. Rose and I have agreed not to see each other until you've had a chance to think it over and let us know how you feel." He squeezed my shoulder. Dad would wait patiently for me to decide, but I detected from his tone that he hoped it wouldn't take me too long.

"Let me sleep on it and I'll let you know." I pushed off from the counter, already knowing that no matter how I ended up feeling about this I was going to say of course they could date. What type of person would I be if I kept someone who obviously made my father happy out of his life? As I watched him, the strange feeling that this was just the beginning of the coming changes crept up my neck.

Three

It was three in the morning and I was tossing and turning. I wanted to sleep, but my mind wouldn't shut off. It just kept going over and over the idea of my dad and my teacher dating. How could this have happened, especially a continent away from home? It just seemed so unbelievable. I sat up and grabbed my phone off the night table. I needed to talk to somebody about it, and I needed that somebody to be Ethan.

I texted Ethan, asking if he was up. Within seconds he'd sent back a reply: For you? Always. I pushed the covers back and texted that I wanted to meet him. He immediately replied that he would be right over. I changed back into jeans and threw a sweater on over my pajama shirt. Once I was dressed I eased open my bedroom door. I didn't need Dad to discover me sneaking out of the house the very first night he was back. That would really raise some questions about what had gone on while he was away.

I tiptoed to the top of the stairs and surveyed them, trying to remember which steps creaked so I could avoid those. I maneuvered my way down, holding my breath at every stray squeak, but luckily no sound came from Dad's room. I was banking on his being exhausted from traveling, and that he wouldn't wake up for anything. At the bottom of the stairs, I peered out the front door to see Ethan's Jeep already in the driveway. I threw on my winter coat, pulled the door open, and slipped out onto the porch.

I had chosen not to turn any lights on in the house, so thankfully my eyes had already adjusted to the dark. I bounded down the stairs and made my way to Ethan's Jeep. He was leaning against the front grill in jeans and his navy pea coat waiting for me.

"Hi," I whispered, still feeling the need to be quiet even though we were outside, well away from Dad's ears.

"Hi." Ethan straightened up.

We looked at each other for a moment, and then my arms were around his neck and his lips were on mine. I sank into the kiss. How could I miss him this much after only a few hours apart? I withdrew before I could completely lose myself in the moment.

His emerald eyes were bright as he slowly let his arms slip away from me back down to his sides. "Do you want to go somewhere?"

"Yeah, I need to clear my head." I walked to the passenger side of the vehicle and climbed in, my lips still tingling.

"Sure." He got in the Jeep too and started the engine. I cringed at the sound, but he backed it out of the driveway slowly and didn't accelerate until we were well away from my house.

We drove in silence; I didn't know what to say. I felt silly being so dramatic over my dad starting to date someone, but I couldn't help it. It felt so wrong. I needed to vent, and it was hard not having Ethan steps away from me at any given moment.

He pulled into a parking space down the road from the main strip of beach, where a grouping of boulders created a small, secluded cove, hidden from the road. The locals of East Halton knew of this private beach area, but it had remained somewhat unclaimed by the tourist set. The moon was full, making our path clear as we walked across the damp, winter-packed sand, towards a flat set of rocks sheltered by larger rocks. I settled onto the edge of one of the cold, hard surfaces, my legs dangling over the side as I faced the frozen Lake Pocotoa. The water still had a thin coat of ice that tempted a person to step out onto it, but with the warm temperatures we'd been having all week, that would likely be a dangerous move.

Ethan matched my movement, lowering himself down next to me and also swinging his legs over the edge of the rock as he gazed out at the lake.

"So, did you hear?" I focused on the moon, hanging low over the icy surface of the lake.

"No, but I saw." I could feel his eyes on me and I glanced up. The compassion in his expression was heavy and I swallowed the lump forming in my throat.

"They're dating." I shook my head in disbelief, and turned to stare at the clouds moving across the moon. The assertion sounded ridiculous in my ears. "I don't know why this is bugging me so much. I mean, Mom's been gone for almost four years, I couldn't expect him to be a monk forever, right? But my teacher? Why did it have to be my teacher? She's one of the only ones I truly like at school." The words came fast now, tumbling out of my mouth before I had a chance to think about whether or not I should say them. "So what now? She's going to come to dinner at my house, and they're going to go out to the movies, and I'm supposed to stand back and say, 'sure that's great, so glad you found each other, oh and by the way Ms. Woods, have you graded my oil color yet?'" I threw my hands up. I was being childish and selfish but I couldn't help it. If I was ever going to accept their being together I needed to get all of this off my chest first. Ethan's hand slid across my shoulders, rubbing them gently, but I was so fired up I barely noticed.

"It's one more thing to deal with, and I'm already feeling overwhelmed. Between people attempting to kill me, and trying to figure out why they're attempting to kill me, continually having images of people from the past and future pop into my brain, plus all the normal senior year of high school stuff—applying to schools and figuring out what I want to do once I've graduated—my dad's love life was not something I wanted to have added to the mix." I ran out of words. And oxygen. Drawing in a deep breath, I met Ethan's intense gaze just in time to catch the look that flashed across his face. He was happy we were together, I was sure of that, but he'd let enough doubt creep into his eyes, and some of the things he'd said to me over the past few months, that it was clear he still debated about putting his own happiness above my safety. Something he would never forgive himself for if things went wrong in any way.

I relaxed against Ethan, and his arm tightened around me. He pulled me close and pressed his lips to the top of my head.

"I know you're trying to recover from the shock of learning about your father and your teacher. If you need space from everything, Simon and I can try to figure this out on our own. I know I can't keep images from popping into your head, but you don't need to be part of searching for threads and patterns. It's been unfair of me to thrust all of that on you." Ethan leaned forward a little so he could look at me. It was hard not to melt right where I sat when he stared at me with those deep green eyes, full of concern.

I shook my head. "No, that's not what any of this is about. As frustrating as it is to not have any answers, I don't want to stop looking. I'll drive myself crazy if I keep getting images and don't know who they are or when they're from. I'm just upset about my dad, that's all. He's been gone for months, and now that he's back it appears that I'm going to be sharing him with someone else. It feels like he's cheating on my mom somehow, and I hate that I know who it's with. I'm going to have to see her every day in class. I hope she doesn't talk to me about him at school, or try to act like a stepmother or big sister or something." I shuddered at the thought of how awkward that would be. "Maybe I should drop art."

Ethan frowned. "Don't do that. I know all of this is hard for you, but you love art class. I get that all the analyzing of your drawings that we're doing is a drag, and I am sorry for that, but I love the way you still light up when you're working on a piece you're really excited about, or the joy that shines through when you complete a picture. Don't give that up. I'm sure she'll be respectful of the relationship the two of you have already established, and keep her personal life separate from that."

Was it that obvious how much I loved my work? Warmth rushed over me at the thought that Ethan had picked up on that.

I sighed. "I guess I should give their relationship a chance. How bad could it be?"

"It's fresh. Let things settle and see how it plays out." Ethan squeezed my shoulder.

I nodded. *That makes sense*. We dropped into silence, both staring out at the water. A car drove by on the road, and Ethan's eyes darted subtly in its direction, and then back to me when the car kept going.

"I already miss you," I whispered. I needed him to know why I had texted so late, and hadn't waited for the morning.

Ethan didn't say anything, just slid his free hand across my cheek until he cupped my face in his palm. Turning me to him, he brought his lips to mine in a soft and sweet kiss. *He misses me too.*

For a moment, I relaxed in his embrace, then I pulled back and stared at him.

"You're sure we can't tell everyone we're dating?" I wrinkled my nose. I was half joking, half hopeful, but I already knew his answer before he said it.

"It's safer this way." Ethan ran his thumb across my cheek gently and I leaned into his hand. He was right, but keeping our relationship a secret was going to be hard now that we didn't have the house to ourselves.

We sat together on the rock a little while longer. He kept his arm wrapped securely around me, until the chill of the winter air started to penetrate my jacket. My feet were cold, and I was sure my cheeks and nose were red. I shivered.

"Maybe we should head back to your house." Ethan tilted his head to look at me.

I stifled a yawn. "Yeah, I guess so." My knees and legs were stiff from sitting on the cold rocks, and Ethan jumped up and held out his arms to help me to my feet. We crossed over to the Jeep and started back towards my house.

As Ethan pulled into the driveway, I remembered my vision at the airport and quickly recapped it for him.

"There's never been a mix of past and present before, has there?" He threw the Jeep into park and cut the engine.

"You know my images as well as I do. It's never happened before." I shook my head.

"It sounds very strange, but I don't think we'll be able to do much until you get it down on paper. Then Simon and I will see what we can figure out."

"Okay. I started it at the airport but I'll finish it up tomorrow and give it to you." I surveyed the house for any sign that lights had been turned on, but the building was still cloaked in darkness. I breathed a small sigh of relief, and climbed out of the vehicle.

Ethan walked me to the front door and we stood for a second on the front porch. *I'll have to sneak back in without making a sound.* It would, after all, be just as bad to get caught coming in as going out. Ethan slipped his arms around my waist and gently tugged me towards him until our bodies were inches from each other. His lips brushed ever so slightly against my forehead.

"Sweet dreams," he whispered.

Tingles of delight ran up and down my spine. "Good night," I breathed as he let go of me. Reluctantly, I pushed open the door and slipped inside. The silhouette of his head and shoulders remained framed in the square of glass until I clicked the lock behind me. Then he disappeared. I stood for a second, soaking up the moment we had just shared, before I slid away from the door and tiptoed up the stairs. I went straight to my room, changed back into my pajama pants, and flopped down onto my bed again.

As I pulled the covers up to my chin, the heaviness in my chest lifted. I could handle Dad dating someone, even my teacher, as long as I had Ethan. And if being together meant sneaking out at night, then I would just have to become nocturnal.

Four

I stared at the note Dad had left on the front hall table as I shimmied into my jacket, preparing to head to school. He had plans with Rose for the evening. Again. And I shouldn't expect him for dinner. I'd told him two days after his return that it was okay with me if he dated my teacher, and the two of them had spent pretty much every evening together since then.

I bit my lip as I climbed into my car to head to school. With the house to myself, could I invite Ethan over tonight? My shoulders slumped. No. Even though Dad was gone a lot, I still worried he could walk in on Ethan and me alone together at any moment, so as always, I would keep from giving in to the temptation to invite Ethan over.

Dad had been back for two weeks, and as I drove the familiar route to school I realized just how much I'd started to look forward to my daily hours at East Halton High. It was my only extended time with Ethan now, a very frustrating concept to accept, especially since Dad seemed happier than ever.

I pulled into the parking lot and waited for Ethan. A couple of minutes later, the familiar green vehicle turned into a parking space four down from where my car was parked. I jumped out and walked towards the school, casually passing by his vehicle so he would see me.

"Good morning." I greeted him as he strode up next to me.

"Good morning to you. You look absolutely beautiful this morning," Ethan murmured. His fingertips brushed against mine.

I stopped dead in my tracks to stare at him. His lips were curved up in an appreciative smile, and I blinked. He never touched me at school, and was usually incredibly cautious anywhere in public, in case someone might be watching us.

"Thank you." Heat crept up my neck as I gazed down at my outfit. The weather had warmed up even more over the past week so I'd switched back to my fall jacket. I wore it over a simple oatmeal-colored sweater, a pair of jeans, and knee-high brown boots. My hair was half pulled back, loosely fastened to keep it from falling in my face. I didn't think I looked any better than any other day, but Ethan must really like the outfit to let his guard down in such a blatant way.

We split off once we were inside the school. I went to my locker to meet up with Katie, while he headed off in the other direction towards his locker. He'd appear again in a matter of minutes, ready to walk to class together. Ethan's second semester schedule matched mine, except for art. He hadn't qualified for that, since it was a continuum of last semester's course, and previous art classes had accidentally been left off of his fake school transcripts.

"Good morning." I sidled up to Katie, Luke and Heather, who were already standing by our lockers.

"You're very happy today." Katie raised an eyebrow as I spun the lock on my locker and tugged it open.

I deposited my backpack inside and grabbed the notebook for my first class. "Am I?" I tried to restrain the grin that was bursting on my lips.

"You look like you just won the lottery or something," Luke said.

Heather glanced up from the notebook she was scribbling in furiously, tilting her head to analyze me.

I shrugged. "I'm just in a good mood, that's all."

Katie and Heather both moved closer, until they were practically inside my locker with me. Katie grabbed my arm. "Did he finally tell you how he feels?"

"No, come on, for the hundredth time, we're just friends." I shook my arm free and tried to sound convincing.

It was hard not to scream it to the world that Ethan and I were in a relationship, but I was willing to do anything if it meant not screwing up what he and I had.

At first it had been easy to fool my friends. Since none of them saw Ethan arrive at the Masks Gala, I told them that he had flaked and never shown up. It had been harder to explain where I had gone with Adam. I'd convinced everyone he had talked me into going somewhere more private to talk, but as soon as he got me away from the country club I'd become uneasy about his intentions and changed my mind about him. Rather than go back to the dance though, I'd just caught a ride home since I was disappointed by Ethan's brush off. It had been a bit of a hard sell to everyone that I would do such a risky thing, but ultimately it had ended up taking the pressure off of the idea of Ethan and I hooking up.

Disappointment crossed Heather's face. "I was sure that the two of you had finally gotten together." She slumped back against the locker.

I was happy that my friends wanted Ethan and I together. "No, I'm just having a good morning." I subtly skimmed the now crowded hallway. Ethan would join us any second and I would have to keep from acting completely infatuated.

After the Gala, Katie, Heather, and Kristen had all banded together to vilify Ethan for ditching me and allowing me to end up with Adam. Ethan had kept his distance for a good month after the dance, which helped maintain our cover, but slowly he'd begun to hang around again. It had taken the better part of the fall for him to earn his way back into our group, but things had eventually gone back to the way they had been, with my friends acting mildly suspicious about Ethan's feelings towards me.

I finished getting my books and closed my locker, but there was no sign of Ethan.

Heather checked her watch. "We really need to get going, guys."

With one last glance down the hallway, I trudged after her and Katie. When we arrived at the classroom we filed into our usual spots as other students came in and settled around us. The teacher came in a minute later, just before the bell rang, but Ethan was still nowhere to be seen. Worry played at the back of my mind. Why wouldn't he show up for class? My gaze kept drifting to the classroom door. *Pay attention, Hannah.* I swung my focus back to Mrs. Morgan, my algebra teacher. There had to be a reasonable explanation for his absence, and besides, Ethan could take care of himself.

Class seemed to drag on forever as I tried to concentrate on complex equations, but finally the bell rang and I packed up my stuff.

Katie fell into step beside me as we exited the classroom. "Where's Ethan?"

I shrugged. "Why? Wasn't he there?"

She rolled her eyes. Katie knew me far too well. Thankfully, she let it slide and didn't press me on it.

We walked back to our lockers and I quickly switched my algebra work for my chemistry notes. "I have some questions for Mr. Jansen. I'm going to head to class early. I'll see you at lunch." I took off in the direction of Ethan's locker before Katie had time to respond. My heart beat faster; I needed to know that he was all right, and that I was being ridiculous.

Ethan wasn't at his locker. I strode past and made my way to the exit. When I got to the parking lot, his Jeep was gone. I scanned the rows of parked cars in a futile effort to see if he'd moved it for some reason. I pulled out my phone and shot him a quick text: Where are you? There was nothing more I could do in the few minutes left between classes so I walked back inside, slipping my phone into my pocket and willing it to vibrate.

Ethan was my study partner in chemistry, so I ended up by myself at my desk, working on a lab that involved mixing chemicals together over a Bunsen burner. I absentmindedly poured different colored chemicals from beaker to beaker, writing down my observations of any changes that occurred as they mixed together. I should have kept my mind on what I was doing, for safety's sake, but instead I was busy conjuring different scenarios of what could have happened to Ethan. None of them were good.

"Ms. Reed, please pay attention to what you're doing. These are chemicals you're working with here." Mr. Jansen, my chemistry teacher, rushed over and turned down my Bunsen burner. I had accidentally overfilled one of the beakers, and it had overflowed and dripped down onto the burner, causing the open flame to sizzle and spark.

"Sorry." My cheeks warmed. I set the beaker down on the table, ignoring the stares from my classmates as I went to the back of the room to grab some paper towels. I forced myself to pay extra close attention for the rest of the class, so there wouldn't be any other incidents.

After chemistry my friends and I made our way to the cafeteria for lunch. I tried to eat the apple and sandwich that I'd brought from home as I kept an eye on the doors for any sign of Ethan's dark head of hair, but my mind was too preoccupied. *Where could he be?*

"Hey, Ethan." Ryan lifted a hand in greeting from the opposite side of the table. I whirled around. Ethan had come in the back entrance to the cafeteria and was walking up behind me.

"You missed an excellent algebra class today. Mrs. Morgan did a quadratic equation rap for us." Katie took a fry and dipped it in ketchup.

I blinked. *She did?* I didn't remember that at all.

Ethan slid into the empty seat beside me. "I had a dentist appointment this morning that I forgot about."

"That's too bad, guy. I had to get three fillings last month; my mouth still hurts." Luke took a big bite of burger, poking a hole in his declaration.

"I got a clean bill of health." Ethan turned to give me a deliberate smile.

"That's good, I'm glad everything is okay." I exhaled slowly, trying to quiet the emotions slamming around in my head, mostly confusion mixed with overwhelming relief that he was all right.

"Me too," he replied. He was sitting closer to me than he normally would and my breath caught in my throat when his fingers lightly grazed the side of my knee under the table as he pulled in his chair. I had to use every ounce of self-control not to snap my head around to stare at him and draw everyone's attention to us. I concentrated on my apple, willing my racing heart to slow down.

"Hannah!"

My head jerked up. I stared at Katie. "Sorry, what were you saying?"

"I asked who was in for a movie night at my house. Everyone else said they were, but you and your apple seem to be having a very meaningful staring contest." Katie pointed at the little red fruit on the table in front of me.

"I have to work, but I can come after." I straightened up in my seat. The sharpness in Katie's voice had yanked me out of the shock I'd been feeling over Ethan's actions.

"I can pick you up on the way if you want," Ethan offered.

I studied him, but his expression was pure innocence.

"That would be good, thanks." I ignored the knowing looks from the others at the table.

"Ethan, come check out these hubcaps I was thinking of getting for the car." Luke held up his phone. "Ryan thinks they're too fancy, but I think they're *classic*."

Ryan made a gagging motion as Ethan joined them on their side of the table. The two boys monopolized Ethan's attention the rest of the lunch hour. It was clear I wasn't going to find out where he took off to for the morning, or figure out what his openly affectionate behavior was all about. I was dying for a chance to talk to him freely, but I would have to be patient.

In my western civilization class, Mr. Henry broke the class up into discussion groups, and Ethan and I were assigned to different groups. After that, I had art class and then it was the end of the school day. I wanted to wait for Ethan but I had to get going to The Patch, the store where I worked part-time. He met up with me just as I reached the door to the parking lot.

"I have to get going, Carmen's waiting for me." I readjusted the straps of my backpack on my shoulders.

"Okay. See you when you get off?" His tone was casual, the way any normal teenage guy, who wasn't going to spend the evening covertly observing me, would talk.

"If not before." I arched an eyebrow. He grinned and headed for his Jeep. I pursed my lips as I climbed into my car. What was going on with Ethan? I would ask him while we were driving to movie night. And neither of us was going into Katie's house until I knew exactly what it was.

Five

When I arrived at work, I jumped on the cash register to relieve Carmen, my boss and good friend. My shift flew by and before I knew it, she was heading over to the door and flipping the sign to closed.

"Hannah, your *friend* is here." Carmen nodded to the front of the store. I narrowed my eyes at her, but then glanced at the front window and smiled. Ethan stood on the other side of the glass. After his disappearing act that morning, I was too glad to see him to even pretend to be indifferent.

"Just go." Carmen grinned.

"You're sure?" I bit my lip and tried not to sound too excited.

"How could I keep you from that?" Carmen waved a hand towards Ethan.

"Thanks." I grabbed my stuff from behind the counter and joined Ethan on the store's outside deck, waving to Carmen as she locked up behind me again.

We headed for his Jeep, parked beside my car in the back parking lot. As soon as we'd climbed in and closed the doors, Ethan slid his hand around the back of my neck and brought his lips to mine. A mixture of relief and pent-up impatience percolated in his kiss. It caught me off guard, and we were both out of breath when he finally pulled away.

"Hi," I murmured.

"Hi." He took my hand in his and kissed the back of it gently. This much affection was surprising. His behavior was usually so restrained. Only when we were alone at my house would he hold me or kiss me. Were all these little moments a response to the time we were being forced to spend apart now that Dad was home?

"All right, what is going on?" I planted both palms against his chest to keep him at a distance. I didn't want to ruin the moment, but I had reached my maximum level of patience. "Where were you this morning?"

"Looking into your latest image. The one from the airport. Franklin, a Hleo stationed in Providence at the moment contacted me. He was pretty sure the image was the girl he's currently protecting, but he wanted my opinion. I raced up there to confirm that he was right."

"You went to Rhode Island this morning?" My eyes widened.

Ethan shrugged. "I figured the unusual mix of past and present in the picture warranted the road trip."

"And?"

"She was dressed up for a costume party."

I flopped back against my seat. "A costume party? Come on. That's ridiculous." I shook my head. "How are we ever going to figure this out if The Metadas is throwing confusing pictures into my head? It's as if I'm intentionally being misled. I wouldn't even mind the visions so much if there was some way to control the nature of them. If I could see them on my terms."

"I agree. Control would help. I'll keep looking into focusing exercises we could try." Ethan put the Jeep in drive and we headed off towards Katie's house.

"Sorry for snapping. I know you're trying." I rubbed my tense neck muscles, wanting to forget my drawing ability for the time being and move on to the other issue weighing on my mind. "I was just worried; I always worry when I don't know where you are."

"It's okay." He shot me a sideways glance. "Is that all?"

"What do you mean?"

"It seemed like something else was on your mind."

How could he read me that well, after the short time we'd been together? I took a deep breath. "Okay, what about…" I wanted to ask about the hand brushing, the grazing my knee, and the incredible kiss we'd just shared, but the words wouldn't come.

Ethan and I had been together for over four months now and in that time we had done little more than kissing. I was totally fine with going slow, since I had virtually no experience in that area.

Does Ethan want more? I assumed he must have quite a bit of experience, considering his age, and his looks, but we'd never actually had a conversation about the physical aspect of our relationship, and I had been too shy to bring up the subject until now.

"What about what?" Ethan's expression was blank, as though he had no idea what I was referring to.

"It's just…" I bit my lip, and then shook my head. "Never mind, it's nothing. I'm just glad you're okay. Now we can relax and have a good evening. I think Ryan is going to bring a romantic comedy. Since he and Trish became official he's doing everything he can to set a romantic mood for his dates with her." I rolled my eyes

"He does know there will be ten other people in the room with him on his date, right?" Ethan propped his elbow on the door's window ledge.

"You know Ryan, that won't stop him. I'm just glad she's into his intense neediness. Then again, she is two years younger so she probably doesn't know better." I laughed.

"Ryan's a good guy, he deserves to find happiness," Ethan said, and I could tell he sincerely meant it.

We pulled into Katie's driveway at the same time as Ryan and Trish, and immediately slipped into *friends* mode as we exited the Jeep, keeping a polite distance from each other and mingling with my friends separately so we didn't seem like a couple. Ethan talked cars and sports with Ryan and Luke, while I chatted with the girls.

After a while we all headed down to Katie's basement for the movie. "Hey, my parents said we could use the cottage next weekend." Kristen flopped down on the loveseat with her new boyfriend, Mark.

"Are you serious? That's awesome. I was just thinking it was about time for the yearly cottage caper." Katie rubbed her hands together as she took a seat in the middle of the couch. Luke grabbed a spot next to her, while I sat on the other side. Ethan dragged a high-backed desk chair up beside me.

"Ha, remember the raccoon?" Luke poked Katie in the arm.

Heather shook her head in disgust at the reminder of the little critter that had wreaked havoc last year when it managed to break its way into the cottage in the middle of the night. "Don't even mention that filthy creature. I still can't believe it made off with my phone." Heather threw a pillow at Luke. The guys had made a valiant effort to chase the animal down to get Heather's device back, but the raccoon had scampered up a tree and disappeared.

"Oh yeah. I forgot about that." Ryan slipped his arm around Trish as they settled on the other couch together. She gazed adoringly at him as he spoke. "Remember the homemade fireworks from two years ago?"

"My dad reminded me again, no fires of any kind." Kristen crossed her arms and glared at Ryan.

Kristen's cottage weekends were legendary. *I can't wait to spend one of them with Ethan.* I looked over at him and he gave me an amused grin.

Katie turned the lights off and started the movie. Every once in a while I could feel Ethan's eyes on me. I peeked over at him a few times, and he would always meet my gaze. *Does he feel this electricity generating between us, too?* The tension grew as the movie played on. I struggled to pay attention, and then I felt Ethan's thumb ever so gently trace a line down the back of my neck. Tingles ran up and down my spine. My heart raced. What was going on with him? Not that I was complaining, but he was definitely not acting like himself. I kept my eyes glued to the screen, and concentrated on keeping my breathing even.

When the movie ended, Katie jumped up and flipped the light switch. The bright track lighting helped to lighten the mood a little, but a force still sparked between us.

Ethan touched my elbow. "Ready to go?"

Another first. He never suggested we leave before everyone else. I raised both eyebrows, but his face was giving nothing away.

We drove in silence towards my house, although the mood was palpable. He had to feel it too; the current between us was escalating. *This time I'm not going to keep him from coming in the house. I don't care if Dad does come back while he's there.*

"My dad went out with Rose tonight." I murmured the words, partly to break the silence, and partly to let Ethan know we would be alone when we arrived at my house. He nodded in silent understanding as he glanced over at me. My heart rate quickened at the intensity in his emerald eyes. As we pulled into the driveway I tried to tell myself to calm down, but the way he was observing me, there was longing there, and my face went warm.

We climbed out of the Jeep and walked up the stairs to the front door. I tugged the keys out of my pocket, nearly dropping them as I did. Ethan caught them before they could fall, closing his hand over the keys and my fingers at the same time. My eyes met his and for a moment neither of us moved. He took a step closer, until our bodies grazed against each other, and brought his lips to mine softly. I wrapped my arms around his waist slowly. His lips went from my mouth to my neck and then back again, while one hand wove its way through my hair and the other circled my back, pulling me closer. I tightened my grasp on him and worked on continuing to breathe. Somehow the door swung open and we stumbled inside in a tangled jumble.

"Ethan, I—" Before I could finish the sentence, Ethan's lips were back on mine. I wasn't even sure what I wanted to say, all of this was happening so fast. We were still in the front foyer, but moving in the direction of the living room, more specifically, towards the couch. We were just about to collapse onto it when Ethan's head snapped back. He thrust an arm around me so I was behind him, and he was in a protective position, blocking me from an unknown danger.

He stared at the dark kitchen. I opened my mouth to ask what was going on, but he put a finger to his lips. I tried to keep my breathing under control as my heart raced with an entirely different type of adrenaline. Fear replaced joy as I waited to find out what was hiding around the corner from us, in the shadows.

Six

Ethan took a careful step in the direction of the kitchen, then froze. Simon came through the doorway, a half-eaten sandwich in his hand, his mouth full of food.

"Hello, you two, I thought I heard you come in." Simon swallowed and took another big bite of sandwich.

"What are you doing here?" Ethan ground the words out through clenched teeth.

Simon strolled past us into the living room and flopped down on a chair. "I believe I was supposed to return the lovely Hannah's car here tonight. I was hungry, and we have nothing good at home. I knew there was a delicious roast chicken from yesterday, and I was hankering for a meat sandwich so I let myself in." I tried to remember if my car had been in the driveway when we arrived, but I had been too preoccupied to notice.

"Simon, you don't just come into her house and help yourself to the food in their refrigerator." Ethan crossed his arms and glared at his partner.

"Hannah, do you mind?" Simon looked at me and cocked his head to the side, blatantly ignoring Ethan.

"Of course not, you just surprised us. I mean, Ethan was about to pulverize you." I shifted my gaze from one to the other, not wanting to take a side in this argument.

Simon just shrugged.

Heat flared up my neck into my cheeks, both from what Ethan and I had been doing, and from the embarrassment of almost getting caught by Simon. He wasn't acting strangely but I was positive he knew exactly what his presence had put an end to.

"I'm going to get a glass of water." I excused myself from the situation, and switched on the lights to remove any trace of the earlier mood. Ethan was still glaring daggers at Simon as I went. No doubt he'd have more to say once I was out of the room. That was fine because I needed a moment to collect my thoughts.

I grabbed a glass from the cupboard and turned on the faucet, my mind spinning. I stared out the window over the sink, into the blackness of the backyard, trying to get my head around the last ten minutes. Ethan was usually so reserved, had so much self-control. If anything, it was me that had tried to move our relationship along further in the physical area. And my fumbling attempts were always met with him retreating, and reminding me it was all right to take things slow. *Maybe I'm not as ready for us to take the next step in our relationship as I'd thought.*

I set the glass gingerly in the sink and started back to the living room, figuring I'd given the boys enough time to hash everything out, but Simon was still speaking in a hushed tone, and I stopped to listen.

"I get it, it's unprofessional for me to sneak into their house and you could have killed me. Next time I'll hang a banner to let you know I'm here," Simon joked.

I strained to catch Ethan's response, but heard only quiet murmuring.

After a moment, Simon spoke again. "Can I talk to you about something, mate?" His tone was serious now, and he had lowered his voice even more. I furrowed my brow and took another cautious step towards the living room, tucking my hair behind my ear and turning my head so I could clearly hear their voices.

"Go ahead." Ethan sounded wary but relatively back to normal; the anger must have dissipated. I had seen Ethan get annoyed with Simon before, but he never stayed mad for too long. Simon was just too lovable.

"I know I promised to keep your relationship with Hannah under wraps, and I have no problem with it, I really don't. You seem to be good for each other, make each other happy and all that, but Ethan, what are you doing?"

I held my breath through the long pause before Ethan answered. "Simon, I don't think—"

"No, clearly you're not thinking. I don't want to come down on you, mate. I'm trying to have your back. You know you can't do what… well I saw the two of you come in before I ducked back into the kitchen, and you really need to be more careful than that. The Three are going to be angry enough if they find out what you've been up to, especially with Hannah being the way she is, but if they think you've slept together… It's just not worth the risk. You're too good at what you do for that sort of fate."

My frown deepened. Sure, Ethan was breaking the rules being with me, but what did Simon mean when he said it would be worse if we slept together? And what exactly would Ethan's fate be if The Three found out about us? I needed to ask Ethan, but I couldn't let him know I'd been eavesdropping. I bit my lip. How would I bring up the subject without driving him away? I'd never gotten to this point with a guy before, never even been remotely close. I had no idea how to proceed.

"I appreciate the warning Simon, I do, but I can handle it. By the way, you've got mustard on your face." Ethan's voice held amusement, but it was clear the subject was closed.

"Mmm, Dijon," Simon responded.

I laughed to myself as I made my way down the hallway to join them again.

"Can I get you guys anything?" I asked as I rounded the corner to the living room. Simon was still sitting in the same chair, and Ethan had settled in on the couch.

"I'm good, love." Simon held up his last bite of sandwich before shoving it in his mouth.

"I'm fine." Ethan gave me his usual warm smile as I made myself comfortable on the armchair across from Simon's, but from the strain in his voice I could tell he was still trying to recover from his conversation with Simon. And probably from having to switch from boyfriend to protector mode so quickly.

Simon snapped his fingers, sending a spray of crumbs across the arm of his chair. He quickly brushed them away. "Hey, before I forget to tell you, I managed to get another ten drawings accounted for. I was finally able to track down two more Hleo, Sergei and Mohinder. Sergei was in a remote part of Russia, and Mohinder was down in Chile. So after the ones they've tagged, we only need to identify seventy-two more."

"And?" Ethan straightened on the couch. "Did Sergei or Mohinder say if they have ever protected anyone with Hannah's ability before?"

Ethan had been systematically going through his list of contacts in the Hleo in an attempt to find out more about my ability. Even after months of gathering information, we had only been able to work out a few key elements about my drawings. The biggest breakthrough had been our discovery that my black and white images were protecteds that Hleo had failed with, and who had been killed. There were only five black and white drawings left that hadn't been claimed, every other one had been confirmed as a Bana hit. All the protecteds in color images had lived. It made me sad to think that people I had drawn had been murdered, even if I had never met them.

"I've already entered the information they gave us into the grid to be analyzed, but no, they haven't protected anyone like Hannah before." Simon drummed his fingers on the armrests of the chair.

I released the breath I didn't even realize I'd been holding. I had hoped for something more useful.

Ethan was losing faith in discovering exactly how my subconscious mind worked, and had focused his attention on finding out if there had ever been another protected like me, someone who had visions of other protecteds. But every Hleo he asked told him the same thing, that the only person they knew with the power to see a protected was Miriam, one of the leaders of the Hleo.

"I'm glad you got a hold of them at least, ten drawings is a fairly substantial amount." Ethan kept his eyes on Simon. *Is he avoiding eye contact with me because of the somewhat disappointing news, or over the awkwardness of what Simon caught us doing?* I sighed, exhausted from the effort of analyzing his every move that day.

I hadn't admitted anything to Ethan but, as annoying as the images invading my head had become, I was frightened they would just stop one day, and Ethan would be ordered to return to Veridan, the North American base where the Hleo stayed and trained, and out of which they were commissioned. My throat tightened. Ethan's departure always seemed to loom in the near future, but neither of us had brought up the subject of what we would do when that time came. The logical solution would be to part ways, but I didn't think I could survive without him; the thought of it caused an unbearable ache in my chest.

Ethan checked his watch. "Hannah's dad will be here soon. We better get going."

Simon got to his feet. "Thanks for the snack, Hannah."

I waved a hand through the air. "Any time." I followed the two of them to the door.

Simon grinned and disappeared out onto the porch. Ethan waited until he was gone and then pulled me close, gently pressing his lips to my forehead, "Sweet dreams," he whispered, his breath warm against my ear. Before I could answer, he let me go and slipped outside.

I closed the door and leaned against it. What was he doing to me? Was he trying to tell me he wanted us to get closer? I headed off to the living room to distract myself with some television as a new, horrifying thought struck me. Maybe he wasn't trying to get closer to me. Maybe he was fighting the inevitable goodbye.

Seven

Katie and I wandered around Randall's Art and Stuff. It had been more than a week since movie night at her house, and I hadn't had a chance to talk to her alone. I'd convinced her to come with me to pick up some new sketching pencils and a sketchbook, since I had filled yet another one with protected images. She had agreed to come, if I would go shopping for dorm stuff with her. She figured it was never too early to start collecting necessities for the room she intended for us to share, necessities like an alarm clock in the shape of a dog that barked a person awake.

I didn't like giving a lot of thought to my uncertain post-secondary future. There were so many unanswered questions surrounding my protected status that it was too discouraging to try and make plans, but I still needed time alone with Katie.

Ethan had been acting a little strange since Simon had startled us. He was completely normal at school, when we were around my friends, but he avoided being alone with me. He would either drop me off at home and take off right away, claiming he had some new lead to look into, or he'd bring Simon along with him so that we were always chaperoned. I didn't know how to talk to him about it, so I'd decided to go to Katie for advice. I couldn't actually confess anything about Ethan, so I had come up with a fake scenario, hoping she wouldn't get suspicious.

"Hey, did you hear about Jill Nesbitt?" I studied the wall of oil paints in front of me so she couldn't see my face.

"No, what about her?"

Jill was in my chemistry class. Katie knew her, but not well, so it was unlikely she'd go to Jill to confirm the fictitious details I was about to share with her.

"I heard that she and Matt Kidman were about to hook up a few weeks ago, but they got interrupted by his older brother, and now Matt is being all weird about it." Matt Kidman was another fellow student Katie sort of knew; again I was hoping he'd be a safe bet.

Katie frowned. "Really? That's weird. I thought she was dating Dylan Torino."

I mentally kicked myself. *Guess I should have checked to make sure Jill and Matt were single before using them for my lie.*

I lifted one shoulder. "I don't know, that's just what I've heard. Apparently since that night Matt's avoided being alone with her; I wonder what that means." I picked up two different shades of green paint, trying to decide which to go for as I waited for Katie to cash in with an opinion.

"It means he thinks hooking up with her is a mistake, and he's trying to subtly tell her." She ran her fingers over the different glitter paints, sounding bored.

"You think so?" I tried to seem nonchalant. I was worried that was what Ethan's behavior meant, but had tried to convince myself there was another explanation; now Katie was confirming my fears.

"What else could it be?" Katie picked up a tube of sparkly blue paint and set it down again.

"I don't know, maybe he's embarrassed about his brother and things are awkward now, or maybe he's worried they were rushing into something and he wants to make sure she doesn't feel things are going too fast," I suggested as we finished with the aisle and rounded the corner to drawing paper and sketchbooks.

"Maybe." Katie's nose wrinkled. "But I'm pretty sure that—" Something flashed in her eyes.

Uh oh. I've said too much.

She grabbed my shoulders and looked me square in the eye. "Hanns, please tell me that if you and Ethan had hooked up you would tell me. I like to think that, as your best friend, you wouldn't feel the need to come up with some lame cover story to get advice from me. Have you guys been together and now he's being weird?

Because if it's you two, scrap what I said. I know he cares, and there is definitely some other explanation for him trying to blow you off."

I worked to keep my features even, which wasn't easy with Katie searching my face as though trying to read a map. I wanted to tell her the truth so badly, but I couldn't risk what Ethan and I had. Or what I hoped we still had. "Katie, if that happened I would tell you. You need to stop trying to make something out of nothing between Ethan and me. I was just sharing some gossip, that's all." I stepped back so she was forced to drop her arms, and reached for a sketchbook.

"Fine." Katie sighed.

She didn't believe me. I lifted my chin. I wasn't going to change my story, so she would just have to accept it.

"So, when is your double date with Ryan and Trish?" I asked, trying to get Katie onto something else. That had been too close. I needed to be more careful around her. In fact, it was probably best to keep silent on the matter of Ethan and me.

Katie chatted about their plans the rest of the time we were in the store. When we were done with art supplies, we browsed the home decor store for a while, and grabbed some supper. I had a pile of homework to do, so I said good-bye to Katie and headed home, ready to work on one of the two major reports due the following week.

Ethan didn't call or text me. I tried to let it go as nothing. He knew I was going out with Katie, and that I had a lot of homework. *He's being considerate, trying not to distract me from the things I have to do.* But as I edited one of my papers, my mind kept drifting back to Simon's ominous words.

From his tone I could tell it was more than just a reminder that Ethan and I weren't supposed to be dating. Something else wasn't being said about the direction we had been heading that night, and part of me wanted to know what it was. The other, more cowardly part, though, felt like we were in our own fragile bubble, and if I poked at it too much it would pop and I would be left standing alone.

Eight

An image appeared in my mind. I sighed and set down my homework. This was the second one in a week. The visions seemed to be coming faster and faster. I was used to one a month, but they had been progressing and now it was up to at least one a week.

The scene was of a family camping out in the mountains. They had pitched tents and there was a campfire pit and picnic table at their site. A wood-paneled station wagon was parked near the campsite. I grabbed a pen and started sketching, closing my eyes to replay the details over and over so I could insert as much information into the picture as possible.

The image remained burned in my brain, like the after-effects of a brilliant light slashing through darkness, its details embedded in my mind until it was fully down on the paper. Once the drawing was complete, I flipped the paper over and started writing out more specific details about the vision. The make and model of the vehicle, the canvas material the tents appeared to be made of, the trees that surrounded the campsite and the style of the parents' and children's clothes.

The front door opened, and I checked my watch. If that was Dad getting home, it was much later than I had thought it was. He and Rose had signed up for ballroom dancing lessons, something he and Mom had always wanted to do but never gotten around to, and he was really enjoying himself. A pang of jealousy for Mom darted across my chest, but I slid off my bed and pasted an approving smile on my face as I headed downstairs. Dad would want to share all the details of the steps they were trying to master, and the elderly couple that could dance circles around the two of them.

When I got downstairs I didn't see anyone, but sounds were coming from the kitchen. I rounded the corner. And stopped. Dad and Rose were kissing passionately in front of our kitchen sink.

"Oh," I exclaimed, before I could stop myself. They immediately broke apart and whirled around to gape at me. *Get out of here. Escape*. I spun on my heel and fled the kitchen.

"Hannah, Hannah, please come back here," Dad called out. From the strain in his voice, he was definitely as mortified by the situation as I was.

"It's okay, I'll just give you two some space." My hand was already on the banister as I was ready to launch myself upstairs. Was this how Simon felt when he saw Ethan and I together the other night? So awkward.

"No, Hannah, please. Come back," Dad repeated.

I shut my eyes tightly, grimacing at the thought of the conversation I was about to suffer through. I inched my way back to the entrance of the kitchen, and leaned a shoulder against the doorframe, staring down at the floor. "It's cool, really, we don't need to talk about this." I kicked at a grout line in the kitchen tile with my toe.

"Hannah." Dad's tone suggested that I better look up. I lifted my head. Dad and Rose stood on opposite sides of the island. Rose's gaze was fixed on the wooden countertop, her arms wrapped around herself.

A deep frown contorted my dad's face. He didn't quite meet my eye. "I'm sorry Hannah; I didn't realize you were here. I thought you were out with Katie for the evening."

"I was. I got in a while ago. I had homework to do, and I really should be getting back to it." I took a step back.

"Our class ended early. I wanted to get Rose's opinion on my study as I've been thinking of redoing the décor in there. We were just about to make a cup of tea when you came in."

Tea, right. "It's fine, really, I get it. It's kind of embarrassing, but let's just forget it and move on." I waved my hands in front of me. Dad was rambling, something he never did, and I needed him to stop talking about this.

"As you wish." His face softened a little at my words. His eyes darted over to Rose, and he gave her a reassuring smile.

"I'll be upstairs, you two feel free to carry on—"

"No! I'm going." Rose grabbed her purse off the island. Clearly the moment between them was over.

Dad straightened the sleeves on his shirt. "I'll walk you out."

"See you later." I had been about to tell her I'd see her at school, but stopped myself. *Definitely wouldn't help this situation.* I flashed them both another smile before practically running up the stairs. I shut my door and rubbed the palms of my hands into my eyes, willing the mental picture of my father and teacher making out in the kitchen out of my head.

I flopped down on my bed and stared up at the ceiling. I wanted to accept this, I wanted to be happy for them, but it felt so wrong, especially in our house, in our kitchen, where mom had prepared meals, made birthday cakes, broken her arm when she'd slipped in a puddle of water that had leaked from the refrigerator.

I was tempted to turn my bedside lamp off so Dad would think I had fallen asleep but I was too emotionally and physically drained to move. When I heard a light knock on my door about ten minutes after our run-in, I silently cursed myself for not giving into that temptation.

"Come in." I dragged myself up into a cross-legged position on my bed.

"Hi." Dad swung my door open and stood in the doorway looking awkward and sheepish.

"Dad, we don't have to do this. I promise I'm o—"

He held up a hand, walked into my room and sat down gingerly at the end of my bed.

"Hannah, what happened tonight, that was a mistake. I told you I would keep what Rose and I have away from you until you felt comfortable enough to be around us, and I certainly didn't want a show of affection to be our first interaction. I'm very sorry you witnessed us, well… I want you to know that tonight was the first time Rose has been in our house. I don't want you thinking that I spend every moment you're not home sneaking around with her here." Dad had been studying his hands, but turned to meet my eyes.

"I know, Dad. I didn't think that. I know you care about my feelings with all of this. I admit that the two of you making out in the kitchen was probably the last thing I expected to see as I rounded the corner, and it does feel a little weird, but I'm not mad or alienated, I promise." I gave him a half-smile.

"This is all so very different and new for me. I never expected to meet anyone after your mom, and I was completely content with that. Rose has been a pleasant surprise, but this dating thing feels so foreign. I just want to make sure I'm doing everything right by you." Dad's frown deepened as he talked.

I rested a hand on his shoulder. "You're being very considerate, really. It's foreign for me too, but I'm glad you're happy, you deserve it." I squeezed his shoulder before letting him go.

"Thank you." Dad stood. "I'll let you get back to your homework. I just wanted to clear the air."

I smoothed out a wrinkle in my bedspread. "Night Dad."

"Good night." He walked out of my room and pulled the door shut, leaving me to the silence of my thoughts once again. I waited thirty seconds before I let out a big sigh, in case he had hesitated on the other side of the door. I grabbed my notebook and starting writing, pressing hard with my pen. It was one thing for him to be dating, but this was… I shuddered. I hated feeling so overwhelmed and trapped, and I hated that a big part of me was upset because Dad seemed so fine with having a physical relationship with someone, while Ethan had put the brakes on ours.

Nine

"Hannah, can I speak to you for a minute?" Ms. Woods walked over to my drawing desk. It had been two days since our embarrassing run-in, and I had managed to avoid both her and Dad, even skipping art the day before. Thankfully, today she had left me alone all class. There were only two minutes left and I had started to gather up my art supplies in hopes of a quick escape once class ended, but now I was stuck. The bell rang before I had a chance to reply and everyone else made their way towards the exit.

I shrugged. "Sure."

"Why don't I let you get your stuff cleaned up? I'll meet you in my office." Ms. Woods gave me a big forced smile before walking back to the front of the room. She had to side-step quickly to avoid crashing into a student who was slam dunking a scrunched up piece of paper through one of the art room's basketball nets, a remnant of the room's former life as a gymnasium.

I groaned inwardly. What did she want to talk to me about? If she tried too hard to explain her actions in the kitchen, I would be forced to stop her.

Ms. Woods looked up when I walked into her office and motioned for me to take a seat in front of her incredibly cluttered desk. *So different from how Dad keeps his.*

"Hannah, I know you're probably worried this is about the other night, but your Dad assured me you guys talked it out so I'm going to leave it at that. We don't need to keep rehashing awkward moments, right?" Ms. Woods slid her hands back and forth on the edge of her desk.

I sank onto the chair, letting my backpack drop to the ground beside me. *Good. Glad we're on the same page.* "May I ask what this is about then?"

"I wanted to talk to you because I'm wondering if anything is wrong." Ms. Woods stuffed a few stray pencils into a cup holder, avoiding eye contact with me.

I blinked. "Um, no. Nothing's wrong."

"It's just that you don't seem to be enjoying art class as much as you used to, and I would hate to think that I had something to do with that." Ms. Woods lifted her head, finally, and looked at me with genuine concern in her grey-blue eyes.

"You? What do you mean?"

"Well, since I've been back from my trip I've noticed a change in your work. It's still as excellent as ever, technically speaking, but there seems to be a spark missing. It's as if the work is missing life, a soul, the passion you used to put into every piece. I know that your father dating must be hard for you, especially with things like the other night happening.

"I'll be honest, I've really enjoyed the past few months with your dad; he's an incredible man. But if our dating is affecting your artwork, that perhaps you aren't as okay with us being a couple as you've let on and it's coming through in your creative expression. If it would help, I…" She stopped and swallowed hard, then lifted her chin. "I would be willing to stop seeing Richard."

I studied her. It meant a lot that she would be willing to make that sort of sacrifice in my best interest. I bit my lip as I processed what she was saying.

"Hannah." Ms. Woods ran a hand through her nutmeg-brown hair. "You are one of the most talented students I have ever had the privilege of teaching, and I would hate to think that I was somehow responsible for the recent change in your work."

I shifted in my seat. I could tell her my drawing issues were her fault, that I didn't want my father dating anyone, or kissing anyone, and it was making me miserable to watch, but I didn't. The truth was, I hadn't seen him this happy since before mom died, and I couldn't take that away from him.

I pushed back my shoulders. "It is hard for me to see Dad with another woman, and there is an added level of weird since it happens to be my favorite teacher, but it's obvious that you make him happy."

"Really?" She beamed. Clearly the feelings my dad had for her were reciprocated.

"Really. He has this light in his eyes that's been missing for a very long time."

Her smile faded. "I like him too, but if our relationship is too much of a strain on you ..." Ms. Woods stood up and began pacing behind her desk.

I held up a hand. "No, it's not that, really it's not. There are a lot of other things going on right now." I refrained from giving any more explanation than that. I straightened the papers on her desk that were closest to me. *Please don't ask for more details than that.*

"Well, if you ever need someone to talk to..." She came around the corner of her desk.

I jumped to my feet. "It's fine, everything will sort itself out, I'm sure."

"I hope so. I think you have a very bright future in the art world Hannah, and if there's anything I can do to keep you headed down that path, just let me know."

I almost laughed. How could I tell her that the path ahead of me was the exact reason my artistic passion was suffering? That the reason my art had lost its life and spark was because every drawing that popped into my mind was a constant reminder that I had no answers about the future. The images sat on the paper, taunting me with their unexplainable presence in my life. Every drawing became more work once it was completed than it ever was to actually draw, and the only things I was getting out of all this effort were more questions.

Since I couldn't say any of that to my teacher, I just waved and headed out the door. I stalked off to my locker on the verge of a terrible mood. Ms. Woods had meant well, but I was sick of hearing about the future. Everywhere I went it was all that anyone discussed. In my senior year classes, with my friends, with Dad and Rose, even with Ethan and Simon. I needed a break.

Katie and Heather were standing by my locker when I got there. Katie was holding a brochure for something and excitedly pointing at pictures.

Heather stood close, appearing to hang on every word.

"Hanns, there you are. Look!" Katie waved the brochure in my direction. "New pictures of Roble Hall. We can check them out over lunch."

A Stanford information brochure. I repressed a groan. Another discussion about the gaping black hole of uncertainty I found myself constantly staring into? I didn't have the energy or the desire to pretend to be excited for it.

"Oh wow, Kate, that's great." I glanced quickly at the brochure, speaking with as much enthusiasm as I could muster. I opened my locker and threw my backpack in.

"Just think, in a few short months, we'll be out of this place and onto our big, bright, west coast lives." Katie thrust the brochure into my hands, forcing me to look at it.

"Sounds good," I agreed, this time without any eagerness.

"Don't worry; you're going to get your acceptance letter. I can't believe you haven't got it already, mine came like two weeks ago. There must be something wrong with your mailman." Katie shook her head.

Or maybe they're going to reject me. One more unanswered question in my life was the last thing I needed. I hadn't heard whether I had been accepted or rejected yet, which wasn't helping my stress level. I had debated about whether or not to even apply, but Ethan had pushed me to do it. He told me I should try to carry on as normally as possible, given the circumstances, to try to make decisions the way I would if I had never discovered I was a protected, and Stanford was one of those decisions. What he said made sense, so I sent in an application, but everything was so confusing now that I didn't even know if I would be able to attend if I did get accepted.

"Katie, can we just stop talking about it for now?" I handed the brochure back to her.

Katie rolled her eyes at Heather, clearly thinking I was being dramatic.

"Why don't you want to talk about next year? Even if you don't get into Stanford, you already got acceptance letters from Brown and Harvard, didn't you? They're not exactly subpar schools." Heather leaned against the locker next to mine and pushed her glasses up on her nose.

"I know, and you're absolutely right. I just really want to know about Stanford." I dug through my bag, searching for my wallet so I could buy something from the cafeteria, although my appetite had suddenly left me. What Heather was saying made sense. Harvard and Brown were both incredible schools and it was an honor to have gotten into them, but Katie and I had been talking about a future on the west coast since before we'd been in high school and it was hard to imagine abandoning that plan.

"If you can get into Brown and Harvard, there's no way you aren't getting into Stanford." Katie waved a dismissive hand.

"Maybe I will, maybe I won't," I responded, trying to keep my voice even.

"Come on, you'll get in. Why aren't you excited?" Katie nudged me in the arm.

"I only got my letter from Columbia last week, I'm sure yours from Stanford is on its way." Heather's enthusiastic tone matched Katie's and I found myself getting more irritated.

"Yeah maybe, I just don't feel like talking about the future right now." I shut my locker, a little harder than necessary. Couldn't they see how frustrated I was and drop the subject?

Katie shifted her weight from one foot to the other and crossed her arms. "What's up with you lately? You're all moody, and every time I bring up our plans for after high school you get all freaked out and want to change the subject."

Heather looked from Katie to me, her brow furrowed.

"I don't freak out." I placed my hands on my hips.

"You do, ever since the Gala. First you take off with that Adam guy you barely knew, and you say nothing happened between you and him, but I'm still confused about why you left the Gala in the first place. How did you know Ethan was going to bail on you? Especially when we had all just gotten there. Going to that dance together as a group was supposed to be a senior year memory, not to mention that it was *your* artwork we went to support."

I took a step back. Guilt pricked my chest. *She's still holding that night against me.* The explanation I'd given my friends for my sudden disappearance with Adam was weak, but I hadn't had much of a choice. I opened my mouth, but Katie's hand flew up and I shut it.

"And then you drop all your extracurricular stuff. You used to love doing set design for the drama club and being on the yearbook committee. Now you take off after school saying you have a lot of homework, and we never hang out anymore. I practically had to force you to apply to Stanford. It's been our dream forever, and now you don't even want to talk about it? What is going on?"

My jaw clenched. "What's going on? Everything, Katie, everything's going on. I'm sick of talking about the future, thinking about the future, trying to figure out the future. How can I get excited for the future when I don't even know if I have a future? I don't know if I'm going to Stanford, I don't know if I'm ever leaving East Halton. My dad's off planning a life with Rose and parading her around our house, my art isn't mine anymore, it's work to be scrutinized and broken apart until it means nothing to me, and all I want is for everyone to get out of my head and give me some space." I flailed my arms as I ranted. It took all my self-control to keep the truth about Ethan, the Hleo, and my calling as a protected from spilling out while I was getting everything off my chest.

"You want some space? Fine, I'll give you some space," Katie shouted back. She slammed her locker and stormed off.

Heather followed her, peering back at me every so often with a small frown on her face until they rounded the corner and disappeared.

I was furious with myself for letting this happen. I grabbed my bag and strode out to the parking lot. I didn't particularly care where I went at the moment, as long as it was nowhere near East Halton. I stopped at the driver's side door and fumbled through my bag, searching for my keys. A shadow fell across the hood of the car. I didn't turn around. "I need to get out of here. I have to get away." I kept my head down and shoved my sketchbook aside, pushing pens and pencils out of the way as I reached down to the bottom of my bag.

"Let's go then. I'll drive." Ethan's fingers fell lightly on my shoulder. I stopped my frantic search.

I drew in a deep breath. "Okay." I yanked my hand out of my bag and trudged over to the Jeep behind Ethan.

He gave me a few minutes, until we were well on the road and the school was no longer in view. Then he shot me a sideways glance. "Want to talk about it?"

I sighed. "I got in a fight with Katie." I stared out the window. Ethan was driving along Lakeshore Road and I kept my eyes on the expansive body of water. A strong breeze blowing across the lake sent choppy waves lapping against the shore. The tossing and pitching felt completely relatable at the moment. *How had life gotten so overwhelming?*

"I know. I ran into her in the cafeteria. She said you started yelling at her for no reason about things she didn't understand." I could feel his eyes on me as he spoke, but I still didn't look over. He'd be wondering how much I had shared. Nothing compromising, thankfully. I did comprehend why Katie wouldn't have understood my rant. I had never told her about Dad and Rose; I didn't like thinking about it and she would have bombarded me with questions. I also had neglected to mention, before it came spewing out during our fight, that my art had become a chore over the past few months instead of my passion, as it had always been in the past. Again, there would have been too many questions I would have had to come up with lies for, and I was tired of continually lying to my best friend.

Silence was always the easiest choice, but that silence was eating away at me. *Probably the real reason I'm feeling so annoyed.* Keeping my mouth shut was a constant reminder that ultimately I was alone in all of this. Ethan was there for me, as much as he could be, but I was still the one being singled out by the mysterious Metadas, it was my mind that received unexplained visions, and me that the Bana were trying to kill.

"Katie was bugging me about Stanford and what we're going to do after high school." I finally twisted in my seat to look at him. He nodded but didn't speak. I pushed my hair off my face, tucking it behind my ears. "Everything about Rose and my Dad and my artwork being picked apart and the uncertainty of Stanford all sort of came pouring out at once. But that was all that came out." I gripped his arm to emphasize that last part, so he would know the secret about the Hleo was still safe. His emerald gaze locked with mine for a moment, and he slid his hand off the wheel, twining his fingers between mine and resting them on the gearshift.

Warmth spread through me at the contact. "I need to get away for awhile, be free from all of it for even just one day."

Ethan threw his signal on and took the next left. "I know a place we could go; it's only a few hours from here."

I narrowed my eyes. "Where?"

"Let me surprise you." Ethan flashed me an adventurous grin, and immediately my mood perked up. Anywhere else would be a nice distraction right now.

"Let's go." I settled back in my seat, ready for whatever he had in mind.

Ten

The warm February weather had melted the last of the snow, revealing the yellowy-green grass of winter. The sun felt warm and comforting on my face as it poured through the Jeep windows. I closed my eyes and tried to leave the fight with Katie behind me. I would apologize and deal with her when I got back.

We cruised east on the I-84, heading roughly in the direction of Boston. We talked about our classes, about Luke's car, and Ryan's new relationship, about Simon and his past. Basically everything except predicting the future and figuring out how I was supposed to impact the world. Ethan expertly maneuvered in and out of traffic. He zipped along well above the speed limit, but I wasn't scared.

"You really love to drive fast, don't you?" I cocked my head to stare at him.

He only grinned and pressed harder on the gas in response. The engine rumbled as we picked up more speed. He seemed so relaxed; it was strange and reassuring at the same time.

We held hands as we traveled, Ethan's thumb tenderly circling mine. I savored the contact.

After an hour and a half, Ethan turned off the interstate and began driving on municipal roads. Then he pulled off the paved roads and we started down a gravel one, lined with thick overgrown trees, that clearly didn't see much traffic.

After about another half a mile the trees thinned and farmland stretched out on either side of us. We passed by a number of fields before Ethan slowed and turned up a long, overgrown laneway that couldn't have been used in years. The grass had grown up to the point where all that remained were remnants of a forgotten path. If we hadn't been in a four-wheel drive vehicle, we would never have made it. A pair of huge old trees towered at the end of the driveway, blocking the view of an old rundown shamble of a farmhouse. Across from the house, a small yard led to the remains of a fair-sized barn.

The house was a two-story structure, covered in rotten wood siding that was missing in sections. The roof was caving in on one side and most of the windows had been smashed. The screen door had fallen off its hinges and now leaned precariously against the house's frame, while vines and bushes had grown up around the building as though slowly trying to devour it.

The barn was almost completely gone too, only the crumbling stone foundation and a pile of collapsed beams that must have been the walls at one point remained.

Ethan parked the Jeep by the porch of the house and shut the engine off.

"So…" I surveyed the property. Why on earth had Ethan brought me here?

"Come on," Ethan said excitedly. He jumped out of the vehicle and came around to help me out too. Pulling me by the hand, he led me towards the porch stairs. We had to walk gingerly since the steps were mostly decayed. The second one was cracked right down the middle and was sinking into the ground, so Ethan practically lifted me up onto the porch. We walked carefully across the old wooden planks. At some point this must have been a charming home. There were a few remaining faded green shutters nailed to the window frames, and beautifully carved spindles lined the railing. Most of the spindles were broken or missing now, but those that were still intact gave a sense that the place would have had real character back in its day.

Ethan turned the knob and tried to push open the front door, but it didn't budge.

Although it appeared to be abandoned, I surveyed the property for any signs of an occupant. "Are you sure we should be—?"

He gave the door a hard shove with his shoulder and it acquiesced, swinging into the house so we could enter. The inside was dark and smelled dank and musty. The cobwebs were thick, and some of the walls had suffered damage from water leaking through the ceiling.

We stood in the front foyer by a staircase leading up to the second floor. I peered through the nearest doorway into what must have been the former parlor of the house. "I think I've been pretty patient; where are we?"

"This is where I grew up." Ethan spread his arms out and motioned to the walls and other rooms we had yet to investigate. "It's the farmhouse my father built when he and my mother immigrated here from Ireland and the house I lived in until I left for the Hleo." A trace of his accent added a lilt to the word 'Ireland.'

My mouth fell open. I looked around again with a whole new appreciation for where I was standing. I couldn't believe he would bring me here, to such a personal place.

"You grew up here?" I echoed back to him as I walked into the parlor. The only furniture in the room was an old settee shoved up against the front wall. Dull-red slashes hinted at an original crimson color, but now it was covered with so many stains and layers of dust it was dirty brown.

The walls were plastered with faded flower-print wallpaper that was peeling badly and ripped off completely in sections. Ethan strode over to one of the pieces hanging from the wall and, in a futile attempt, rolled it back into place. "Yeah. When we first moved to this property my father built a small cabin for the four of us to share, just an open room with two beds and a small cooking area, but as soon as we had enough shelter to survive he set to work on this place. We didn't know anybody in the area, no family or friends, but the neighboring farmers and some of the people from town soon introduced themselves and offered to pitch in with the construction. With their help he was able to build both the barn and the rest of the house in less than two years."

"That's amazing. My parents were in the process of fixing up our house my whole life. I can't imagine getting it all done in two years." I drifted out of the parlor to the next room. The only clue that this had been the dining area was the low-hanging chandelier in the center.

"The people in this area had a real sense of community. Quite a few of them were immigrant families, and I think the fact that most didn't have any extended family to rely on motivated them to reach out to neighbors."

I stepped on an old floorboard with a loose nail and it creaked under my feet. "That makes sense."

From the dining room, we wandered into a huge farmhouse-style kitchen, a large horseshoe area of cabinets with most of the doors either hanging from a hinge or missing altogether. The food prep area of the room flowed into a large open space, the perfect spot for a dining table. Wooden chairs were strewn haphazardly around the room, two against a wall, two in the center of the room, and one tipped over near a door that led out to the backyard.

"This is a huge kitchen. Oh the meals that could have been made here." I ran a hand along the old wooden countertop.

"My mother loved to cook, so my father wanted to give her a kitchen big enough that she would have all the space she would ever need."

"Mission accomplished."

"I remember he even splurged and bought her a six-plate cast iron stove. I guess it's long gone now." Ethan had a far-off look in his eyes as he walked over to an area on the other side of the kitchen that had a large dark stain on the floor, likely the original location of the stove.

"It sounds like your father was a really good man." I tried to imagine what the house must have looked like back when Ethan's father had built it.

"He was," Ethan murmured.

We walked around the first floor a little longer, through a living room with deep green walls, and passed another small room that Ethan explained was a sewing room, until we were back in the front hall where we had started. The living room had two more couches that looked in roughly the same condition as the one we had seen in the parlor. I was tempted to sit on one to get a feel for what it must have been like to live in the house, but didn't out of fear that it would collapse beneath me.

"You'll want to be careful on the staircase, the risers are a bit deeper than ordinary stairs." Ethan held out a hand—no doubt assuming he would have to catch me—as we carefully made our way up the narrow winding stairs that led to the second floor. Four small bedrooms were located off of a large landing area.

"So which bedroom was yours?" I raised an eyebrow as we stood in the middle of the landing.

Ethan pointed to one of the bedrooms to the left of the stairs. "Mary's was that one there, and mine was this one." He took a step over to the room across from his sister's.

I hurried to join him, curious to see if there were any items remaining from when he had used the room. My face fell when I saw that it was empty. The walls were white plaster, although one of the exterior walls had a large dark brown water stain running down from the ceiling. The window in the room was broken and glass lay scattered on the old wooden floor below the frame.

"The house has been sitting empty for so long. At some point someone cleared out the upstairs. I'm not really sure why they left everything downstairs. So there's not much to see, unfortunately, but the bed used to be there." Ethan motioned to the area under the window. "It had a great view of the back orchard."

I moved closer to him and peered out through the gaping space between the dirt and cobweb-encrusted window frame. The orchard now consisted of rows and rows of overgrown trees.

"Mary and I would climb the trees in the summer and make ourselves sick on apples and pears. She used to get so mad at me because I could swing myself up into the branches no problem, but she always had trouble in long skirts and dresses." Ethan stared outside for a few seconds, grinning as he reminisced.

"I wish I could have met her."

"She could always make me laugh." Ethan turned away from the window and we made our way out of his old room again. A broken bed frame sat in the biggest bedroom, with an old mattress on top it. "My parents' room." Ethan sighed as we walked through the dusty space.

I peeked outside as I passed by the window and saw the old barn. Fields overtaken by weeds stretched out behind it. *Another beautiful view.* The property must have been spectacular back when Ethan and his family lived here. My chest tightened. He'd lost so much over the years, so many people he had loved were gone while he lived on. Losing my mother had been almost more than I could bear. What must it be like to lose everyone close to you?

The roof had caved in over Mary's room so we avoided checking it out and went downstairs. Back on the front porch, we sank down on the top step and gazed out over the yard.

"This house holds so many memories." Ethan pointed to the corner of the porch, "I used to sleep on a swing hanging over there in the summer, when it was too hot inside."

I squinted, trying to envision what that would have looked like.

"My mother always had my father set up our Christmas tree in the window of the parlor, so it could be seen from outside. She loved the Christmas season. Every year we would host a party for all the neighbors. One particularly harsh winter, a terrible blizzard blew in the evening of the Christmas party. Most of the neighbors were still here and my parents declared that everyone should stay until it was safe to go back to their own homes again.

"Unfortunately, one of the families had set out early, trying to get ahead of the storm. Just as everyone else was settling in on different beds and couches in our house, the eldest son of that family rode up on horseback. Their carriage had gotten stuck in the snow and, with three small girls, they were worried about trying to make it back to their farm on foot."

I studied Ethan's expression. He stared straight ahead, a faraway look on his face, as though he had gone back to that night and was re-living it.

He took a deep breath. "My father immediately formed a search party and about ten of us made our way through the blinding snow until we found the carriage. It was half-buried by windblown drifts by the time we arrived, but we dug the family out, bundled them up, and brought them back to get warmed up.

"Our neighbors ended up staying almost three days before the weather was clear enough for them to go home." There was a mixture of warmth and sadness in Ethan's voice that tugged at my heart. I could feel how much he missed his family.

"I wish I could have seen it, any of it. I'm sure the house was really beautiful back then." I slipped my hand into his, sorry that I had missed so much of Ethan's life. We sat for a while, content to be in silence.

"This is the first time I've ever brought anyone here." Ethan kept his gaze on the wild, overgrown yard.

"Really?" The corners of my mouth turned up a little. What a special privilege it was to be here at this dilapidated old house.

"When I first became a Hleo I stayed away so no one could trace me back to my family and they would be safe. After they passed it was hard to come back. My father had always dreamed of giving me this place as an inheritance one day, and when I 'died' he and my mother were heartbroken. He couldn't bear to sell the property, so the two of them stayed here the rest of their lives. Most of my family was still back in Ireland so they ended up willing the land to a distant cousin in Boston so it would stay in the Flynn family.

"My father's cousin wasn't interested in farming, but he held onto the property. For a time his family would come up here and use the property as a vacation home, until finally, sometime in the mid 1950s, the house and land were simply abandoned. The property continues to be willed to the next family member in the line, but no one is ever interested in living here or trying to fix it up. I've come back occasionally over the years to see how the house is doing. I even tried to do some maintenance and upkeep for a while, but as time has passed it's just become too much to keep up. My father would cry if he saw what has become of all his hard work." Ethan looked down at our linked hands. The sadness and regret in his voice brought tears to my eyes.

I blinked them away. "I'm glad you brought me here," I murmured. I lifted his hand to my lips and kissed the back of it. He cupped my face in his palm and leaned in for a long, comforting kiss.

"I have one more thing to show you." Ethan broke away from the kiss, but only pulled back a few inches.

I searched his eyes. What else could he possibly have to show me?

For a moment he didn't move, then he grinned and tapped my nose with one finger. "Come on." He stood and bounded down the porch stairs, then stopped and held out a hand for me.

We climbed back into the Jeep and drove off in the opposite direction we had come from. After a few twists and turns on back roads we came to a highway that led into a quaint little village, *Essex*, according to the sign. We drove through the town, past little shops, a town hall and library, a public school, and two old-looking churches. When we reached the outskirts on the other side of the town, Ethan turned down a quiet, tree-lined residential street. There were a few houses dotted along it, with expansive yards separating each. The road ended at a small gravel parking lot and Ethan pulled in and stopped the Jeep.

I figured we were at some sort of park, but as I climbed out and met Ethan at the front of the vehicle I realized it was actually a small cemetery. We made our way past rows of graves until we reached the last one where there were only four small tombstones. They were faded and cracked. A big piece had broken off the corner of one of them and was now lying in the grass. Words were etched across the front of each stone, but time and weather had rendered them almost unreadable. It took me a moment to make out what they said, but then I understood why Ethan had brought me here.

The first tombstone read Cameron Flynn 1840-1901, the next Moira Flynn 1843-1910, followed by Mary Catherine Flynn 1871-1889. My breath caught in my throat as my gaze fell on the last tombstone, Ethan Douglas Flynn 1869-1890. This was Ethan's family's final resting place, and there with the graves of his father, mother, and sister, was his own. A shudder worked its way through me. How did that feel, looking at a tombstone with your name engraved across the front of it? I reached out and touched the cold stone.

"My parents wanted to have a place they could come and remember their son, as well as their daughter, so they had a grave marker made for me and placed it beside Mary's." Ethan glanced from me to the stone.

I did the math in my head. "It's from the year you became a Hleo."

"The year I died, as far as they knew. When I told Mary's fiancé Stanley that I was going to stay with my Hleo mentor Lucien he agreed to return to the farm and undertake the difficult task of telling them I was gone. The story we decided on was that I had succumbed to illness while on our hunt for Mary's murderer. It was the simplest explanation for my disappearance. Once Stanley and I parted ways, I knew I was severing my last tie to this place. It was a decision I had been willing to make, but every once in a while I think of my old life and question whether I made the right decision."

Ethan fell into silence again. He was still as he stared at the graves, his expression unreadable.

His words tugged at my heart. I wanted to tell him how happy I was he had chosen the path he had. It had brought him to me, and I couldn't imagine my world without him. Somehow, though, the words wouldn't come.

After a moment, he seemed to shake himself, as though pulling himself back out of the past. "For a while I would come once a year to put flowers on their graves, but it's been years since I've been back here. With the time restraints that come with what I do, it's just been easier to stay away."

The sadness was back in his voice. I moved closer, until my shoulder touched his arm.

Ethan drew me close and kissed the top of my head lightly.

It was a sunny day, but the wind had picked up and the long grass around us rustled. Puffy white clouds scuttled across the sky overhead, but in the distance a sheet of dark grey threatened to envelope the sky. The temperature had dropped and snow appeared to be on its way. I would have been cold if it hadn't been for Ethan's arm around me.

After a couple of minutes, Ethan released me and we walked hand in hand back to his Jeep. He pulled open the passenger door and held it until I had settled on the front seat. Then he closed it behind me and rounded the front of the vehicle and slid behind the wheel to start the engine.

Ethan looked at me. "Hannah, it's not in my nature to open up to people, which I think you know by now. But you have to understand I was extensively trained not to reveal anything about who I am—or was—for the safety of myself and for the people I'm protecting. I've simply adopted each new identity and become that person. For years that strategy has kept me alive. But I want you to know, for your sake, I'm working on doing what doesn't come naturally to me. I know you must get frustrated with me sometimes for pulling away, or giving you silence when you want openness, but I want you to see every part of me, and to know every part of me. That's why I brought you here, so I could show you that I'm trying, even when it might seem that I'm not." Ethan kept his eyes locked on mine.

My heart melted. I reached for his hand and held it tightly. "You have no idea how much it means to me that you showed me a glimpse of your old life, the house you grew up in, and this place." I motioned to the cemetery.

He squeezed my hand. "Hannah, you are my life. After years of following orders and watching the future happen for other people, protecting them until their destiny moment came, I'm finally starting to feel as though there could be a future for me, for us. I haven't felt that in an incredibly long time. I know you're sick of hearing about the future, but when I look at you, all I see is the future and I am reassured about it." Ethan's eyes glowed. Warmth crept into my cheeks. He reached up and stroked my cheek gently, then tucked a strand of hair behind my ear.

"Thank you," I whispered as he pulled his hand away and smiled.

Ethan sat back and shifted the Jeep into reverse, and we started on our way home, driving in a comfortable silence. The sun was beginning to set; orange and pink hues streaked across the sky and stained the dark clouds. *What time is it?* I started to check my watch then lowered my arm. I didn't really care. All that mattered was this moment, not the past or even the future that suddenly seemed a lot brighter. I rested against Ethan's warm, strong arm. Peace flooded through me, a feeling I hoped would never end.

Eleven

By the time we arrived back in East Halton it was well after seven in the evening. My house was completely dark and the porch light wasn't on, which signaled that dad wasn't home yet. I checked the garage to be certain, but his usual parking spot was empty.

Once we were inside, Ethan called Simon to come over with a report on the day. I went to the kitchen to make us something to eat. We had the ingredients for roast beef sandwiches and I made one for Simon too. By the time I had the sandwiches ready and a pot of coffee brewed Simon had arrived, and I could hear the two guys talking in the other room.

"So he wasn't sure if it was his protected?" Ethan asked as I brought the sandwiches in on a platter for the guys. Ethan sat on the couch and Simon had grabbed his usual spot in the armchair.

"No. Dominic said the picture was a bit fuzzy. He wondered if we could resend it, maybe zoom in a bit of the woman's face so the facial features are clearer. I looked through our stuff at home, but it looks like it's one of Hannah's more recent images so it must still be here. Well, hello love." Simon gave me his usual customary greeting of anyone of the female sex.

"Hi Simon, sandwich?" I held up the tray.

"How did you know?" Simon happily took one off of the tray and proceeded to take a big bite.

Ethan turned to look at me. "Is your dad working late this evening? One of our Hleo contacts recognized a few of your images but there's a newer one he's not sure about. It must be in the sketchbooks that we have here. I can look for it, but I don't want to pull anything out if you dad will be back soon. It can always wait for another day."

"I'm not sure. He didn't mention anything about staying late, but then he doesn't always tell me his plans. It's possible he got delayed at work, but it is getting kind of late. He didn't leave a note, so I don't think he was seeing Rose tonight." I set the tray down on the side table. "I'll call him and see where he is." I picked up the phone and punched in his office number.

"Great idea." Ethan stood up and came around the couch to stand beside me.

The phone rang and rang. Finally Dad's voicemail picked up with the familiar message that he was currently out of the office, and would respond to the call as soon as he could. I hung up without leaving a message and dialed his cell number instead; again it rang through to his voicemail. This time I left a quick message that I was just checking in and if he could call me when he got this message it would make me feel better. "That's odd; he's been so good about being reachable lately." I frowned as I slipped my phone back into my pocket. I probably had nothing to worry about, but couldn't shake the anxious feeling in the back of my mind.

"How about if Simon does a quick scan of the school's security camera footage, just to make sure everything is all right?" Ethan squeezed my shoulder gently.

I nodded. "That would be great, thanks."

Simon stuffed the last bite of his sandwich into his mouth. "I'm on it, love," he said, his voice muffled. In spite of my concern, I smiled. As I'd learned more about the Hleo, I'd found out that Ethan was technically Simon's superior, as the Hleo who took on a persona in a protected's life was always above the technical support person. That meant Simon had to do what Ethan asked, but he never resisted or grumbled about any given request. He always seemed happy to oblige.

Simon grabbed the tablet he always carried with him out of his shoulder bag and slid it onto the coffee table. Within seconds he'd pulled up GPS coordinates and live satellite imagery of the university. He zoomed in until we could see that my father's car was still parked in its usual spot in the school parking lot. It had a dusting of snow on it and I looked out the window to see that large flakes were now swirling to the ground outside.

"There's his car, right where it should be." Simon pointed to my dad's Lexus.

"Good. Now can you tap into the school's security system and check the footage? Then we can make sure Mr. Reed is safe and just working late in his office." Ethan drummed his fingers along the back of the couch.

"Sure, I love breaking the law in the name of protection. Let's see what we've got." Simon punched away at the keyboard until he was able to bring up a menu that listed different cameras located across Hartford University's campus. He scrolled through the list and brought up the feed of a camera that showed the hallway outside of my dad's office and gave a clear shot of his door. Ethan and I crowded in on either side of Simon so the three of us could see the video clearly. It looked as though the light in Dad's office was off. The room appeared to be dark with no reflection shining through the glass or from under the door.

"Simon, can you rewind the security footage to see if it shows Hannah's dad exiting his office? Maybe he left to go to a meeting or something."

I studied Ethan, my chest tightening. There was a trace of worry in his voice. Did he think something had happened to my father?

"Just give me one moment and we'll be going in reverse." Simon's fingers flew over the keyboard again.

The time stamp on the footage started to move backwards. For a while nothing happened, but then we could see people walking backwards down the hall. Different professors and students filed past, going in and out of various offices down the hall from my father's. If I hadn't been concerned, I would have found it funny, watching them move so quickly in reverse. After about two minutes we saw what we were looking for, my father and a man retreating from the exit at the end of the hallway back into his office. The time stamp on the footage was 6:33 pm.

Simon clicked on the stop button.

Ethan circled a finger in the air. "Replay that section in the right direction now."

Simon clicked on another button.

We watched as this time my father, followed by a man I didn't recognize, left his office and hurried down the hallway. The man was a head taller than my father, with very broad shoulders and short dark hair. He looked like a football player, or maybe a bouncer. Something in their body language made my stomach lurch a little. My dad was frowning, and kept glancing back over his shoulder at the man, while the guy appeared to be subtly pushing my father forward.

"Can you rewind it, Simon, and replay it slower?" Ethan eyes were fixed on the screen.

We watched the footage three more times, each time progressively slower, before Ethan got Simon to freeze the footage right at the point the man was coming out of Dad's office.

"Simon stop, right there. Look." Ethan pointed to the man's waist.

Before Simon said anything I saw it, the muzzle of a handgun pointed at my father's back. The man had almost fully concealed the weapon, but it showed for a second on the footage. The average observer would simply see this as two colleagues leaving together instead of what is was, my father being taken at gunpoint out of his office to who knows where.

"Ethan, what…?" A wave of dizziness washed over me and I reached out to grab his arm. I needed him to explain what was going on, even though I knew he had no idea.

"It's okay, Hannah, we'll figure this out. Simon, rewind the footage further." Ethan's jaw was tight and his brow was furrowed as he stared at the screen.

Simon sent the video into reverse again, and once again my father and the horrible man moved backwards from the exit of the hallway into his office. About five minutes went by on the time stamp, and then the man came out of my father's office by himself and back-pedaled in the same direction he and Dad had gone. The man kept his head down and his face hidden, obviously aware that there were security cameras. Ethan had Simon play the footage over and over as they studied it intensely. The replays all looked the same to me; nothing stuck out as an important clue to who this guy was or what his plans were.

Ethan obviously had more experience analyzing videotape footage than I did. "Looks like he's scanning a badge to get into the faculty hallway here." He pointed to the top edge of the screen.

I narrowed my eyes to study the frozen shot. Through the window in the door that led to the faculty office hallway, I could see the guy holding something up to the wall on the other side of the door before pushing it open. "That makes sense; you need a badge to get onto the floor after regular school hours."

"Okay, we need to find out whose badge he used. It's likely the guy just lifted it off some unsuspecting professor, but there's a chance that person could give us a clue to who he is. We can check that out once we get to the university, but for now, Simon, I need you to pull the footage of them coming out of the building. Maybe we'll see them get into a vehicle, or at least find out which direction they went."

I could tell from the lines on Ethan's face that he was anxious to figure out what had happened to my dad, but he spoke with his usual composure. I forced myself to take several deep, calming breaths. Freaking out wouldn't help anyone, especially my dad.

Simon kept fiddling around with the video footage, finding a different camera to tap into, and eventually we saw my dad and the man exit out to the nearest parking lot. The man directed my father to a dark, non-descript sedan with tinted windows. My fists clenched as he stuffed my father into the front seat, pushing his head down in a manner similar to that of a police officer putting a criminal into a cruiser. How dare he manhandle my dad like that? Once Dad was in the car, the guy walked around to the driver's side, climbed in and drove off in the opposite direction my father would normally take home.

"Ethan, where do you think that guy took him? I mean, my dad doesn't even have his coat on." My heart pounded. Why would someone abduct my dad? He'd never hurt anyone in his life.

"I don't know, but I'll find out, and I will bring him back safely." Ethan wrapped his arms around me.

What would I do if something happened to my father? I didn't understand any of this. Tears welled in my eyes, but I swiped them away with the back of my sleeve. *Get a hold of yourself, Hannah.* I needed to be stronger than this; my father needed me to be stronger than this. I swallowed down the remaining emotion and pulled myself away from Ethan.

"So, what's the next step?" I asked him in a controlled voice, ready to take action.

"Simon and I need to go to the university and get into your father's office. There might be some clue there as to where this guy could have taken your father," Ethan said.

Simon stood and shoved his tablet back into the bag. The two of them strode towards the front door.

I started after them. "Wait. I'm coming too." Ethan wouldn't like it, but there was no way I was sitting at home doing nothing while my father was out there somewhere, likely completely confused and frightened.

Ethan stopped and looked at me, his green eyes dark with concern. Even before he spoke, I knew what he was going to say. "Hannah, I'm pretty sure this guy is using your father to get to you. I can't be certain what his plan is, but there is no way I am taking you anywhere near him. There are too many unknowns in all of this."

"But I don't want to be home alone. What if the guy shows up here or he has a partner?" Adam's face flashed through my mind.

Ethan drove his fingers through his hair. "Could you go to Katie's?"

"Katie and I… our fight, I don't know if I can go there." My cheeks warmed. Our argument seemed so trivial now, in light of my father's situation. I yanked my phone out of my pocket. "I'm not sure if Katie will talk to me, but I'll try." I quickly punched in her number and waited. Would she pick up when she saw it was me?

"Yes?" Katie's voice was as cold as ice.

"Hi, I was wondering if I could come over so we could talk. I need to apologize to you, but I'd really like to do it in person." I held my breath, hoping she'd immediately cave, instead of drawing the conversation out as she sometimes did when we fought.

"I don't know Hanns, I mean you really hurt my feelings," Katie muttered. Her voice had softened; she sounded like a wounded puppy. Relief flowed through me. I hated that I'd hurt her, but now that her anger had passed, I knew everything would be okay. I made my way out the front door with Ethan and Simon close behind.

"I promise I'll explain everything when I get over there." I met Ethan's gaze as we climbed into the Jeep and shook my head slightly to let him know I wasn't really going to share the truth about what was going on with Katie.

"Fine. For a little while." Katie's curiosity about why I had freaked out on her clearly outweighed her desire to sulk.

"Thanks Kate, I'll be right over." My house was already out of view behind us by the time I hung up. I gripped the seat as Ethan tore across town towards Katie's house, not because I was afraid of his driving but because I needed to hold onto something real at the moment, something solid.

My dad was missing. My world had been rocked.

Twelve

It was a tense, quiet drive as each of us was occupied with our own thoughts. The snow fell harder now, building up on the road instead of melting away. I was worried about Dad. What could this man want with him?

"Hannah, I know this is going to be difficult, but when you get to Katie's you have to act like everything is fine." Ethan was grasping the steering wheel so tightly his knuckles were white as we turned onto Katie's street.

"I think I can do that." I took a deep breath to fully compose myself.

"It's really important Katie doesn't know that anything is wrong. Once we know something, I'll call you, so try not to worry. I'm going to figure out what this guy's plan is and get your dad back. Just stay with Katie until you hear from me, okay?" A tremor worked its way through Ethan's words. Was he stressed about my dad, or at the thought of being separated from me? There hadn't been any threats in the last few months so I'd almost forgotten to worry that anything could happen to me. Now that sense of calm had been shattered.

We pulled into Katie's driveway. I reached for the door handle, but Ethan leaned over to stop me. His hand slid from my arm to the back of my head and he drew me close for an intense kiss. "Please be careful," he whispered as he broke away.

"You too." I pressed my forehead against his, hating the thought of getting out of the vehicle.

Simon cleared his throat softly in the backseat, and I pulled myself away from Ethan.

"Don't worry, love, I have his back." The steadiness in Simon's voice helped ease some of the tension tightening up my muscles and I pushed open the door and climbed out. Before I could change my mind and insist on going with them, I shut the door and plowed through the blowing snow to Katie's front porch.

Ethan's Jeep remained in park as I rang the bell, but he backed it down Katie's driveway as soon as she opened the door. Katie glanced past me to the Jeep, and lifted an eyebrow.

"My car's been acting up, and Ethan was over working on an assignment, so he offered to give me a ride." I repeated the rehearsed excuse I'd come up with on the drive over.

"An assignment, huh." Katie crossed her arms and stood in the doorway. Her voice was as cool as it had been on the phone. Would she let me in the house? After a moment, she moved back so I could step into her front hallway.

"Look Katie, I owe you a huge apology. I've been completely stressed out about the future, and some other things, and I sort of took it out on you. I'm sorry. Can you forgive me?" I held out my hands, palms up, wanting this sorted out before I even took my coat off.

Katie studied me for a second. She wasn't one to hold a grudge, and I knew my persistence in coming over to apologize in person would be hard for her to resist, but she held her original position, arms crossed with annoyed coolness on her face.

"Hannah, we have been best friends practically forever, I will completely forgive you and we can just forget your little meltdown if you answer one question for me, and I want the truth." Katie locked her dark brown eyes with mine.

I cringed inwardly. *What is she going to ask me?* Whatever it was, I would likely have to boldface lie to my best friend, since there was no way I could tell her about my ability, or why Ethan had shown up in East Halton. I desperately wanted to, but my father was missing because of all of this. That only confirmed that the less Katie knew the safer she was.

"Are you and Ethan dating?" Katie asked. She locked her jaw and stared at me as she waited for my answer.

I hesitated, but I'd been keeping this massive secret from my best friend for too long. "Yes." My voice was so low it was barely a whisper.

As soon as the word was out of my mouth, Katie jumped up in the air, grabbed my arms, and shook me. "I knew it, I knew it. Everyone else said that if something was going on you would tell people, but I knew from the way he looks at you and the way you are around him that the two of you had a secret thing going on." She squealed, releasing me for a moment, only to yank me into a hug that almost lifted me off the ground. After she let me go, I shrugged my coat off and we headed down to her basement.

As I hit the last step, something she had said struck me and I tensed. "What do you mean, the way I act around him?" I thought I had been doing a pretty good job of concealing my true feelings for Ethan, all things considered.

"Hanns, you've always been a bit closed off. Hard to read, I guess you could say, and we all accept that it's just who you are, but you seem completely open with Ethan. It's as though you've known him your whole life and you're completely comfortable allowing him inside your head." Katie placed a hand on my arm. "That's all I meant."

My muscles relaxed. I hadn't really noticed, but she was right, I had allowed Ethan into my head.

"So, why aren't the two of you telling anybody? I would have hired a skywriter to spread the word if I had snagged a guy like Ethan Flynn." Katie flopped onto the couch and propped her head on her hand.

I scrambled to come up with a good reason. I couldn't very well tell her it was because Ethan was part of an ancient organization of protectors, and that I was one of the people they were trying to protect.

"Because his parents don't want us to date." I wrinkled my nose, deciding on a distorted version of the truth. I hoped it sounded convincing, because it didn't feel convincing.

"What? Why would they have a problem with him dating someone, especially someone like you? You're smart, caring, nice, and don't forget gorgeous." Katie threw her arms up in the air as she leapt to defend my honor.

"They don't think he needs to date until he goes away to college. They're super strict, and think school should be Ethan's only focus," I explained, amazed at how easy it was to lie once I had started.

"But he's in his last year of high school, he's eighteen years old, what do they expect him to do?" Katie sounded completely shocked at the idea that anyone's parents could be so strict. I knew it was a bit of a stretch, since Ethan, even by normal standards, was an adult.

"Yeah, I know. It's not really that bad though. I'm sure they will eventually be all right with the idea, and school will be over before we know it. It's just easier this way." I shrugged.

"I guess so," Katie said finally, sounding like she was absorbing the idea, but still finding it hard to comprehend.

"Look Katie, I told you because you are my best friend and I hate the thought of keeping anything from you, but it is incredibly important that you not tell anybody. And I mean anybody, not Kristen or Heather, or even Luke." I ticked them off with my fingers as I named them.

"Hey, what are best friends for? I won't tell anybody, don't worry. I wouldn't want to do anything to jeopardize what you've got going on with Ethan. I just wanted to know the truth." Katie picked at a loose string on her sweater.

We'd been friends too long for her feigned nonchalance to fool me. She was hurt that I had held this secret from her for so long. I touched her arm. "I'm sorry I didn't tell you earlier. I've wanted to ever since we got together, but I didn't know what to do, and it seemed easier just to not tell anyone."

"It's okay, I understand." Katie nodded slowly.

We talked for another hour about Ethan and my relationship with him, and I explained why I had freaked on her. I told her about Rose and Dad, and how strange it was for him to be dating, especially my teacher. We talked about the pressure of not being sure what we wanted to go through school for, and what life after East Halton High would hold. I shared my worries about what might happen between Ethan and me, and that, although we hadn't been together that long, I couldn't imagine my life without him, which would have an impact on any decision I made. She told me she had the same worries about her and Luke.

Under different circumstances I would have loved spending time with Katie, talking through everything with her, but it was hard not to be preoccupied waiting for Ethan to contact me.

It was almost midnight when I finally felt the phone in my pocket vibrate. By that time Katie and I were watching a late night talk show in her room. She had insisted that I sleep over, and I was glad I hadn't needed to ask. I jumped off her bed. "It's Ethan," I mouthed. I ignored her teasing whistle as I left, and ducked into the dark empty office next to Katie's room. I kept the light off and sank down onto the floor by the window, the dim moonlight the only illumination in the room.

"Hello," I murmured, trying to respect that Katie's parents had already gone to bed.

"Hannah, are you okay? You're still at Katie's right?" The concern was thick in Ethan's voice.

"Yes, I'm still here, why? What happened at the university? Did you find Dad? Did you find out who this guy is?" I was firing questions off faster than he could answer, but I couldn't help myself.

"We didn't find your dad, but we did find out who took him. His name is Uri Volkov, he's a Bana."

My heart felt cold and hard suddenly, like a rock. The Bana. That possibility had been in the back of my mind, but I hadn't wanted to seriously consider it. I pressed a hand to my chest. *So all of this is my fault.*

"Hannah?" The urgency in Ethan's voice called me back.

"I'm here." The words came out in a raspy whisper and I cleared my throat. "What do you know about him?"

"Just that he's only been involved with them for about fifteen years, which is still rookie status. Probably why Simon and I didn't recognize him. From what we found out it looks like he's trying to make a name for himself within the organization."

"Do you know where he took Dad?" I tapped my fingers on my knee nervously.

"Not exactly. Simon found a list of aliases in Uri's file. He used one of them on a long-term rental at a dive motel halfway between Hartford and New Haven just off the highway, about forty miles away. We're on the interstate headed there right now." A whooshing sound, as if they were passing another vehicle, sounded in the background. Was Simon driving or was Ethan using hands free as he spoke to me?

"Well, that's a start. Was there much else at the university to help you? Do you know whose key card the guy used?"

Ethan sighed. "We do. It belonged to Paige White."

"Paige," I breathed in a terrified whisper. Adam's mysterious and deadly partner, the one who had posed as my dad's teaching assistant in order to get to me, was back. And if she was back then there was a good chance that Adam was back. That was something I had been dreading. No wonder Ethan wanted to make sure I was at Katie's house. A sudden thought sent chills through me. Was I putting my best friend in danger too? It would be just like Adam to cause a distraction so he could get to me. I peered out the office window into Katie's dark backyard, and shivered at the thought of someone waiting in the shadows for the right opportunity to strike.

"Do you think Adam–?"

"I don't know, there haven't been any signs that he's part of this, but after what happened at the Masks Gala he may have chosen to play it safe and stick close to the sidelines on this one," Ethan replied.

"But for sure Paige is involved?" A sick feeling churned in my stomach. Paige was evil. Those silver eyes flashed in my mind. If she had something to do with my father's disappearance, he could be in even greater danger than I'd thought.

"Yeah, she must be. I guess the security at the school isn't the most efficient at updating their system, so her card from when she was your dad's teaching assistant was still active."

"What is her issue with you? Why did she come back? Adam said you and she have bad blood between you." I suddenly remembered that when he had me trapped in the library Adam mentioned Paige had her own reasons for helping him seek revenge on Ethan.

"Hannah, that's ancient history, and we don't really have time—"

"Actually we've got a good twenty miles to go mate, and I have to say I'm curious too." Simon's voice came over the phone, confirming that I was on speaker phone.

I held my tongue, waiting to see what Ethan would do. He sighed. "There are two types of Bana. There are those that used to be

Hleo and switched over, like Adam. These we call pure Bana, because they are branded with Hleo serum. Then there are those that started out as Bana. We call these synthetic Bana because they are branded with the serum that Isaac, the original leader of the Bana, came up with. His serum is a very close facsimile to the Hleo's. Bana don't age, don't need air or food to survive, and won't succumb to disease like Hleo, but there is a slight difference in the copied serum in that it makes the synthetic Bana vulnerable to one thing the Hleo aren't – poison."

I blinked, trying to absorb this new information. What did it have to do with Ethan and Paige?

"Paige was romantically involved with another member of the Bana, Julian Monteiro. The two of them helped Adam track down Lucien so he could kill him. After I dealt with Adam, I went looking for them, still seeking to avenge Lucien's unjust death. I began tracking them, hunting them like the animals they were, and eventually found them hiding out on a private tropical island together." Ethan paused for a moment and I swallowed hard, my mouth dry as I took in the anger in his voice, the horror of the story.

"They had let their guards down, thinking they had managed to disappear off the grid completely. I broke into their vacation villa one night, and found the perfect opportunity to deal with them. A fancy meal was laid out on the table. There were lit candles and glasses of wine, it was all very romantic.

"I had managed to obtain a vile of very strong poison from a tribe in New Guinea. While they were otherwise occupied in the bedroom, I divided the vile of poison between their wine glasses and returned to my hiding place in the ceiling. I waited for them to come and drink so I could be sure the poison worked. I watched as they arrogantly toasted each other and the life they had established together, and took a sip of the wine. Julian immediately clutched his throat and began coughing and choking, but Paige wasn't affected by the poison. She tried desperately to revive him, but Julian was dead within seconds. I escaped from the building just as she began tearing it apart, trying to discover who the intruder was and what had happened."

Ethan paused. The engine of the Jeep revved in the background. *Is he passing someone again or is the emotion of reliving this memory causing him to drive more aggressively?*

"It wasn't until I got back to Veridan that I learned a crucial and well-buried bit of truth. Paige had been a Hleo at one point, many years before I ever entered the society. After Paige assisted in Lucien's death, her former partner, out of loyalty to her, tampered with her file. He made it look as though Paige was a synthetic Bana in order to draw me out, knowing that I would likely come after her and attempt to poison her. That Hleo was removed from service after his misconduct was discovered, but it was too late for me. It didn't take Paige long to discover who had killed Julian, and she is now as determined to kill me as I am to kill her."

It took me a moment to find my voice. When I did, all that would come out was a whispered, "Ethan." I hoped he could hear in that one word how much I cared about him, how worried I was that he could be hurt. I was glad that, as a pure Hleo, he couldn't be poisoned, but the Hleo did have other weaknesses. Although they weren't susceptible to death by natural causes, they could still be murdered, and I shuddered at the thought of him being shot, beaten, or stabbed.

"Hannah, I love the people in my life fiercely. I can't bear to let injustice against them go unanswered, it's just who I am. I know that what I've told you probably seems extreme…" The words spilled out, as though Ethan was rushing to justify how he could act so ruthlessly.

"I see why Paige has it in for you." I tried to make my voice light so he would know I was trying to accept what he was telling me. I was still getting my head around the Hleo world. I had come to realize that killing was an unfortunate but necessary part of the job. It was still hard for me to think of my wonderful, sweet, caring Ethan as capable of such calculated and violent acts though.

"You don't think less of me?" Ethan asked quietly.

"Ethan, everyone should have someone in their lives as completely devoted to them, and willing to fight for them, as you are."

"Thank you." He sounded relieved, almost grateful.

"I don't think less of you either, mate." Simon chimed in through the speaker and a small grin spread across my lips. *Good old Simon.*

"Thanks, Simon." Amusement softened the strain in Ethan's voice a little.

"No problem. By the way, you're going to want to take the next exit," Simon said, and I knew that storytelling time was over.

"We have to go, we're getting close to the motel," Ethan's tone had made an abrupt transition to professional

"Let me know as soon as you can if you find my dad, and please be careful." I took a deep breath; I didn't want to hang up. As long as I was in contact with Ethan I felt like we were both secure, but when we were separated from each other a sense of vulnerability enveloped me like a cloud.

"You too. Stay with Katie." Ethan voice's softened again.

"I will." I hung up and sat for a second, trying to compose myself and compartmentalize the story Ethan had just told me before I joined Katie again. Switching from the world of secrets, revenge, and murder to the world of typical high school senior was difficult, but I squared my shoulders and plastered a smile on my face as I went to rejoin Katie.

"He just wanted to wish me a good night, and let me know he probably won't be at school tomorrow." I settled in on the foam mattress Katie had set up for me while I was talking to Ethan, but kept my phone securely in my hand.

"Awww, Hanns. That's so cute. I'm glad we can finally talk about it." Katie tugged the ponytail holder from her crazy blonde curls and shook them out before lowering her head onto her pillow.

"Me too." I clutched the covers across my chest, needing to feel some sense of security.

We called it a night shortly after, but I ended up staring at Katie's ceiling in the dark, unable to drift off to sleep. Ethan's story kept playing over in my mind. He had gone to extreme lengths to punish Paige for her actions, and it seemed she was just as determined to repay him for his. It was all so much more intense than I was used to and I was worried about how her vendetta would play into the treatment of my dad. I flopped onto my side and punched my pillow. *If anything happens to him I'll never forgive myself.* Why did Paige and this thug need to kidnap him in the first place? What could they possibly hope to accomplish?

Ethan hadn't said as much, but I could tell this new development troubled him too. Paige should be coming after me for revenge, not my father. None of this made any sense.

Thirteen

I awoke to the sound of Katie's alarm clock buzzing just above my head. I had dozed off at some point in the night, and I jolted upright to flip it off. Katie groaned and mumbled under her pillow—something about needing just five more minutes of sleep—while I felt around for my cell phone. I had fallen asleep with it in my hand in case Ethan called or texted, and found it under my pillow. I glanced at the screen. No new messages. My heart beat faster. Why hadn't he gotten in touch with me? Was that a good sign or a bad one? I fired off a text, asking him for an update.

His reply came within seconds: Still looking and didn't want to wake you unnecessarily. We will find him. Stay with Katie for now!

I didn't want to stay with Katie. I wanted to be with Ethan and Simon on the hunt for my dad. I texted back: Why don't you come get me? I could help with the search.

Ethan's response was immediate: NO, you need to go to school. It's the safest place for you right now.

I inhaled slowly, my fingers on the screen ready to type in an argument, but then I stopped. *I don't want to add to his stress.* I sighed as I typed: You win, but please keep me in the loop.

I promise, was Ethan's reply.

I set my phone down and started getting ready for school. Katie got up not long after I finished dressing. She threw on some clothes and pulled her unruly hair into a ponytail. I followed her downstairs to grab a bite to eat before leaving for school, amazed at how good Katie could look with such little effort.

It felt as though time were moving backwards. Lunchtime couldn't come fast enough. When it finally did, I found a quiet corner in the library to text Ethan for an update. Ethan and Simon had arrived at the small, dingy motel Uri had checked into. It looked as though he had been staying there as he prepared whatever plan he had for my dad. They discovered from the desk clerk that Uri had been renting the room for over two weeks, but he hadn't returned to the room the night before. Ethan and Simon had found a few clues within Uri's belongings and now they were on their way to check out another lead.

Ethan and I texted through most of the lunch hour. I asked question after question. trying to get a feel for how close they really were to finding my dad, but Ethan just kept reassuring me that they would find him.

I bit my lip. Why was he being so vague? I shoved back my frustration. *Trust him, Hannah. If anyone in the world can find Dad, it's Ethan.*

I kept my head down during art class, silently pleading that Ms. Woods wouldn't ask me where my father was. Thankfully she was busy with other students and she left me alone. I managed to get out of class without exchanging a word with her.

By the end of the day I was exhausted from worry. I knew that it couldn't be a good thing my dad had been missing for almost twenty-four hours, and I couldn't help but start to think the worst. What would I do if I was officially an orphan? The thought terrified me, and I took a steadying breath as I tried to push it away.

"So, what time are you coming tonight?" Ryan sidled up to my locker.

I leapt in the air. I had been staring blankly down the hall, and hadn't noticed him walk up.

"Whoa, you're jumpy today Hanns, what's up?" Ryan's eyes were wide as he took a step back.

"Sorry, I wasn't paying attention, what were you saying?"

"I asked what time you're coming tonight. You know, to Kristen's cottage."

"Oh right, well I don't know if I can make it tonight…"

"What! You have to come. There is no other option here." Katie strode up to us from down the hallway, opened her locker, and tossed her books in carelessly.

"It's just that–"

She waved a hand to cut me off. "I gave you a ride to school today. I won't drive you home unless you promise to come tonight. If I have to, I will throw you in the back of my car, drive you up there right now, and leave you there until everyone else shows up."

I held both palms up to her. "Okay Katie, you win." I didn't want to go, but I knew Ethan wouldn't be pleased with the idea of me sitting at home waiting for a call or text from him, especially if all of my friends had gone off to some cabin and weren't close by for safety in numbers.

"Just drop me off at my place to grab some clothes and my car, and then I'll head back over to your house and I can drive us both to the cottage." I reached into my locker, pulled out the books I would need for the weekend, and shut the door before following her and Ryan down the hallway.

"I thought your car was giving you issues. I can drive if you want. My mom said it's not a big deal to borrow her car." Katie pushed through the door leading out to the parking lot and she, Ryan, and I walked towards her mom's black Chevy sedan.

"I'll see you guys up there." Ryan took off for the bus stop while Katie unlocked the car doors.

"My car can handle the trip up there," I insisted. I wouldn't tell Katie, but I wanted a vehicle in case I heard from Ethan and needed to make a quick exit.

"Okay, if you're sure."

We drove the short distance to my house, Katie chatting the entire way. When she pulled up to the curb, I jumped out. One hand gripping the top of the door, I turned to lean back in. "I should be at your house in twenty minutes or so. If I'm going to be any longer than that, I'll call you." I couldn't explain to her that I needed her to know that, on the off chance someone was waiting to attack me at home. She nodded, apparently not picking up on any undercurrent of meaning in my words.

Once Katie was gone, I ran to my room and packed a bag. *I hate that I no longer feel safe in my own home.* It was too quiet, almost eerie, as though there was danger lurking around every corner, although that could easily have been my imagination playing tricks on me. I texted Ethan again: Any luck finding him? If you came and picked me up, I might be able to help.

Ethan's response was almost immediate: We are over two hours away, looks like we're closing in on him. You're still with Katie, right?

I winced. Could he sense, somehow, that I wasn't following his very strict instructions at the moment? His text wasn't an outright refusal to my request, but clearly he wasn't coming for me.

I bit my lip as my fingers tapped quickly across the screen: I'm just packing a bag and then picking up Katie. It's Kristen's cottage weekend. I forgot all about it, but we'll be up there if you need me for any reason.

Ethan's response: Please meet up with Katie as quickly as possible. I'll text when I know more. Try to have fun with everybody.

It was a fine recommendation, but until Dad was home and safe there was no way I would be able to relax and have fun. I looked out my window. The sun was shining, but it had snowed all night and the backyard glistened with a fresh blanket of white.

Please be careful, I sent back to him.

You too, was his instant reply.

I frowned as I slipped my phone back into my pocket. The longer Ethan and I were separated, the stronger the feeling of being exposed grew. I finished throwing a change of clothes into my overnight bag and ran back downstairs.

I drummed my fingers along the top of steering wheel as I drove over to Katie's house, my forehead creased. It felt as though Ethan and Simon were falling further and further down a rabbit hole. I just hoped that my father would be safely waiting at the other end.

The cottage we were heading to sat on the opposite side of Lake Pocotoa from East Halton, a little over a half hour drive along the shoreline. The woods were thicker and the cottages sparser on that side of the lake, with more land stretching between each one. Kristen's parents' cottage had been in her father's family for three or four generations, and each generation had added their own addition to the structure so that it was now a substantially-sized building with a patchwork configuration.

Katie and I pulled into the driveway and grabbed our bags, then made our way down the stone path and into the post and beam building. The living room had a cathedral ceiling and a wall of windows that looked out over the lake.

Carly, Megan, and Samantha, three other school friends, stood in the kitchen with Heather, preparing various snacks.

"Hey guys, where is everyone?" Katie asked as she and I walked through the sunken living room space to the kitchen area.

"The boys have already hooked up some video game in the den, and Kristen's giving Mark a tour." Heather pointed towards the French doors that led out to the backyard. Kristen and Mark stood together on the deck, looking very cozy with his arm around her waist. Mark was a year younger than the rest of us, and at first we had given Kristen a hard time about that, since she usually had her sights set on older guys, but he was really nice, and fit in with our group well.

From her hand gestures I could tell she was explaining to him how big the property was. Off the deck the backyard sloped down at a fairly sharp angle to meet up with the lake. Wooden steps had been constructed into the side of the hill and led right onto a long dock used to moor Kristen's parents' boat, and for jumping off of into the water in the summer.

Katie and I made our way down one of the hallways that broke off from the main area, towards the guest bedrooms. We passed by the guys. Ryan and Luke were there, as well as Tristan and Bradley, two of their friends from the school's volleyball team. None of the four of them even looked up as we lugged our bags by them.

"Isn't he so romantic?" Katie rolled her eyes at her boyfriend's inattentiveness.

"It must be an interesting game." I followed her into the last bedroom in the hall, since the rest already had stuff in them, and dumped my overnight bag on the bed.

"That wouldn't matter. I need a relationship like you have with Ethan. He's completely wrapped up in you."

"Katie!" I shot a look at the open doorway, hoping no one had heard her.

She winced and pursed her lips. "Oops, sorry. Not another word from here on out, I promise." She held up her fingers in a scout's honor fashion, and I shook my head.

After we dropped our things in the guest room we wandered back out into the hallway. Katie breezed by the room where the guys were, obviously trying to show Luke she was annoyed, but I stopped and poked my head in the door. "Hey guys, how's the game going?"

"Tristan must seriously have no life because he is killing us," Ryan said as he jammed and mashed the buttons on the controller, his eyes glued to the television screen.

I looked over to see that it was a shooting game, and laughed. "Literally." I motioned to the screen.

"Is Ethan coming?" Luke hit the pause button and all four guys looked up at me expectantly.

"Um no, his grandma's sick, so his family's gone to be with her for the day." I tapped my finger on the doorframe. *Really hate lying to my friends*. "What about Trish?"

Ryan's face fell. "Her parents wouldn't let her come because it was an overnight with guys and girls."

"That's too bad; we'll have to do something all together when we get back," I suggested, and he perked up.

I let the guys get back to their game and walked out to the living room area where the girls were milling around. Heather had two big bowls of chips in her hands and was making her way towards the couches. Samantha and Carly followed her, carrying salsa, dip, and a huge bowl of popcorn.

Kristen and Mark came back inside shortly after we'd sat down. Kristen flopped down on the couch beside me while Mark went off to find the boys. I tried to stay in the conversation, but now that the sun had set, and we were heading into the second night of not having any idea where my father could be, or whether he was unharmed, I found it nearly impossible not to obsess. I wanted to call Ethan, to hear his voice, but I also didn't want to bother him since he had told me he and Simon were closing in on their target. I kept my fingers tightly clasped around the phone in my pocket, on the off chance he tried to contact me.

Half an hour later, I was ready to scream from the effort of making small talk when my dad was in danger. *Why hasn't Ethan called or texted me? I have to call him*. I was about to stand up and go to my bedroom when the guys all stampeded past us, heading for the back deck.

"What's going on?" Kristen demanded to know as we whirled around in our seats and watched them run outside.

"Luke dared Tristan to go jump in the lake, and now they're all going." Mark stopped by the French doors, as the rest started down the deck stairs in the direction of the lake.

"Are you serious? The lake is practically frozen over, what are they thinking?" Heather pushed her glasses up on her nose.

We all scrambled off the couches and ran to the windows for a better view. Luke, Tristan, and Bradley had stripped down to their boxers and were running to the end of the wooden dock. Ryan was still struggling out of his sweater at the bottom of the stairs.

"Luke, don't be stupid, I'm not taking you to the hospital when you get hypothermia," Katie yelled out the door. The guys all stopped just at the edge of the dock; clearly no one was willing to be the first to leap.

"Looks like you're having a little trouble, Ryan," Heather called out. We all laughed as he finally got stripped down enough to join the rest of the guys.

We watched for a few minutes, waiting to see if anyone would be brave—or stupid—enough to jump in. It looked like they were going to chicken out, and I couldn't blame them. I hated being cold, and the thought of even touching a toe in that icy water gave me shivers.

"Come on, they're not going to do it." Katie walked away from the window.

I was about to follow when the guys all let out a huge war cry and jumped into the water at the same time. No sooner had they hit the surface than they let out a simultaneous yelp, scrambled out of the lake, and ran back up to the cottage.

Kristen wouldn't let them back inside until she'd given them towels to dry off with, but soon we were all gathered in the living room. The guys had thrown their clothes back on, but were still shivering, even under blankets. Katie rubbed Luke's arms, while the other guys tried to convince the girls to help them warm up too.

"I can't believe you didn't join us, man," Luke said to Mark, who had curled up comfortably on a love seat with his arm casually slung around Kristen.

"That's because he's not an idiot." Kristen narrowed her eyes and cocked her head to the side. Mark just grinned.

While my female friends all took turns giving the guys little jabs over their stupidity, I willed the phone in my pocket to vibrate.

"Hey Hanns, I didn't know your dad was in the Mafia." Ryan reached a hand through the blanket he had tucked tightly around him. He grabbed a handful of popcorn and began munching on it.

My head snapped up at the mention of my dad, but I worked to keep my voice even. "What do you mean?"

"Calm down Hanns, I'm just joking. Kristen, Heather, Mark, and I saw your dad heading toward that cottage at the end of Bayer's Road with this tough-looking guy. You know that big, creepy cottage we joked had been bought by the Mafia last year? The one where the renovations were done so quickly and the only vehicles we ever see drive up there are those town cars with the tinted windows? That's all I meant."

I did know the cottage he was talking about. It was located on the dead end road that connected to the one Kristen's cottage was on. It was a huge, two-story building that looked well over a hundred years old. There had always been something ominous about the property and since it had sold in the fall my friends and I had all speculated about who could have bought it.

"When did you see him?" I leaned against the back of the couch, attempting to appear relaxed.

"The four of us came up yesterday to air out the cottage and drop off food and stuff, and he drove by sometime last night, just as we were about to head home, so maybe around eight? Why, did he tell you he was doing something else?" Ryan's eyebrows rose.

I looked around and realized all my friends were watching our exchange with obvious interest. "No, I knew that he was busy with another professor, I just didn't realize they were going to be in this area." I waved my hand dismissively, hoping my excuse sounded legit. I couldn't get up now without arousing suspicion, but I was desperate to go call Ethan to let him know where my dad was, or had been last night, so he could come and save him.

"It's funny that he was right up the road. It's sort of comforting to know that the house isn't owned by the Mafia. I mean, your dad would never be mixed up in anything scandalous, he's such a gentleman." Kristen tugged Mark's arms around her a little tighter and snuggled against him.

"That's true." I pictured my Dad. *Please let him be okay.*

Luckily the topic of conversation changed, and I was able to excuse myself to go to the bedroom Katie and I shared. I kept the lights off and sank down on the edge of the bed. My leg jiggled nervously as I dialed Ethan's number and waited for him to pick up. Instead, the phone beeped to signal the call couldn't be completed due to no cell phone reception. I stared at the screen, hoping I had heard wrong. I hadn't.

Pacing at the end of the bed, I bit my lip and tried to decide what to do. For all I knew, Ethan and Simon had already found my dad but weren't able to communicate that to me because I couldn't receive texts. But what if Ethan hadn't discovered where Dad was being held yet? He said he and Simon were two hours away, but if Ryan was right, my dad was just down the road. I couldn't very well sit around and do nothing when he might be minutes away from me.

Ethan would be angry, but I had to go check out the property myself. I would be extremely careful to make sure no one saw me, but if I could confirm that my dad was actually being held there, then I would find a way to pass that information along to Ethan. No sense in dragging him away from his search efforts if my dad had been moved somewhere else and he and Simon were about to track him down.

I came back into the living room, where everyone was now watching a movie. The guys all seemed to have finally recovered from their swim, and were happily munching on snacks as they stared at the screen.

"Hey everybody, I've just been hit with a really bad headache, I think I'm going to go home." I walked into the living room, rubbing my temples to sell the excuse.

Katie jumped up. "Are you sure? What if you just laid down for awhile? Maybe it will pass." She rubbed my arm lightly, her voice full of concern.

"It's pounding pretty badly; I think it would be better if I slept in my own bed tonight. I'll call you as soon as I get home, and I'll come back tomorrow if I feel better, I promise." Once again, I needed Katie to expect my call. That way if something went wrong, someone would be wondering where I was.

"Well… I guess, if you're sure." Katie took a small step back.

"Thanks Kate." I grabbed my bag and said good-bye to everyone. They all waved from their places on the couches, while Katie walked me to the door.

“This isn’t about Ethan, is it?” Katie grabbed my elbow to stop me. She spoke in hushed tones but I looked past her to make sure no one was listening to us.

My eyes widened. “What are you talking about?”

“I mean, you don’t have like a secret plan to meet up with him or something, do you? Because you could just tell everyone, you honestly don’t need to be sneaking around. No one here will let it get back to Ethan’s parents.” Katie’s dark eyes studied my face intently.

“No, Ethan’s a couple hours away from here, honest. I just have a headache, like I said.”

“If you say so.” She didn’t sound convinced as she let go of my elbow and gripped both of my shoulders. “Come back tomorrow, please.”

“As long as my head stops pounding, I’ll be back.” I kept my eyes locked with hers and she nodded.

Once Katie let me go, I climbed into my car and sat for a moment, working up the courage I needed for what I was about to do. I tried Ethan’s cell phone again, maybe there would be at least a little reception outside, closer to the lake, but the annoying out of range beep let me know that there was no way of getting a hold of him.

This is it. I started the car, silently praying that I wasn’t about to make the worst mistake of my life.

Fourteen

I pulled out of the driveway, hoping that Katie wasn't watching from the door and could see me turning in the opposite direction of home. I drove, headlights off, towards Bayers Road, trying to decide what to do. It was dark in the forest, but the moon was out. *Just like the night Adam dragged me through the woods to the library.* I shuddered as I remembered the fear coursing through my veins at the thought that I was going to die.

Thinking of Adam made me wonder again if he was connected to all of this. We hadn't seen or heard anything from him, but now that Paige had resurfaced it seemed certain Adam couldn't be far behind. Ethan had assured me there was no way Adam was going to get to me. He and Simon were being extra vigilant in their protection duties. Still, as I maneuvered down the gravel road I wondered if I should be more worried.

I tried to force Adam out of my head and focus on where I was, and what I had to do. I didn't want to needlessly put myself in danger, but this was my father. I couldn't just sit around doing nothing if there was anything I could do to help him. I drove up the dirt road—really more of a path—slowly, the car bumping and shuddering as it rolled over loose gravel. When the house came into view I veered onto the shoulder, climbed out of the car, and popped the trunk to look for something I could use to defend myself, should the need arise. I rooted around and found a tire iron. I had never actually had to use it before, especially not as a weapon, but it had a good weight and felt like it could do some damage. I quietly lifted it out of the trunk and started up the road, staying close to the edge of the forest and as hidden by the trees as possible. My car's dashboard thermometer had read twenty-nine degrees, and I wished I'd worn a proper winter coat instead of the lightweight pea coat I'd thrown on earlier.

Two stone pillars rose up on either side of the end of the driveway, lamps positioned on the top of them. Thankfully they weren't lit, and I was still shrouded in darkness as I started up the long driveway.

The house was built into the hillside, set back a ways from the road on a steep incline. I took a deep breath and headed to the edge of the yard where there was a scattering of overgrown trees, brush, and rocky mini-embankments. I scampered from one tree to the next, hoping to avoid any surveillance that might be on the property. As I got closer to the house, I slowed down and watched my feet, careful to avoid walking on any branches or twigs that would snap and echo. It took me a bit, but I finally made it near the house. The trees grew thicker here, as if to shelter the building, or keep it from being seen, and I was able to stay hidden in the woods while getting really close to the house.

A soft glow shone from the window on the side of the house I was approaching, and I made my way towards it. When I reached the window ledge, I stood on my tippy toes and carefully peered in, hoping to see my father. I slapped my hand over my mouth, and still had to use all my self-control not to gasp. Dad wasn't there but the man who had held a gun to him, Uri Volkov, stood in the middle of the room, a cell phone pressed to his ear. He was playing with a lighter, clicking the metal cover open and closed as he talked. I don't know why, but I hadn't actually expected to see him. I was sure Ryan must have been mistaken.

The room Uri stood in looked like a parlor. A window to my right looked out onto the front yard, and a fireplace had been built against the wall to my left. Two cream-colored antique sofas in front of it created a sitting area. The light came from a lamp sitting on a table against the wall behind Uri. A doorway in that wall led into a hallway and a set of stairs.

He was alone. What did that mean? Was my father in a different part of the house, or had he been moved? *Please let it be the first one.* I backed away from the window. What should I do now? A slight movement of air behind me lifted the hair on the back of my neck. *Someone's here.*

I didn't think. I just swung the tire iron around as hard as I could, making direct contact with the person behind me. The figure yelped in pain and stumbled forward, into the glow of the window.

"Simon!" I gasped and dropped the tire iron.

He doubled over, clutching his arm.

I reached out a hand, but he shifted away from me.

"Hannah, what in the world are you doing here?" Simon hissed, as he straightened up to look at me.

"Kristen's parents' cottage is just down the road. Ryan thought he saw my dad drive by there last night, and I had to come see if he was here. How did you find this place?" I lowered my voice to a whisper to match his, worried that we may have been heard.

"We found out that the Bana bought this property last fall. They have so many shell companies that look legitimate from the surface that it's hard to keep track of them all. If we'd known about this place right from the start we could have saved a lot of time and just come here, but it took a while to track down the information. Hannah, do you know how incredibly dangerous this is? Ethan is going to kill you." Simon rubbed his arm. "Nice shot, by the way."

I winced. "I'm sorry. I know coming here wasn't my most brilliant move, but I had to do something. Where is Ethan?" I scanned the surrounding woods, figuring he must be close by. I wasn't exactly sure how he was going to react to seeing me, but I had a feeling he wouldn't jump for joy.

"He's on the other side of the house, trying to spot where they are keeping your dad." He'd barely gotten the words out before there was a slight rustling in the bushes. Simon sidestepped so that he was between me and the source of the sound. I appreciated his attempt to protect me, but my heart began to race. A second after we heard the noise, Ethan's face appeared in the dim light from the window, and from the look on it I could tell he was not pleased.

"Hi," I whispered, shifting my gaze to the surrounding woods. The intensity of his stare was too much for me, and my face grew warm.

I could feel his eyes on me, forcing me to look at him again. "Hannah, what were you thinking?"

"I found out Dad was being held here and I tried to call you and tell you but I couldn't get a hold of you because there's no reception out here…" *Lame, Hannah.* How could I possibly justify why I had decided to take on this extremely dangerous bad guy by myself?

"Hannah." Ethan exhaled slowly. He drove his fingers through his dark hair in frustration. Clearly he would have loved to tell me off for my reckless decision, but it would be unprofessional to do so in front of Simon. Besides, he needed to stay focused on the task at hand, getting my father back safely.

"Have they hurt him?" I glanced up at the window. My forehead creased. Even though we were talking in hushed tones I was worried that Uri could hear us.

"I'm not sure. They obviously took him for a reason, so they must need him alive. I don't think we'll find out their motive for capturing him, though, until we talk to your dad." Ethan's gaze darted towards the window and then back to me. His tone still carried a controlled anger, and I swallowed hard.

"Um guys, I hate to interrupt, but it looks like Mr. Macho is on the move; he's not in the room anymore." Simon pointed at the window. I stood on my tiptoes again and stared into the now-empty parlor room.

Ethan tugged me to him, so that I was tightly secured against his chest with his arm around me. He and Simon did a quick scan of our surroundings, presumably to make sure the guy hadn't crept up to us in the dark. I strained to hear a sound but the woods were quiet. Ethan released me, but still stood so that we were within inches of each other.

"I didn't see anyone else in the house. I think we can slip inside undetected if we go through the back entrance off the kitchen." Ethan took my hand and started walking around to the other side of the house.

"Assuming he hasn't gone to make himself a cup of tea." Simon fell in step behind us.

"Right." Ethan gave him a wry nod.

We made it to the back door and I watched as he silently jimmied the lock and the door swung open. I bit my lip. Would an alarm go off and give us away? We waited for a moment. Obviously Ethan was wondering the same thing, but the house remained silent.

Ethan and Simon signaled to each other with their hands what the plan was to be as we entered into the empty kitchen. Ethan led the way, keeping me just behind him so that I was always within arm's reach. Simon brought up the rear, also staying close, so that we created a sandwich-type configuration. All the lights were off in the back half of the house, with only a dim glow coming from down the hallway where the front room was. The creepiness level of the situation was off the charts. *I really hope this Uri guy isn't waiting in the shadows to attack us.*

We cautiously made our way from the kitchen out into the hallway. The first door we passed on our left led into an empty living room. Straight in front of us was the entryway. A set of stairs on the right, the same stairs I had seen through the window, ran alongside the hallway. That meant the parlor was just ahead on the right. The room the light was coming from.

We crept to the edge of the stairs and crouched down so we were still out of sight from the parlor. Ethan signaled to Simon that he would check out the room, and Simon should go upstairs to look for my father. Simon gave a slight nod, and slipped past us to sneak up the stairs. I stayed right behind Ethan as he moved to the doorway and scanned the room before taking a cursory step into the parlor.

I peered around him. The room was empty and Ethan's shoulders relaxed. I exhaled in relief. I wasn't exactly sure what I had been expecting but I *was* sure that I didn't want to get involved in a confrontation with that scary-looking guy.

An arm suddenly wrapped around my waist and yanked me backwards, ripping my hand from Ethan's. A small cry of surprise and fear escaped from my lips as Ethan whirled around and instantly assumed attack stance.

Something cold and sharp pressed against my neck.

"It is a rookie mistake bringing the girl here. I had heard that the great Ethan Flynn was a far more worthy adversary than this. It is Ethan, isn't it?" The man who had kidnapped my father held me close enough that his breath was warm on my neck. I detected a Russian accent in his sneering tone.

My heart pounded. "I'm sorry, Ethan." The words came out in a raspy whisper. I stood frozen, terrified to move in case the knife dug farther into my skin. Uri's grasp tightened around me, and fear rose up from the pit of my stomach into my throat.

"Let her go," Ethan demanded through gritted teeth.

"I don't think so. You have made this very easy for me. I thought I was going to have to ransom her father to have a chance at getting close to her, but instead you have delivered her right into my hands. Besides, she seems like a girl you could have a little fun with." Uri's hand slipped under my jacket and slid ever so slightly up my stomach, closer to my chest. I tried not to be sick as I thought of the possible activities he could have in mind for me.

"Don't you dare touch her, you piece of garbage," Ethan growled and took a step towards us.

"Temper, temper. I think you are more to this man than just a protected, aren't you? Another mistake on his part," Uri taunted in my ear. "This is fun, but we should get going. Alexander is very interested in meeting you." Uri backed into the doorway, dragging me along with him. I worked to stay on my feet.

"Don't take another step or it will be the last move you ever make." Ethan advanced slowly, keeping the gap between us tight, his green eyes blazing. But it was an empty threat. I knew it, and no doubt the guy behind me knew it too. Ethan would never risk my life by lunging at Uri, especially when he had a knife to my throat.

I desperately looked around for anything I could use to distract him or fight him off, but besides the lamp on the table there was nothing.

"I really can't see why I should listen to you. I have all the chips and you have nothing." Uri laughed menacingly and continued backing up, so that we were in the hallway.

"He has me," a voice declared from behind us.

Uri jolted hard against me. The knife slipped from my throat and the arm that had held me tight went slack.

I lunged away from him and spun around.

Uri's left arm flailed as he attempted to reach for the blade sticking out of his shoulder, rendering his right arm useless.

I caught a glimpse of Simon behind him.

Before Uri had a chance to pull the knife out, Ethan rushed him, pushing me to the side in one motion and attacking the big Russian with the next. With his useless arm, the guy couldn't put up much of a fight, and in seconds Ethan and Simon had wrestled him to the ground. Ethan clambered on top of him, pinning both arms down at his sides with his knees, apparently unconcerned by the man's groan of pain.

He clutched Uri's hair tight in his fist and pounded his head against the old wooden floor. "Where is Richard Reed? What does Alexander want with Hannah?"

I tensed, ready to run to wherever my father was being held the second Uri disclosed the location, but with every sickening thump of his head Uri simply laughed and refused to answer.

Ethan had delivered quite a few good blows while they were fighting, and Uri was bleeding from his forehead and his mouth. His eyes rolled up. Clearly he was only one or two blows away from blacking out altogether. A movement at his side caught my eye. His left hand crept toward the pocket of his pants.

"Ethan, watch out!"

Before Ethan could stop him, Uri had tugged his lighter from his pocket. He wrenched his arm out from under Ethan's knee, clicked open the lighter, and held it to the corner of the sheer lacy curtains that framed the window. They caught fire immediately, as though they had been dosed in lighter fluid.

Uri lay on the floor laughing a menacing, half-crazed cackle, as flames danced above his head and spread to the fading wallpaper. Ethan gave him one more hard knock and he went silent. Even so, Ethan eyed him suspiciously, as though skeptical that Uri really was unconscious, before getting up and stalking across the room to join Simon and me in the doorway.

"Ethan, what are we going to do?" The fire worked to consume the parlor. He slid a protective arm around me to shield me from the flames.

"We have to get out of here." He directed me towards the hallway.

"But Ethan, my dad." I turned to Simon, hoping he had found him.

Simon shook his head. "He wasn't upstairs," he shouted. The flames were crackling loudly, and it wouldn't be long before they spread to the other rooms of the house.

We had to get out, but if there was a chance my father was in the house somewhere we needed to find him before it was too late. Ethan strode over to the fireplace.

"Simon, look at the smoke; it should be drawn up the chimney but it's not. It looks like it's being sucked down behind the hearth stones." Ethan motioned for Simon to check out what he had noticed. I followed his gesture, and it did look as though the smoke was being drawn down into the floor around the fireplace. Ethan coughed into his sleeve before running a hand along the stones where the smoke was disappearing.

"There's cold air running along here. The fireplace must be a fake panel." Ethan started looking around frantically, clearly trying to find a trigger that would open it up. Simon did the same thing on the other side, pushing and twisting stones that might release the door.

I searched beside the fireplace, hoping something would stand out. *Think, Hannah.* What about all those old black and white mystery movies I had watched with my parents as a kid with secret passageways and fake panels? How had the characters gotten them to open? The room was so hot and smoky now that I could hardly see or breathe. I had my coat sleeve over my mouth trying to keep from inhaling too much smoke, but we were all coughing as we searched for a way to get the hearth open. My gaze skimmed over the wall beside the hearth. *The lights!* One of sconces hung slightly askew. I bounded over to it and wrenched down its brass arm. There was a muffled clicking sound and the entire fireplace swung forward. Behind the panel, a stone passageway with large wide stairs led down into blackness.

"Well done, Hannah." Simon patted me on the back as we stood in the opening.

"Yes, excellent thinking." Ethan turned his gaze to Uri. A frown creased his forehead and I knew what he was thinking. Evil or not, burning to death would be a horrific way to go. We couldn't just leave the man to that fate.

"Stay here." Ethan crossed back over to where Uri's still-limp body lay. He crouched down at Uri's head and shoved his arms under Uri's. A large cracking sound echoed through the room and one of the beams that ran across the ceiling came crashing down, separating Ethan from Simon and me.

"Ethan!" I started forward, ready to jump over the flames to get to him, but Simon's arms wrapped around my waist, planting me firmly to my spot.

"You can't do it love, it's too dangerous." Simon's voice rang in my ear. He and I watched helplessly through a wall of flame as Ethan tried to lift Uri, but the Russian was just too heavy.

"Come on mate, you tried. You have to leave him." Simon waved an arm towards Ethan.

Ethan looked from the man on the floor to us one more time before dropping Uri, pressing his arm to his mouth and taking a running leap over the burning beam.

I inspected him anxiously as he joined us in the entrance of the passageway, but, thankfully, none of his clothes had caught on fire. Ethan shot one last glance at the hulking Russian and then he, Simon, and I hurried into the darkness. Ethan slammed the panel shut behind us.

I took a deep breath, trying to get my stomach to stop reeling. *Uri brought it on himself; he was the one that lit the curtain on fire.* Maybe if I told myself that enough I would stop feeling so guilty for just leaving him.

Ethan slipped the phone from his pocket and the glow from the screen lit the space enough for us to see our way down the stairs.

"I hope that's not the only exit," Simon murmured grimly.

My mouth gaped open. I hadn't thought of that. I prayed that we would find some other exit down in this blackness.

Ethan led the way and I followed closely behind him, while Simon brought up the rear again. The passageway looked to be fairly new, and was made out of a stone and mortar mix. The construction trucks we had witnessed in the fall must have been carrying in the supplies to create this space. I trailed my fingers along one of the stones. It was cool to the touch, a refreshing change from the intense heat of the fiery room above us.

We reached the end of the stairs and a tunnel stretched out before us. It was hard to see very far into the distance, but we had to keep going. *Dad has to be here somewhere.* I shivered at the thought of him trapped underground. We'd walked about the length of the house when Ethan stopped.

"What is it?" I peered around him. In the glow of the screen, the walkway forked off in either direction.

Ethan pointed to the left. "Simon, can you head that way? I'll take Hannah the other way with me. Yell if you find anything."

"No problem." Simon grabbed his cell phone from his pocket. His face shone in the glow of the screen, and he squinted.

"If you don't find anything, come back and meet us here," Ethan instructed. Simon saluted and took off down the tunnel to the left, while Ethan and I continued on to the right. My arm brushed the wall and I pulled it back. The stone was damp, and small puddles dotted the floor. The water was soaking through my shoes and the temperature was dropping as we walked. I shivered at the change. "It's wet."

"We aren't under the house anymore, so the dampness of the ground is seeping through into this passageway."

"Where do you think we are?" I frowned a little and tried to figure out which direction we were moving in.

"We're heading down in the direction of the lake at the front of the property, if I've calculated our location correctly."

The stiffness in his voice let me know he was definitely still angry with me for putting myself in such a dangerous position. I didn't know what to say to make it better, because he was right.

"I'm sorry." I gripped his arm to stop him and force him to look at me.

"Hannah, let's just find your dad, all right?" Ethan met my gaze, his tone softening a little.

"Do you think he's okay?" I asked as we started walking again. My stomach was in knots with the fear that he might not be.

"We'll find him." Ethan took my hand and gave it a reassuring squeeze. I was grateful for the contact.

We reached another fork in the tunnel. This time there was a faint bit of light coming from the left, so we headed in that direction. We had only walked a few feet when it became apparent the glow was coming from a small barred window at the end of the corridor. The tunnel must have been built into the hill and we were coming out above ground. Between us and the window were four heavy-looking wooden doors, two on either side of the tunnel. Ethan tried the handles. The first three were unlocked and opened onto small empty concrete cells. When he tried to open the fourth door, it wouldn't budge. Ethan reefed on the handle, but the door was locked.

My heart beat faster. I stepped around him. "Dad, Dad, can you hear me? Are you in there?" I pounded my fists against the thick wood.

"Hannah?" A weak voice came from the other side of the door.

"Yes, it's me. I'm here with Ethan and we're going to get you out of there." I craned my neck to look back at Ethan. A ring with four brass keys hung on a hook just beside the window frame, and Ethan grabbed it. The second one he tried twisted in the lock, and he yanked open the door.

Another small window set into the far wall of the cell allowed a small amount of moonlight to filter into the room. My father sat on a metal chair looking beaten and bruised, hands tied behind his back. His head was down against his chest but he raised it when I ran into the cell. His face was dirty and stained with blood and he blinked, clearly disoriented.

I gasped. "Dad, what have they done to you?" Dropping to my knees behind the chair, I clawed at the ropes around his wrists with trembling fingers. His hands were bloody too. His hair was disheveled, and his clothes were dirty.

My fingers shook so badly I couldn't work out the knots in the rope.

Ethan grasped my shoulder. "I've got it, Hannah." He slid a knife from the sheath strapped to his calf.

I stumbled to my feet and went around to the front of the chair.

"Hannah, you shouldn't be here, it's not safe. You need to get out of here." Dad tried to focus on my face. There was fear in his eyes, and although it was hard to tell in the dim light, it looked as though his left eye was black and swollen.

"It's all right. Ethan stopped that guy, he can't hurt us anymore. We just need to get you out of here." I ran a hand over his head to smooth down his hair.

The ropes from my dad's ankles and wrists fell to the ground. "Mr. Reed, do you think you can stand?" Ethan came around and held out his hand to help Dad out of the chair.

"Ethan?" Dad looked up at him, his brow furrowed. Clearly he was out of it, and I was pretty sure that, even if he could stand, he wouldn't be able to walk very far.

"Yes, Mr. Reed, we need to get out of here. Do you think you can walk if I help you?" Ethan asked, his voice calm. He pulled on my dad's arm, lifting him partway out of the chair.

"Hannah." Dad glanced over at me, his mouth open as though he wanted to try to say something, or maybe get some answers, but Ethan already had his arm around Dad's waist, ready to carry the bulk of his weight.

"We'll talk later, Dad."

He nodded and rested heavily against Ethan as we made our way to the door. Ethan handed me his phone to light the way. We had just started back down the tunnel when Simon rounded the corner.

"You found him, very good. I discovered the way out, it's back this way." Simon jerked his head to indicate the way he had come, and then circled around to my dad's other side and slipped an arm of support around his waist. It took a few minutes but we made it back to where we had originally split from Simon. The air smelled strongly of smoke. *Is the whole house on fire now?*

Simon led us down a tunnel similar to the one we had just come from, except twice as long. At the end was a set of stairs that led up to what looked like nowhere. Simon released my father, bounded up the steps, and pushed on the ceiling. After a few hard shoves that lifted the wood above his head, I realized that the ceiling was actually two heavy doors, similar to those that open up into farmhouse cellars. The doors swung open to reveal the night sky and a thick canopy of forest.

We made our way up the stairs and outside. We were actually quite a distance from the house, which was now completely ablaze. It had begun to snow again and thick white flakes fell silently to the ground, their icy coolness a stark contrast to the flames and smoke that billowed from the structure.

Sirens wailed in the distance as we made our way through the woods and back to Bayers Road. Ethan's Jeep was parked a little ways down the road. My car was out of sight in the opposite direction, but we all walked over to the Jeep. Ethan practically lifted my dad into the vehicle and helped him settle into the passenger seat.

"Simon, take Mr. Reed to the hospital, we'll follow behind in Hannah's car." Ethan tossed his keys to Simon.

"You got it." Simon jumped into the driver's seat so eagerly, I wondered how often Ethan let him drive.

Simon and my dad sped past us as Ethan and I walked to my car in silence. Ethan was still angry with me, I could feel it, and now that my father was safe, there was nothing to keep us from discussing it. We were back to my car before I knew it, standing by the passenger door, and we still hadn't said a word to each other.

The tension was mounting. I opened my mouth to say something, but Ethan cut me off. "Hannah, what were you thinking?" His voice was carefully controlled, but he was clearly fighting hard to contain his emotions.

"I wasn't thinking about anything, except saving my dad. It was stupid, I know," I murmured sheepishly, staring down at the loose gravel on the road.

"You could have been taken away tonight. From me." Ethan paused before adding the last part, and I glanced up to see anguish in his eyes. The events of this evening had shaken him up more than I realized, and it made my heart ache.

"I know," I breathed, my eyes locked with his.

"I couldn't bear it if that happened." He wrapped his arms around my waist and lowered his lips to mine. His kiss was intense and passionate, and he held me so tight I started to feel lightheaded. He pulled back after a moment but kept his arms around me.

"I will not lose you, Hannah Reed, do you hear me? Don't make my job harder than it is." His emerald eyes shone as he held me.

"I'll try not to."

A light dusting of snow covered his head and shoulders. He looked so cute that I couldn't help but slip my arms around his neck to pull him in for one more kiss.

As we finally broke away from each other, Ethan lifted an eyebrow. "What exactly did you think you were going to do anyway?"

I shrugged. "I didn't know for sure, but I had my tire iron. I could have done some damage with that. Just ask Simon." I gave him an impish smile.

He shook his head in disbelief and opened the passenger door for me to climb in.

By this time the sirens were right around the corner and we had to get out of there. The Hleo world didn't mix with proper authorities if it could possibly be avoided; there would be too many questions that couldn't be answered. I quickly brushed the snow off of myself, jumped into the car, and handed Ethan my keys.

As we drove to the hospital, Ethan held my hand again. I gazed down at our interlocked fingers, contemplating how the same action could take on different meanings. On the trip to see his family's homestead holding hands had been about tenderness, wanting to touch and connect. This time I could tell by the intensity of his grasp that it was about security, that Ethan was physically holding onto what he was willing to give his life to protect.

Fifteen

It was still dark outside as we pulled into the East Halton District Hospital emergency room parking lot.

We quickly made our way to a registration desk where a clerk was busily typing away at a computer. "Excuse me, but my father Richard Reed was just brought in."

She looked up from the computer for a moment, then she dropped her gaze back to the screen and began to type again. "Richard Reed. It looks like he was admitted immediately. I'll go check and make sure it's okay for you to see him." She stood up and disappeared behind a set of double doors.

I paced in front of the desk until finally, after what seemed like hours but was probably only a few minutes, she returned. "He's been moved to the third floor. Room 3072. You can go sit with him if you like. Take this hallway to the elevators at the end. Go to the third floor and his room will be on the left." She pointed to the hallway behind us.

"Thank you." I headed for the elevators, with Ethan close behind me. I followed the directions the clerk had given and entered the room quietly so we wouldn't wake my dad, but he wasn't there. Simon sat in a chair beside an empty bed, his eyes closed. I gently touched his shoulder and he jerked awake.

"Hannah." Simon shot up, then, no doubt realizing how loud he had been, amended his voice and spoke in hushed tones. "Hannah, hi."

"Simon, where's my dad?" I motioned to the rumpled covers on the bed.

"They've taken him down for some x-rays. The doctor believes his arm could be broken." Simon rubbed his eyes with his palms, as though trying to wipe away the tiredness that was clear on his face.

"Broken," I breathed and sank down in the chair beside Simon. How had this happened? I stared at the plugs and buttons on the hospital wall. Dad had looked so weak when Simon and Ethan and had lifted him into the Jeep.

I glanced over at the guys. In the dim fluorescent glow of the hospital room, Simon and Ethan, soot and dirt smeared across their faces, hands, and clothes, didn't look a whole lot better. I rubbed at the black streaks on the arms of my coat. I'm sure I didn't either.

"Did Mr. Reed mention anything to you on the ride over?" Ethan leaned against the windowsill in the room.

"Not really. He seemed to drift in and out of consciousness as we drove here, and then they whisked him away for x-rays as soon as we arrived." Simon shifted in his seat.

I studied him. He looked uncomfortable, as though he was in some pain.

"Thanks Simon, for getting him here so quickly." I rested a hand on his shoulder.

"No problem." Simon reached up and squeezed my fingers, offering me a small smile, as though he'd read my thoughts and wanted to reassure me that he was fine.

Ethan opened his mouth to speak, but Dad came rolling in at that very moment, pushed on a gurney by a pair of male orderlies.

His eyes were closed. His left arm was in a cast, he was hooked up to an IV, and he had an oxygen tube running across his nose. The orderly closer to the wall flipped on the overhead light. In the harsh lighting, I could see more clearly the bruises and cuts on his face and my chest squeezed.

The orderlies rolled the gurney into position beside the hospital bed and locked the wheels in place. In one swift motion the two of them lifted my dad and slid him onto the bed. The orderly closer to me, an older gentleman, gave me a sympathetic smile as he pulled up the covers, while the other orderly switched the IV bag that had been attached to the gurney over to a pole in the room. Then they left the four of us alone.

I stood up and took Dad's hand gently in mine.

He stirred and his eyelids fluttered as he tried to open them.

"Hannah?" His voice was hoarse, as though he had been yelling. The look and sound of him made me want to cry. My father didn't deserve this. How could the security Ethan and Simon had worked so hard to build around me have been breached so easily?

"I'm here, Dad. It's okay, just rest, we'll talk later." I squeezed his hand gently.

"You bet we will," he mumbled as his eyes shut again and he settled back into a deep sleep.

I glanced from Ethan to Simon, my eyebrows raised. I had known that I was going to have to talk to Dad about what had happened, but I hadn't expected him to be with it enough to respond to what I was saying.

A young gentleman wearing navy scrubs entered the room. "Good evening, everyone. I'm Dr. Lau. Are you relatives of Mr. Reed's?"

"I'm his daughter." I squared my shoulders, preparing myself for whatever prognosis the doctor had to share.

"Okay. First off, your dad's going to be fine." He gave me nod, as though he could sense my anxiety.

My muscles relaxed. "Good."

"He is pretty dehydrated, suffering from mild smoke inhalation, and his body temperature is low. The x-rays showed that his left arm is broken, but I'm not too concerned about the cuts and bruises. I know they don't look great, but they're actually just superficial wounds. I've given him some pain meds, so he'll be pretty groggy for the next little bit. I am going to keep him overnight for observation, partly to watch for signs of a concussion, which is likely, given the gash on his forehead, and partly to get his fluid levels up."

I exhaled slowly. "All right. Thank you so much for taking care of him."

"We'll do our best." Dr. Lau gripped the stethoscope around his neck and glanced from the guys to me. "I'll have a colleague check on him in the morning and we can go forward from there."

"Sounds good." I replied, fighting to control the tremble in my lips as the realization of the amount of damage Uri had inflicted on my father threatened to overwhelm me.

Dr. Lau exited the room, and I turned my attention to the guys. "He looks awful." I touched my dad's arm, pale and frail-looking against the white sheet pulled up to his chin. He didn't respond.

From the lines in his forehead, Ethan had clearly picked up on my agitation. He gestured toward the hallway and Simon and I followed him as he opened the door and went out.

We dropped onto a row of gray plastic chairs just down from dad's room. I didn't want to take any chances on leaving Dad alone again, and I knew Ethan and Simon felt the same way.

I lowered my head into my hands. I felt completely responsible for what had happened. I hated that I was at the mercy of whatever plan the Metadas had for me, and that, so far, I hadn't been able to figure out what that plan could be. I needed answers so that my family and my friends could be safe.

"This is not your fault, please don't blame yourself." Ethan placed a comforting hand on my shoulder and gave it a light squeeze.

I straightened up and stared at him. "How is this not my fault? If it wasn't for the stupid broken slideshow in my head, and whatever use destiny has for it, there wouldn't be Russian assassins coming after my family." I struggled to keep my voice down so people passing by wouldn't hear me.

Ethan glanced down the hallway at a couple of nurses, but they didn't even look up from the charts in their hands. "Hannah, you never asked to be dragged into any of this. This should never have happened. I let my guard down and took myself off duty. That was a mistake, and I'm sorry. Simon and I will make sure nothing like this ever happens again, to you or anyone you care about." The strain of regret was thick in his voice. "My first responsibility should always be to protect you and the people you care about. It was foolish of me to take you away and leave your dad on his own."

I shook my head. This wasn't his fault. How could he have known that some guy was planning to kidnap my Dad? "Ethan, stop. I don't blame you, and I don't want you to blame yourself. So we left for a bit. You have to do things for yourself every once and awhile, you're only human." The last part slipped out before I could stop myself. Ethan wasn't only human, not entirely, and he held himself to different standards because of it. I just hoped he wouldn't be too hard on himself.

Simon rested his ankle on one knee. "I'm fine to sit here and keep an eye on your dad's room, why don't you guys go get some air, or a coffee or something."

I nodded and Ethan and I stood up and ambled off towards the stairwell that would take us back outside to the main entrance of the hospital.

The whole thing was so incredibly frustrating and terrifying. It was one thing when people were coming after me, since I trusted Ethan completely to keep me safe, but if they were going to come after my family or my friends—my stomach tightened at the thought—as a way to get to me, that was not okay. Ethan couldn't be in more than one place at a time, how would he ever effectively be able to divide his focus?

Sixteen

We settled on a bench in a little grove just outside the hospital. I rubbed my hand hard across my forehead. *Why is all of this happening?* I turned in my seat to face Ethan. "How did you find him?"

"It was Paige. She was leading us farther and farther away. She and Uri switched vehicles just outside of East Halton, under a bridge so satellite tracking wouldn't catch the exchange. Then she headed off in one direction while Uri doubled back to the cottage. They were fast and it took us a while to discover our error. Simon had put out feelers to all his contacts to see if anyone knew of the Bana owning any property in this area, and one of them mentioned the purchase of a cottage last fall on Lake Pocotoa. It didn't take us long to track down which cottage and we quickly headed back there.

"My guess is she was trying to get us away from you, knowing I wouldn't bring you along at the risk of putting you in danger. I think she was going to get Uri to make a quick ransom video showing your father bruised and beaten up and send it to you electronically, banking on the hope that you'd be willing to sacrifice yourself to save your father."

"Which I would have."

He grinned wryly. "Obviously."

I sighed. "But why would they take my father in the first place? I mean, if the goal is for me to be dead, why would they bother kidnapping him, and try to lure me to them with a ransom video? Why not just attack me directly?"

He grimaced. "I don't know. But I'm not going to give them the opportunity again to make that attempt."

I touched his arm. "Who is Alexander?" I had wanted to ask ever since Uri had mentioned this mysterious person, but knew there was no point until we found Dad and everything had settled down again.

Ethan sat for a minute, staring at the ground, as though he wasn't sure how to respond. "Alexander Mathieus is the Bana's leader. He is to the Bana what The Three are to the Hleo, except his leadership is a vicious dictatorship where anyone who steps out of line is swiftly and brutally executed." Ethan's jaw clenched. "Do you remember when I told you the story of how the Bana came to be? About Isaac, the one of The Three who dissented and started the Bana? Well, Alexander is his grandson. Isaac ruled the Bana for roughly five hundred years before his son Eric overthrew his regime and took over. Eric then ruled for the next five hundred years, before Alexander did the same thing to him. Alexander has been the leader of the Bana for almost one hundred years now, and he's at least as horrifying as his father and grandfather, if not more so."

I swallowed hard. "What do you think he wants with me?"

Again Ethan took a moment before responding. "I've been trying to come up with an answer for that question myself, and I have a few thoughts, but honestly I'm not entirely sure what the Bana's game plan is."

"What are your theories?" A strong breeze began to blow and I flipped up the collar of my coat as flakes of snow lifted off the branches of the trees we were sitting under and swirled around us.

"It hasn't happened very often, perhaps a handful of times in the years that I have been a Hleo, but occasionally a protected will surface who, for whatever reason, the members of the Bana are interested in using in some way. They decide that person would be more valuable to them alive than dead." Ethan's mouth was drawn in a hard line.

I let the weight of his words sink in. If what Ethan was saying was true, the Bana must have discovered my talent for seeing protecteds and wanted to use it for their own gain. His theory made sense. Why else would they try to barter my father for me? But how had they found out about my ability? Something must have happened since Adam's visit to East Halton to change their minds about killing me.

"You think Alexander knows I can see protecteds?" A chill ran up my spine, but I knew it was from fear, not the cold. The idea of the Bana's leader wanting to kidnap me was far more terrifying than the thought that he wanted to kill me.

Ethan straightened up and slid an arm around my shoulders. "We don't know anything for sure. I need to dig deeper before we jump to any conclusions. For now you just concentrate on making sure your dad gets better, and I'll work on figuring out our next step."

I rested my head on his shoulder. I didn't want to think about this anymore, and Ethan was right, I should focus on Dad. I was so glad he was okay, and that we had found him before Uri could hurt him any more than he had.

Before I could say anything more, my phone vibrated in my coat pocket. I pulled it out to see an unknown number. Who would be calling me so late? I pressed the device to my ear. "Hello?"

"Where have you been?" Katie's voice came over the line, shrill and loud, and I moved the phone a couple of inches away from my ear. "I've been trying to get a hold of you for like the last hour and a half. The house down the road caught fire, the one Ryan saw your dad going to, and I tried to call you on my cell phone but there's no stupid reception here, so I had Luke drive me to the corner store down the road so I could use the payphone. I used like three dollars worth of quarters trying to call you, but I kept getting your voicemail. Why weren't you answering your phone?"

"Well, Katie, I'm sort of at the hospital. Dad did get injured." I squeezed my eyes shut, trying to remain calm. I hadn't thought about my friends seeing the fire down the road. I should have called Katie earlier.

"I knew it. I knew something was wrong. Is he okay? What happened? We saw the smoke and flames coming out of the cottage so we called 911 from the payphone before I called you, but I was so worried your dad was in trouble. And then when I couldn't get a hold of you, I thought that something had to be wrong." Katie was fully rambling and wouldn't let me get a word in edgewise, so I just waited for her to finish.

When she finally stopped for breath, I jumped in. "It's all good, Katie. Dad was at the house. They were there for some sort of retreat, and I guess there was a gas leak or something. Anyway, the house caught fire, and Dad ended up getting a little banged up on his escape, but he'll recover. The doctors are keeping him overnight for observation, and we'll go from there."

"Do you want me to come and sit with you at the hospital? I can be there right away with coffee, snacks, whatever you need."

"No, I'm good, thanks. Ethan's here, and Dad's sleeping, so I'll probably head home in a bit. I'm not going to be able to come back to Kristen's tomorrow, given the circumstances, but I'll call you tomorrow and let you know how everything is." I appreciated that Katie would think to check in on me, but I was starting to feel very tired from the events that had transpired, and all I wanted to do was curl up in my bed.

"We'll miss you, but I totally get it. And if Ethan's there and you're sure you'll be fine…" Katie didn't sound too certain.

"I'll call you tomorrow," I promised. After disconnecting the call, I motioned to the hospital. "I should go in and see how Dad's doing."

Ethan rose and held out his hand to help me to my feet. He didn't let go as we went in and started up the stairs. When we arrived back on the third floor Simon was still posted outside Dad's room.

When he saw us, he yawned and stretched before getting to his feet. "No action since you left, mates."

The poor guy was clearly in need of rest and a shower. I jerked my thumb toward the exit. "Why don't you guys go? I'll stay with my dad."

Ethan's grip on my hand tightened. "No way. I'm not letting you out of my sight. And you need rest as much or more than either of us does."

Simon ran a hand through his disheveled brown hair. "He's right, love. I'm fine. You two go home and get some sleep."

I was too tired and emotionally drained to argue. I checked on my dad one more time before we left. He was still fast asleep, so I just gave his hand a little squeeze and quietly left him to rest. As we made our way out of the hospital and headed for my house, I couldn't help but silently obsess about the fact that the Bana's objective regarding me had changed. The way Ethan gripped the steering wheel suggested that he was worried too.

I only hoped we could figure out what this Alexander person wanted from me before it was too late.

Seventeen

We were on our way to the hospital. Ethan had let me sleep in and I hadn't managed to wake myself up until almost ten o'clock. I had an afternoon shift at The Patch, but I wanted to stop by and see how Dad was doing before going to work. Nervous butterflies fluttered in my stomach as we drove. *What am I going to tell him?* I was going to have to admit that I had learned the truth about myself and my adoption, and tell him I knew that he had knowledge of my family and past. He was the one who had kept the truth from me all these years, but I had been deceiving him the last few months too, and I wasn't sure how to start the conversation.

Dad's room was empty when we arrived at the hospital. I stepped back and glanced up and down the hallway, but he and Simon were nowhere in sight. My pulse jumped when I walked in and saw the empty bed.

Ethan squeezed my arm. "Don't worry. They have to be close by. Stay here and I'll find them."

I went back into the room and sank onto the chair beside Dad's bed. Where was he? Had the Bana tracked him down here and taken him again? My hands tightened into fists in my lap. *I have to go find him.* I pushed to my feet and strode across the room, almost bumping into Ethan when he came through the door. Simon trailed along after him.

"Simon! Where were you? Where's my dad? Did something happen to—"

He held up a hand. “Your dad’s fine, Hannah. They took him down for a CT scan to make sure his head injury wasn’t more serious than it looked.”

“Do they think it could be?”

“No, they’re pretty sure it’s nothing, but they don’t like to fool around with these things. They want to make sure he’s all right.”

Ethan rested a hand on my shoulder. “He’s fine, Hannah.” His eyes searched mine, as though he knew I needed the reassurance.

The thudding in my chest slowly subsided and I blew out a breath. “Okay. Good.” My knees were a little weak and I walked around the two of them and back out to the plastic chairs in the hallway, so I’d be able to see my dad as soon as he was nearing his room again.

They followed me and we all took the same spots we’d sat in before. “So, how was your night?” I asked Simon, as he took a long sip of the very large coffee he was holding.

“Oh, you know, sleeping in a chair all night has its perks. For instance, I can’t feel my back anymore.” Simon shrugged and grinned.

“Well, thank you for staying with him. I slept better knowing you were watching over him.” I set a hand on Simon’s arm, truly grateful that he was here to help Ethan.

“No problem. It’s what I’m here for, love.”

Once again, I was struck by Simon’s humility and sincerity. Ethan had definitely lucked out, getting him for a partner.

“Is Mr. Reed more lucid today?” Ethan leaned forward in his chair. “Has he been able to give you any information on his kidnapping?”

“Between nurses coming in and out of the room, and his going off for tests, we haven’t had much of a chance to chat, I’m afraid. He did thank me for saving his life, so he definitely remembers what happened last night.” Simon ran a hand across the stubble on his chin.

Before I could respond, Dad rounded the corner, pushed in a wheelchair by a broad-shouldered male orderly.

“Good morning.” I clambered out of my seat to stand beside him. I was glad to see that his coloring was better than it had been last night.

"Hannah." He held out his un-casted hand to me and I grasped hold tightly. "You're okay." The relief was clear on his face.

"Yes, Dad. I'm fine, just happy to see you up and moving." I released him so the orderly could take him to his room.

Ethan, Simon and I followed them into dad's room. The orderly helped him get back into the hospital bed. "You're all set, Mr. Reed."

"Thanks, Peter," Dad said to the hospital worker, who gave us a smile before leaving the room.

"How are you feeling?" I moved to stand beside the bed.

"Pretty good, relatively speaking, and mostly grateful." He turned his attention to Ethan, giving him a knowing look.

"Sir—" Ethan began, but a gray-haired gentleman wearing a lab coat and a stethoscope entered the room, a chart in his hands.

"Good morning, Mr. Reed, I'm Dr. Kauffman. It looks like you've had quite the accident. You're very lucky; usually when someone's deck collapses and they take a tumble, the injuries are far more serious. It's fortunate your daughter decided to head up to your cottage a day early and found you, or you might really have been in trouble." Dr. Kauffman consulted the chart as he spoke, and I frowned at the unfamiliar version of what had transpired. Simon coughed, and I glanced over at him. He nodded his head slightly. *Ah.* That must be the story he had given when Dad had first arrived in the Emergency Room.

"I am definitely fortunate my daughter came when she did." Dad looked up at me and took my hand in his. He gave it a tight squeeze, and another wave of gratitude that he had been spared washed over me.

"The CT results show that you did indeed suffer a rather nasty concussion, but your fluid levels are coming up nicely, and the break in your arm is a simple hairline fracture. I want to keep you here for observation for a little while longer, but if you get some rest today, I'm sure we can release you tonight." The doctor examined Dad as he spoke, listening to his heart and lungs, and shining a light in his eyes. He made some notes on the chart, reminded Dad to get some rest, gave us a somewhat reproachful look, and wished us all a good day. Then he was gone.

"I guess that was his not-so-subtle way of suggesting that we shouldn't all be here." I fiddled with the adjustable tray table beside

Dad's bed, making sure the glass of water sitting on top of it was easily accessible for him.

"Perhaps, but Hannah, we need to talk." Dad's expression was solemn.

I swallowed hard. I just wasn't ready to get into it. "I know, and we will, but I don't have time right now, I need to get to work. I'll come back when I get off and take you home if they release you. Let's talk when you're settled there. That way we'll have time and privacy and can get everything out in the open, okay?"

I held my breath until he nodded.

Simon came up beside me, resting his hands on the metal bed rails. "I'll stay with him."

I shook my head. "You need to go home and get some rest."

"No, really Hannah." His voice was firm. "What I need is to be here until your dad is completely out of the woods. If it hadn't been for me..."

My chest squeezed. I hadn't realized he felt so responsible for what happened to my father, since he was in charge while Ethan and I were away with me visiting Ethan's family home.

Dad reached over and gripped Simon's forearm. "If it hadn't been for you, all of you," he nodded at Ethan and me, "I would be dead. I owe you a great deal."

"Just rest and get better, Mr. Reed. That's all the thanks we want." Ethan checked his watch. "Hannah, we better go if you want to get to work on time. I'll drop you off at The Patch and then do some digging around, try to find out where Paige could be hiding."

"All right." I turned back to my dad. "I'll see you after work?"

He managed a weak smile. "Count on it."

Eighteen

Ethan and I arrived at The Patch. I'd been quiet on the car ride over, too busy with my thoughts to make conversation, and as I reached for the Jeep's door handle ready to jump out, Ethan put a hand on my arm to stop me. "He's going to be fine."

"Yeah. I know his injuries look worse than they are." I exhaled slowly.

"No, I mean with the truth. I know you're worried about getting everything out in the open, but clearing the air will be good for the two of you. He's going to be okay with it, trust me."

He always seems to know what I need to hear. I leaned forward and pressed my lips to his. It was a soft kiss, the kind I could easily have gotten lost in, but I forced myself to end it after a moment and rest my forehead against his. "Thank you."

"You're welcome." He slid back in his seat, and I climbed out of the vehicle. As I passed by the old wooden sleds and skis Carmen had displayed in the store's front yard, I determined to clear my head of all the stress from the past few days and just focus on my job. It would be a welcome distraction. I could always count on Carmen to keep things lighthearted.

"Hey, can you come give me a hand?" Carmen called out as soon as I walked through the door. The store was empty for the moment, and Carmen stood a few feet up on a ladder trying to reach down to a pile of silk screen printed t-shirts sitting on one of the display tables just out of her reach.

"You know, you could climb off the ladder to get these." I walked over and handed her half the pile.

"Yes, but where is the fun in that?" Carmen set the shirts on an empty shelf and reached for more. I laughed and handed her the rest of the pile, then walked to the counter to stash my bag and winter coat.

I got down to work, re-stocking shelves, tidying areas that looked like they needed attention, and assisting any customers that came into the store. The shift flew by, and before I knew it I only had half an hour left before I could leave and go back to the hospital. I hadn't told Carmen about my Dad—mainly to avoid having to answer endless questions—and it was nice to be away from the situation for a while.

I was busy re-folding a pair of jeans when someone tapped my shoulder. "Excuse me, I was wondering if I could get your opinion on something," a girl's voice rang out. I turned around to see a petite, college-age blonde holding a dress in each hand and gazing expectantly at me. "What can I do for you?" I asked, putting on my best helpful salesclerk voice.

"I can't decide between these two dresses. Which one do you like better? I'm supposed to be shopping with my mom but she went into a store down the street and I haven't seen her in a while or I'd get her opinion." She gave me a sheepish smile.

I tapped a finger on my chin as I studied the two garments. "Well, the blue dress brings out the blue in your eyes nicely, but the burgundy one is a good color for your complexion."

"Yeah, I'm not sure; maybe I should try them on and see what you think." The girl held the dresses up to her chin, one at a time, trying to look down at them as she did.

"If you want to. The change rooms are just over there." I pointed to the back of the store.

"Thanks, I'll be right back." She draped the garments over her arm and made her way to the change rooms.

I went back to re-organizing the jeans, hoping her mother would come soon to give a more informed opinion. *If she's really here with her mother*. The thought popped into my head before I could stop it, and I worked to squash it away.

A minute later, the lock clicked open on the wooden change room door and the girl emerged. "What do you think?" she asked, walking towards me wearing the dark-blue floral wrap dress. It fit her perfectly, and really did make her eyes pop.

"It looks great. It's a very flattering style." *Why are you so suspicious of her?* Maybe if I knew a little more about her I would relax.

"So, do you live around here?" I asked her as we walked back to the changing area.

"Actually, I just moved here with my mom. It seems like a really nice little town." She stepped back into the change room and pulled the door closed behind her.

"Oh, so you're new to town. Are you working anywhere?"

"No, I'm still in high school so I don't have a job, but maybe I'll look for a part-time one. Are you hiring here?" she laughed lightly.

My brow furrowed. Why was she laughing? Was she joking about wanting to work here? "You're in high school? I haven't seen you around."

"Um, that's probably because I go to Wellington Collegiate, the private school in Hartford. Plus I've only been here in East Halton for like two weeks." She stammered a little as she spoke.

I frowned. *New in town, just happens to not go to my school? It's all a little too convenient.*

"What do you think of this one?" She asked, coming out in the burgundy dress.

"It's nice too, but I'd go with the blue." I waved a dismissive hand towards the garment she was wearing.

She gave me a funny look, as though she was starting to think I was a little strange. "Okay, sure, if you think it looks better, thanks."

"I'll just let you get changed. I'll be at the cash if you need anything." I left her to get dressed in her own clothes again and walked over to the counter, but kept the change room in sight the whole time. If she was going to try anything, I would to be ready. *I won't be taken in by a member of the Bana ever again. I will not be that naïve.* My head shot up. Wait, what? The Bana? Where had that come from? The chances of the girl in the change room having anything to do with the Bana were extremely slim. Everything that had happened in the last few months, especially dad's abduction, had obviously shaken me more than I'd realized, and now I was seeing bad guys everywhere. I shook my head. I couldn't allow the Bana to do that to me either. If I started living my life in fear, unable to trust anyone, they would have already won.

After a few minutes the girl came out of the change room with the blue dress, leaving the other one for me to put away, and walked over to the cash register. I rang her through, determined to be as friendly with her as I usually was with customers so she wouldn't leave here thinking I was a complete nut case and stop shopping at The Patch.

"I really think you'll be happy with the blue one." I slipped the dress into a brown paper bag.

"Me too. Thanks for the advice, maybe I'll see you around." The girl took her change and the bag.

"Maybe." I smiled.

As she left, a gust of wind caught the door and sent it crashing into an ill-positioned display of scarves. "I'm sorry." She looked at me apologetically.

"No problem." I waved a hand, indicating that I would take care of the mess, and crossed over to pick up the scarves as she went out the door.

From my vantage point by the front window, I saw a middle-aged woman who looked a lot like the girl would in about twenty-five years, come out of Lynette's Furniture and Home Goods Store, just down the street and across the block from us. The woman walked over to the girl, who pulled the blue dress out of her bag, and pointed to The Patch.

I quickly moved away from the window so I wouldn't be caught spying on them, and headed back to the cash register. She had been telling the truth, and why wouldn't she? *I'm getting paranoid.* I went to the change room to grab the dress she had left.

This was no good. I couldn't go around thinking every new person I met was a potential assassin; I would drive myself crazy. We had to do something, I couldn't just keep sitting around waiting for a revelation to strike and give me some sort of clue as to what to do next, while my father had so easily ended up in harm's way.

I thought about it for the rest of my shift, trying to come up with some sort of answer. Finally, an idea came to me, something Ethan and I could do that might, finally, make everything clear.

Now I just had to get Ethan to agree to do it.

Nineteen

"I think we should go see The Three," I declared as soon as I climbed in Ethan's Jeep.

"What?" Ethan's eyebrows shot up.

"I've been thinking about it, and we can't keep waiting for the answers to come to us. The information we've gathered doesn't seem to be shedding any light on my ability. We need to start being proactive and go to where we can find some answers. If anyone will be able to give us some sort of direction it has to be The Three. They know more than anyone about the future of this world and the ways of the Metadas." I used my hands to emphasize my argument.

Ethan looked at me thoughtfully for a moment, before shifting the Jeep into drive and pulling away from the curb. "Hannah, I don't want to be the one who tells you no, but I don't think it's a good idea. No one ever goes to see The Three, ever. I can't predict how they would react to this request."

I wasn't ready to give up yet. "What do you mean, react? You think they would get mad that I want to come to them for answers? That would be a little ridiculous. If they want to keep me alive, wouldn't they want to help me find out what I'm supposed to do so I can just do it and we can all move on?" I tried not to raise my voice in frustration.

Distress flickered across Ethan's face. "Move on," he echoed softly.

I immediately regretted my choice of words. I hadn't meant that *he* should move on, but that reality was one more thing casting a shadow over the future that we refused to let ourselves talk about.

"Not like that. I mean, wouldn't it be good to feel safe, to not always have to watch over my shoulder to make sure no one is following me? Wouldn't it be nice to be able to just relax together, and not worry that something is going to happen to me or my family? The Three can give me answers, I know they can, and then we can take the next step, together." I willed his deep green eyes to meet mine, desperately wanting to convince him to go along with my plan.

Ethan glanced over at me before focusing on the road. He sighed. "What you're saying makes sense, and you're probably right, they could give you some sort of direction. I'm just not convinced they would. The Three adhere completely to the rules of the Hleo. One of the foundational pillars of the society is that we don't get directly involved in the lives of protecteds unless absolutely necessary, and if we do, it is imperative that the protecteds still make their own decisions and lead their own lives as though our presence were invisible. If we try to influence their decisions, then we are no better than the Bana, because we're taking steps to make destiny move the way we want it to. The Hleo's only concern is to keep outside forces from interfering with protecteds so that they are free to live their lives."

We pulled up to a stoplight and a couple from my chemistry class crossed in front of us. They were laughing and leaning into each other, and I fought the urge to glare at them, envying their carefree demeanor.

"The Three have never agreed with my decision to tell you about who I am, and what I am doing in your life. They feel I've interfered too much, and have possibly jeopardized what you are meant to do. They've admitted that they are perplexed and intrigued by your ability, but they still feel it is up to you to discover its purpose. I know that's not what you want to hear, but I think that if we were to go, you would only end up disappointed." He shot me a pained look.

I knew it was hard for him, not being able to give me the answer I wanted, so I decided not to press the point. I flopped back against the seat. "So we won't go, but what can we do then? Because we have to do something, I'm starting to get paranoid. I think every new person that comes into my life is evil, like this poor girl who came into the store this afternoon to buy a dress."

Ethan's head whipped toward me. "Why did you think she was evil? Did she do something to make you suspicious?"

I shook my head. "No, not at all. I was just acting crazy."

Ethan gripped the steering wheel tightly as he took a quick corner onto the street the hospital was on. "Don't underestimate your gut reaction to a situation, Hannah. If you ever feel like something is off with someone, call me and I'll come right away."

"All right, I will. But in this case nothing was really off. I think what happened with Dad was making me see things that weren't there."

He didn't look convinced. "That doesn't mean you shouldn't continue to be vigilant. In the meantime, I'll start looking through old cases from Hleo I haven't been able to contact and see if I can find anything that resembles your circumstances; maybe we can find an answer there."

I reached over and gave his hand a squeeze, wanting to convey how much I appreciated his desire to make me happy. "Okay."

He held my fingers in his for a moment before releasing them so that he would be able to turn into the hospital's parking lot.

I thought of the girl who'd come into the store that afternoon and her mother, and my cheeks warmed as I recalled how odd my behavior toward her had been.

Then I straightened in my seat. Just because I couldn't let fear and suspicion take over my life, didn't mean I should let my guard down. Maybe that girl wasn't a threat, but the Bana were out there, and if one of them did suddenly come back into my life, I needed to be ready.

Twenty

Dad had been more than ready to leave by the time we arrived at the hospital. An orderly pushed him to the main doors in a wheelchair, but Dad insisted on getting out and walking to the Jeep from there.

The ride back to our house was fairly quiet. Ethan switched on the radio for a few minutes, presumably to fill the gaps in conversation. During a brief news update, the broadcaster mentioned the fire at the cottage where my dad had been taken. He said the building was abandoned and thankfully no one had been injured. Ethan's eyes met mine briefly in the rearview mirror. That meant Uri had escaped somehow and was out there somewhere, likely arranging his next plan of attack with Paige. Ethan switched off the radio. I wasn't sure if my dad picked up on it, but I was deeply aware of the underlying tension of the things not being said as we drove home.

After what seemed an interminable length of time, Ethan maneuvered the Jeep into our driveway. He helped Dad get settled in the living room, but then went back outside.

I followed him to the door.

"I'm going to go so you two can talk." Ethan pulled the collar of his coat up as the wind cut across the porch.

"That's probably for the best. I'll call you later." I propped a shoulder against the doorframe, barely resisting the urge to grab him and kiss him. So many thoughts swirled through my head, I needed to focus on my talk with my dad and not get distracted.

He waved as he climbed in the Jeep and then I was alone with Dad. I squared my shoulders and forced a smile as I walked inside and plunked down on the couch beside him. "How are you feeling? Can I get you anything?" I picked a pillow up off the couch, ready to prop his arm up if needed.

He shook his head. "I'm fine, really, I don't need anything." His voice shook a little, as though he was as uncomfortable and unsure about how to start this conversation as I was. His gaze dropped down to his cast. "Hannah, I owe you an apology."

"What? Why?" I blinked rapidly.

He met my eyes. "Well, you've obviously learned a lot more about who you are in the last few months, and I'm sorry that I didn't try to explain everything before you found out in whatever manner you did." Dad sounded sheepish.

I rested a hand on his good arm. "It's funny, I was going to apologize to you. I've known the truth since just after you left for England, and I've been acting as though I didn't. I've pretty much been lying to you for the last few months."

"Technically speaking, I've been lying to you for years, so you have no need to feel guilty. I did a terrible thing last year when you brought up finding your real parents. I lied and told you I didn't have any information on them because I didn't want to risk you finding out the truth and putting yourself in any sort of danger." He shifted on the couch.

"So, you do know the whole truth about my biological parents then?" My heart rate jumped. I'd been dying to learn more about my parents, but with everything else that was going on, it had been easy to push my curiosity to the side. Still, somewhere along the way I had begun to think learning more about them might be able to give me some clues about my ability, and how I was supposed to use it.

"I do." Dad took a deep breath. "When I was in college I fell in love with history. I'd had a fascination with the past from the time I was a boy, especially the idea of lost civilizations and secret societies. If it wasn't for your mother I would probably have gone off and been an archaeologist, but once I met her I was happy to put down roots and settle into a teaching role instead.

"In university, I stumbled across some old documents that referred to a secret organization of individuals who were called the 'guardians of destiny'. They were people who had accepted a call of duty to protect others whom fate had touched with a higher calling.

The references were very speculative and mysterious. There didn't seem to be any concrete evidence of the group's existence, but I was hooked." Dad twisted his casted arm and winced. I held up the pillow and he nodded.

Once his arm was propped up, he relaxed against the back of the couch. "After months of poring over old documents, I had only managed to discover that they went by the name Hleo, and that it appeared the organization was still active. Then one night when I got back to my apartment, a beautiful young woman with dark hair and dark eyes was waiting for me. Elizabeth Seaton. She told me that she was a member of the Hleo. The society had heard of my investigation and had sent someone to explain the danger in stirring up information that had long been buried. Elizabeth ended up staying most of the night talking with me, until I confirmed that I had told no one else about the Hleo and agreed, reluctantly, to stop researching the organization.

"I thought that was the end of it, but after that night Elizabeth would come to see me from time to time. The Hleo exist in shadows and secrets—the less people know about them the better—but I think talking to me was a release for her. She opened up and told me about the group and their abilities. She revealed to me that a faction had splintered off from the Hleo—the Bana—and described their dark and ugly objectives. I guess you already know who they are though, don't you?" Dad stopped to look at me.

I nodded. "Uri, the guy who took you, is Bana."

"A most unpleasant gentleman." Dad grimaced.

"Agreed." I glanced out the front window and a chill ran over me. I knew Ethan would be close by, but with Uri and Paige on the loose it was hard not to feel vulnerable. I reached over and pressed the switch on the lamp on the table beside me.

Dad ran his fingers through his hair. "I appreciated Elizabeth's friendship, although I did worry about her. I knew the risks of what she was doing, and the possibility that every time I saw her it would be the last. It had been almost three years since I had seen her, and I had accepted the fact that she must have died in the line of duty, when she suddenly appeared again, with you."

I straightened up on the couch. "She brought me to you?"

"Yes. I remember very clearly the day you came. I arrived home from a long day at work, and as I walked up the steps I could hear a baby's cry. When I got inside I saw Julia sitting on the couch. Elizabeth was beside her, holding a young baby. A man I'd never seen before, your father Noah, stood by the fireplace, looking very serious and uncomfortable." Dad hunched forward and coughed.

I realized I was holding my breath. I exhaled slowly and reached a hand towards him. "Are you okay?"

"Yes. I'm sorry to stop; my throat's bothering me a bit. I think I need a glass of water."

"I'll get it." I jumped up and practically ran to the kitchen, desperate for him to continue now that I was finally getting a picture of what my life looked like at the time of my adoption.

I handed him the glass and he took a big swig before setting it on the end table beside him. "Thank you, that's much better. Elizabeth had fallen in love with the man, Noah Carter, one of the Bana's more notorious assassins and your father. She didn't give me a lot of details of how that happened, but told me that they had decided to leave their life of destiny behind, and run away together. While on the run she had become pregnant and given birth to a baby girl. Elizabeth and Noah wanted more than anything to be left alone so they could raise you in peace, but certain members of their former allegiances, especially the Bana, weren't satisfied to just let them leave. The two of them realized that they were in danger and were being followed.

"I was the one person Elizabeth felt she could trust in this world who wasn't caught up directly with the Hleo. She came to me hoping that your mother and I might be willing to take care of you for a little while, until they were sure the coast was clear. Then the three of you would make a life together, somewhere off the grid where no one would be able to find you. Julia didn't hesitate, even after learning the truth about Elizabeth's identity. We had been married for three years, and had been unsuccessful in having our own baby. She fell in love with you instantly.

"Elizabeth and Noah stayed with us for a few more days, trying to come up with the best exit strategy and to get you settled. Julia felt uncomfortable with simply taking you without any sort of documentation. You had no birth certificate, no birth registry, and she was worried if we ever took you to the hospital it would somehow be discovered that we weren't your biological parents and it would create many questions we didn't have answers to. That's why your parents set up your adoption through The Crestwood Adoption Agency, an organization Noah knew of that could make it happen quickly and quietly. As soon as that was taken care of, the two of them left. A few years later we found out they had died."

Dad rested a hand on my shoulder. "I know you've questioned if your birth parents loved you, or if they were simply burdened with you. Hannah, from my observation of them, saying good-bye to you was the hardest thing either of them ever did. I think somehow they knew it was the last time they would ever see you."

I wiped at a stray tear as the overwhelming emotion of it all threatened to spill over. My birth parents hadn't just given me up to keep living their glamorous life of adventure; they had wanted to come back for me.

"Do you have a picture of them?" My voice was barely a whisper.

"I'm sorry, I don't. The people that were after your parents were so dangerous, Elizabeth and Noah didn't want to give them any way of tracing you back to them. Then, if they did get captured, at least you would be safe. They even took a baby doll in your car seat with them when they left in case someone was watching them. And they asked us not to take you out of the house for at least two weeks after their departure. I never did know whether that was necessary or not, but those were the lengths they went to, to make sure you were safe," Dad explained.

I swallowed the lump in my throat away. "Thank you for telling me all of that." I gave him a gentle hug so as not to press on his injuries. We sat silently together on the couch for a second, each lost in our own thoughts.

"I'm sure you probably have lots of questions for me, but I actually have one for you." Dad sat up straighter and kept his gaze on me.

I pushed back my shoulders. "Go ahead."

"As I understand it, Hleo exist to look after special chosen people, protecteds. I don't know a lot about the society but I thought that was their only… I guess I'm just… why are Ethan and Simon here?" Dad stumbled over his words as though he wasn't exactly sure what he wanted to ask. "Obviously there is some sort of danger. I was assured a long time ago that you were safe, that the Bana that had gone after Elizabeth and Noah had been dealt with, but has something changed? Are the Bana coming after you, even after all this time?" His frown deepened as he spoke.

I rubbed my hands back and forth a little. "As it turns out, *I* am a protected."

"A protected." As though he needed a little time to process that, he took his glasses off and fiddled with them, trying to wipe them on his shirt, a difficult task with one arm.

I clasped my hands in my lap. "It seems that sometime shortly after Mom's car accident, Miriam, the leader of the Hleo who sees protecteds, was given a vision of me as a protected. They started a file on me and right before my senior year Ethan showed up here in East Halton to shadow me." I bit my lip.

"Because of Elizabeth?" Dad slipped his glasses back on but the frown remained on his face.

"We aren't sure. We haven't found any connection between the two things. Ethan said protecteds are usually ordinary people, not affiliated with either the Hleo or the Bana in any way. As far as anyone can tell it's a coincidence." I shrugged, feeling as unconvinced as he looked.

He shook his head. "But from all of my studies of the society, the Hleo world holds no coincidences."

"I know." I sighed.

Dad tapped his chin with a finger. "Hmm."

"What? Is there something else I should know?"

"On one of her visits, Elizabeth explained the process a Hleo goes through, and the differences that had made to her physical nature. Neither Elizabeth nor Noah had remained completely human, both had been changed into different versions of themselves. I wondered how their altered states would affect your genetics and development. I explained all of this to Julia, and at first we were worried you wouldn't age, as they didn't, but thankfully you were right in the average percentile for weight and height all of your childhood.

"There was one thing that stood out when you were younger, though, your health. You were never sick, never had a cold or an earache. When all the other children in your grade were passing around germs and missing school from sickness you were healthy. We knew it was more than average good health when you accidentally ingested window cleaner, mistaking it for blue Kool-Aid, when you were about five, and it didn't even phase you. It wasn't until you broke your arm skating when you were eight that we were convinced you were fully human." Dad pointed at a framed photo on the mantle, of Mom and me eating ice cream in our kitchen. I had a hot pink cast on my arm.

I slid off the couch and drifted towards the picture to examine it closer. I hurt myself all the time—clumsiness being one of my endearing qualities—so I'd never noticed my capacity to stay healthy before, but now that he pointed out, I couldn't remember a time when I had been truly sick. Was I more like Ethan than I had realized?

Dad adjusted the sleeve of his shirt that met at the top edge of his cast. "And you had one other peculiar trait, your drawing ability. From an early age your drawing skills far exceeded what a normal child would be capable of drawing. As an art teacher, your mom recognized that, which is why she encouraged you as much as she did." His eyes were still on the photo of me and mom. He sounded wistful and it made the familiar ache of missing her sharper than normal.

My finger traced her outline. *I wish she was here now.* I could have used her guidance and support while dealing with this whole mess.

"The drawing thing I can explain a little. Since I was about twelve years old most of my drawings have come from images that pop into my head like photographs. It turns out that these images are of real people that exist, either in the past or in the future. And from what Ethan, Simon, and I have discovered so far, the images seem to be solely of people Hleo have protected, or will protect, I suppose." I joined Dad on the couch again.

He studied me for a moment. "So, you have a clairvoyant ability?"

"I guess so. Although it feels more like a disability. The three of us have been trying to come up with a way for me to control the visions, but so far no luck. Most of the time we can't even distinguish if an image is of something that has already happened or something that is yet to be, so for right now I'm not much use to anybody." I tried not to let too much frustration slip out as I spoke.

"But still, Hannah, that is an incredible gift. I'm sure you'll figure out how it works. If it's only protecteds that you envision, there must be a very important reason. It's probably why you're a protected."

"Yeah. Maybe. Again it appears to be a coincidence."

His encouraging words made me feel better. I could tell he had absolute faith in the Hleo society and what they were fighting so hard to protect.

"So, when did you learn about the Hleo and your drawing ability?"

Here we go. Time to confess. "Do you remember when I introduced you to Ethan?"

"Ah yes, of course." His smile was a little sheepish, as though he'd just remembered how he had treated Ethan with cool suspicion when they first met. "I suppose I should apologize to Ethan for my behavior that day. I was very leery about a young man, a perfect stranger, just showing up in your life. In the back of my mind I've always worried the Bana could come for you, and he looked so much older than a high school student."

"You don't need to worry, he wasn't offended. To answer your question though, it was shortly after you met Ethan. You had been in England for just over a week when Ethan saved my life in such a way that he was forced to tell me who he was, and why he was in East Halton." I thought back to that time, and how disappointed I had been to learn that I was just a job to him.

"What happened?" The fatherly concern was thick in Dad's voice.

"I was working on a painting in the art room at school, and a member of the Bana tried to kill me with a basketball backboard. Ethan arrived just in time to push me out of the way and take out the assassin."

"And since then, have there been any more attacks, besides my getting kidnapped?" Dad narrowed his eyes.

I tried to keep my face expressionless as I debated whether or not to tell him the truth. I didn't want him to be needlessly worrying about me, but I also wanted to be honest. "There have been a few attempts, but Ethan has handled them well. It's not something you should be worried about. Your getting kidnapped was probably the worst thing that is going to happen." I patted his good arm gently.

"I will worry. I always have and always will, it's my job as your dad, but at least now that we're all on the same page I can work at not being an extra security liability for Ethan and Simon as they focus on you."

"I'm sure they will both appreciate that. You can trust them; they're very good at what they do." I smiled.

"It certainly seems that way." A strange look crossed his face. "From all that I have learned about the Hleo and the way they operate, I'm a little surprised you and Ethan are as close as you are."

I shrugged, trying to play it cool.

"I was always told by Elizabeth that a Hleo's role was to stay in the shadows of people's lives, never to admit the truth of who they are unless absolutely necessary."

It was my turn to shift on the couch a little, uncomfortable. "It's like I said, Ethan was forced to tell me who he was after he killed a guy in front of me. It was that or I was going to call the cops and have him arrested, or locked up for being crazy. Even after he told me the truth I wasn't sure if I should believe him or not." My cheeks grew warm.

"And since that time he has openly attached himself to you?" Dad arched an eyebrow.

"I think he feels it's easier to guard me if he is with me, and since I know the truth, that's possible."

"I guess." Dad sounded a little skeptical. "What do your friends think of the two of you?"

"They think we're friends."

"Just friends?"

My stomach tightened. I wanted to tell him, but I couldn't jeopardize what Ethan and I had. Besides, I wasn't sure how Dad would take learning that his little girl was dating a 146-year-old, half-human who protected people for a living, even if that meant killing someone along the way.

I locked my eyes with his. "Just friends."

"Okay, good." The relief in his voice was unmistakable. I had made the right call, not telling him the truth about me and Ethan. He gripped the arm of the couch and pushed himself to his feet. "The painkillers are wearing off; my arm is starting to throb. I think I'll give Rose a call and then go lie down for a while." He pursed his lips. "I'm sure she'll be wondering where I've been, and I'll have to explain to her how I hurt my arm. I suppose falling down the stairs wasn't my smoothest move ever, was it?" Dad gave me a conspiratorial look.

I was glad to see that he seemed to have reconciled himself to the fact that I had been keeping secrets from him. Of course, he couldn't really be too upset with me, since he'd been keeping secrets of his own for a long time now.

Twenty-One

It had been over two weeks since Dad's accident, and we still didn't have any answers. Uri and Paige seemed to have dropped off the face of the earth. In order to focus on finding the deadly pair, Ethan and Simon had put a temporary hold on the ever-consuming quest to figure out the meaning behind my drawing ability. We still had no clue why the Bana had changed their directive, and were now trying to kidnap me.

Dad's arm seemed to be healing quickly. I continued to feel terrible that he had gotten hurt, and I knew Ethan did too, since he had let his guard down to share some of his past with me.

It was Saturday afternoon, and I was in the kitchen peeling potatoes for supper. Ethan was in the living room going over the newest information Simon had been able to dig up on Paige and her known hideouts in the New England area and on the east coast.

Dad walked into the kitchen just as I was peeling the last potato and gave me a funny look. "Oh Hannah, did I forget to mention that I was going to take Rose out to dinner tonight?" He looked sheepishly down at the sink full of potatoes. I had planned on making a roast beef dinner for the three guys, and already had the meat cooking in the oven.

"You did, but that's okay." I turned back to the sink so he wouldn't see the annoyance on my face. Since his injury I'd been trying to cut him some slack. Besides, it would be fine; Simon was coming, and he would eat Dad's portion of the meal.

"Are you sure? It looks as though you've gone to some trouble here. I can cancel my plans." Dad pressed his hands to the counter. His eyes suddenly lit up. "Or, what if Rose came over here for dinner?"

Since the night I had walked in on them kissing in the kitchen Dad had kept Ms. Woods away from me. I would see Dad leave for his dates, and occasionally hear about them, but I never actually witnessed any interactions between the two of them. I was starting to feel more comfortable with the idea of them as a couple, but bringing her into the home my mother raised me in would be hard. Of course, I couldn't very well tell him that while he was standing there, his face practically glowing with expectant hope.

"I guess that would work." I forced myself to keep the reluctance out of my voice. "The guys are going to be here, though, how would we explain them to her?" I bit my thumb as I waited for his response.

"Ethan and Simon can be brothers, family friends that we invited for dinner, since their parents are out of town," Dad suggested. I blinked. Since when had he become so proficient at lying?

"Great, that's great. You call Ms. Woods, and I'll keep working on dinner." I picked up a potato and started peeling it.

"Excellent, I'm sure she'll be thrilled. She's wanted the three of us to spend more time together for quite awhile now." Dad grinned and headed off to his study to make the call.

I better add a dessert to the menu if we're going to have actual company. I threw the potato back into the sink and grabbed a can of filling and the rest of the ingredients for a pumpkin pie from the cupboard and set to work.

As I worked I deliberated; I needed to watch how I acted this evening. I had to be the supportive, approving daughter, even though I wanted to scream out that this was wrong. My art teacher in my house, cuddling up to my father, was wrong. I tried to push the image of the two of them out of my mind. In my anxious mental state I had begun unintentionally slamming bowls and utensils around harder than normal. Ethan walked into the kitchen, a concerned look on his face, just as I was dumping the pie mixture into the waiting crust.

"Is everything all right?" He surveyed the mess I had made of the kitchen.

"Yeah. Ms. Woods is coming to dinner, isn't that just great?" I forced a fake smile as I spoke.

"I thought that was what I heard your dad say. Are you okay?" He came over to stand beside me. I'd have thrown my arms around him if there wasn't a good possibility Dad would come into the room at any moment.

I sighed. "I'll be fine. It's just going to be hard seeing her in my mom's house. It feels so intrusive, but I guess this moment was coming. It will be good to get it done and over with." I picked up the pie and set it in the oven gingerly, fighting the desire to slam the door shut after it.

"I'll be right by your side all night. If things get too tough just give me a signal, and I'll remind you we need to pick up some books at the library or something." I was still grasping the oven door's handle and he gently closed his fingers over mine. I glanced up at him. He was so caring, his eyes full of compassion and understanding. Suddenly I didn't care who walked into the kitchen. I reached up, slid my hands around his shoulders, and pulled his lips to mine. He kissed me back softly, but we quickly broke off to separate sides of the kitchen island when footsteps sounded in the hall.

"I just got off the phone with Rose. She is delighted to accept our invitation for dinner. She asked if there was anything she could bring and I told her I would call her back if there was." Dad beamed.

"Just herself," I replied cheerfully.

"Great, well I'll leave you to it. Oh, Ethan, you have a little flour on your shoulder." He pointed towards the spot I had just had my hands.

"Thanks. I was assisting Hannah, but I'm not nearly as competent in the kitchen as she is," Ethan replied, an innocent look on his face as he wiped his shoulder.

I kept my head down, hoping dad wouldn't notice my flushed cheeks.

"She is a good cook. I'm sure we're in for a treat." Dad left us to it, and I let out the breath I'd been holding in a whoosh.

"Sorry." I held up both hands, palms up. "You're just too kissable." I raised an eyebrow mischievously.

Ethan rolled his eyes but grinned. He helped me prepare the rest of the meal and get the dining room ready for company. We hadn't eaten in there in quite awhile, so there were papers, reports and sketches everywhere. Ethan cleaned them all up, making sure they were out of sight so Ms. Woods wouldn't stumble across them, and then set the table.

Dinner was just about ready when the doorbell rang. Simon had already arrived. Ethan had met him at the door and told him they would have to pretend to be brothers for the evening, and that Simon would have to talk with an American accent so Ms. Woods wouldn't suspect anything. Simon wasn't used to taking on different personas the way Ethan was, since he was usually the background tech Hleo on a mission, so listening to him practice his accent was downright hilarious.

I took a deep breath and mentally reminded myself to be on my best behavior or my life would become even more complicated, both at home and school. Dad opened the front door and ushered Ms. Woods into the living room. "Rose brought ice cream." Dad held up the container of vanilla swirl.

I stood from my spot on the couch. "That's great. It will go well with the pumpkin pie."

Ethan and Simon got up as well.

"Oh, hello." Ms. Woods eyebrows shot up. "It's… Ethan, isn't it?"

Ethan nodded. "That's right. Good to see you, Ms. Woods. And this is my brother, Simon." Ethan put a hand on Simon's shoulder.

"Hi there." Simon waved.

"Ethan and Simon are old family friends. Their parents are out of town at the moment so we offered to feed them," Dad explained.

"That's nice," Ms. Woods said, but shot me a conspiratorial grin when he looked away.

My cheeks warmed. "Which I guess we should get to." I took the ice cream from Dad and ducked into the kitchen to grab the food. Ethan and Simon helped while Ms. Woods and Dad walked into the dining room. Once we were all settled, with Dad at the head of the table, Ms. Woods on his left, Simon on the other side of her, and me on the other side of the table with Ethan, we dug into the meal.

"This roast is delicious, Hannah." Ms. Woods took another bite of food.

"Thanks. Roast is always my default meal for company." I speared a carrot with my fork.

"I wish I could cook. My recipe books might as well be takeout menus for the amount of skill I have in the kitchen." Ms. Woods laughed lightly.

"It takes lots of practice, and lots of burnt or ruined meals, but it's definitely a skill worth having. At least, that's what my… er, what I've always been told." I reached for my glass of water and took a big gulp. Under the table, Ethan nudged my leg with his knee. I glanced over at him and he gave me a sympathetic smile.

"So you two seem a little far apart in age." Ms. Woods turned her attention to Simon and Ethan, and I sighed with relief. When Dad had come up with the backstory, I'd hoped Ms. Woods wouldn't find the age difference between the thirty-three year old Simon and twenty-one year old Ethan odd. *How will you handle this one, boys*?

"We're actually half-brothers. We share a mother." Simon reached across the oak dining room table to grab the salt.

"Oh." Ms. Woods took a sip of water.

"Yes. My father died when I was just a baby. My dear mother was a sweet but lonely woman. Then on one fateful trip to Yellowstone she met the man who would father Ethan." Simon's 'American' accent was getting more southern as he spoke. "You see, I was a precocious little boy and I accidentally wandered a tad too close to old faithful. Well, if Walt—Ethan's Dad—hadn't been there, I don't know what would have happened."

My mouth fell open as I listened to Simon's melodramatic account.

Ethan rolled his eyes. "You slipped and fell off one of the viewing benches."

"I scraped my knee pretty good." Simon shoveled a forkful of potato into his mouth. "And how do you know what happened? You weren't there. It was still a good six years before you came along."

"I highly doubt Dad's version of the story is wrong, and I've heard that one at least a hundred times." Ethan shook the buttered roll in his hand at Simon. They were naturals. With their easy rapport, no one would ever question they were brothers.

Everyone was pretty much finished with their meals, and it hadn't been nearly as painful as I'd expected. I stood to start gathering plates, just as an image flashed before my eyes. It was a guy, crouching in the corner of a sophisticate-looking office, with dark mahogany paneling and large picture windows with huge drapery panels framing them. It was dark outside the glass, but a light shone towards the guy, possibly from some kind of lamp. The guy looked to be in his mid-thirties with dark hair and glasses; he was dressed in a dark suit, and had the appearance of a businessman, or perhaps a scholar. Books lining the wall behind him reinforced that idea. The man had a terrified look on his face and he held both arms in the air, as though protecting himself from an assault of some kind. The image was so graphic and filled with fear, I gasped.

"Hannah?" My dad's voice was thick with concern.

The image faded as quickly as it had come, into the back of my mind to be pulled out at another time. I looked around to see my four dinner companions staring at me, all looking as concerned as Dad sounded.

"I'm sorry; I just got… a headache all of a sudden." I rubbed my temples and shot a knowing look at the guys.

"Are you all right?" Ms. Woods stood and reached out to touch my arm. Little worry lines creased her usually smooth forehead.

"I'm fine, it's gone now."

"Well, you sit. We can do the dishes. I may not be able to cook, but I certainly know how to clean." Ms. Woods started to gather dirty plates together.

"Oh no, that's okay, you're our guest. I'm fine, really."

Ms. Woods lifted a hand. "I insist, now sit."

I obeyed and let her and the guys take everything off the table.

"We'll get the dessert and coffee ready." Dad gave me an understanding nod as he and Ms. Woods exited the dining room.

Once Dad and Ms. Woods were safely out of earshot in the kitchen, Ethan and Simon both leaned in closer, waiting for me to explain my flash.

"Sorry I didn't hide that reaction very well; the image was just sort of dark." My eyebrows furrowed as I explained what I'd seen to Ethan and Simon. It didn't happen often, but occasionally my visions would be of this nature, as though I was catching a protected during a moment of attack against him or her. I always felt shaken up after having this kind of flash. It was hard enough to have images of real people popping into my head without them being dark, violent ones.

"How do you feel now?" Ethan asked. He knew I didn't like these flashes. As of yet only two of the handful of violent images I had seen were accounted for, which meant there was a good possibility the rest were of the future. That knowledge added a great deal of pressure to Ethan and Simon's mission to discover who these people were and make sure a Hleo found them before my images had a chance to play out.

"I'm fine, it was just a little startling. He wasn't being beaten or anything, but it looked like he was just about to be." I shook my head.

"As soon as Ms. Woods goes we'll give you a chance to get it down on paper." Ethan rubbed my back reassuringly.

I took a deep breath, trying to compose myself so Ms. Woods wouldn't think anything was wrong with me.

She and Dad came back in shortly after with the pie already cut into pieces and a fresh pot of coffee. After a minute or so Dad cleared his throat and spoke up. "I've been considering your drawing talent, Hannah, and I was thinking you could really use the Glain Neidr." The humor in his tone suggested he was trying to make one of his history jokes.

I narrowed my eyes. "The what?" I'd never heard of the Glain Neidr before.

"The Glain Neidr. It's an ancient mythical necklace full of great power. It's said to have assisted many historical figures rise to power in different ways," he explained.

"So, how exactly would that help me?" I frowned as Ms. Woods' eyebrows shot up.

"Well, as the story goes, when a person wears the Glain Neidr, it heightens whatever their greatest natural ability is to the point where they become unstoppable in that particular area. The first person believed to have worn it was Sir William Gray, a knight during the Middle Ages, around 1300 AD. If I recall correctly he was on some sort of quest bestowed on him by King Edward the first, and he ended up on what is now The Isle of Man. When a storm blew in, he sought shelter in one of the seaside caves that run deep underground. While there, a luminescent glow in the earth caught his eye. It was the stone of the Glain Neidr calling to him. He picked up the smooth round dark stone, with the bizarre, perfectly circular hole in the middle of it, and knew that he had found something special.

The legend goes that he slipped the stone onto a gold chain and wore it around his neck for luck in battle. Sir William Gray already had a reputation as a talented swordsman, but apparently, once the Glain Neidr was around his neck, he was invincible. He was unyielding and undefeated until his death, which occurred when a rival knight stole the Glain Neidr and challenged him to a duel." Dad thrust his casted arm forward as though he were holding a sword.

"Dad, be careful!" I warned.

"Yes, Richard, you don't want to do any damage to that wrist of yours." Ms. Woods rested a hand on his good arm.

"I'm fine." He straightened up in his seat. His voice was fully animated, now that he was in history sharing mode. "After Sir William, the Glain Neidr ended up in the possession of Gwendolyn the Fair. Apparently the knight who stole the necklace from Sir William offered it to Lady Gwendolyn as a token of his love, not realizing the extraordinary power the necklace possessed. Once the necklace was around her neck news spread throughout the known world of her matchless beauty. It seems that she radiated a natural charm that caused men to lose their senses. Her powers of seduction were so great that she caused royal brothers to become enemies, and eventually brought down an entire nation." Dad brought his cup of coffee to his lips.

"I met a girl like that in Amsterdam once." Simon took a bite of his pie.

"Mmm." Dad gave him a knowing nod.

"Richard!" Ms. Woods' eyes were wide, but Dad just grinned into his mug.

Ethan and I exchanged a bewildered look. Dad was downright giddy, for him.

He scratched his chin. "Let's see. After her there was Hanns Gyorhab, known to have had the strength of twenty men, who once lifted an entire building from the foundation on which it stood. Then came Nicholas Rye, the man with the swiftest feet on earth who ran the length of Ireland in only one day. There are plenty of historical figures whose great feats have been credited to the Glain Neidr. Of course no one has ever proven the artifact actually exists. There's a good possibility it doesn't. It's just one of those teaser items of folklore people use to try to explain how a figure in history could have done something extraordinary. Believe me, I have many a colleague that has tried to track down the stone and they always end up frustrated and give up the search. It's in the same league as the Holy Grail, or the lost city and gold of Paititi. It may have at one point existed, but now it has been lost to us forever." He tipped back in his chair.

I waved my fork at him. "A lost, potentially fictional necklace of power is somehow supposed to help me with my art? How about if we keep the suggestions to things that would actually be useful for me, okay Dad?" I scrunched my nose up, pretending to be annoyed. In reality I loved listening to his stories. I looked over at Ethan to see what he thought of Dad's tale.

He had a strange look on his face, as though he was deep in thought. *What's that about?*

"I can't really help you then; my suggestions are patently unuseful." Dad shoveled the last bite of pie into his mouth.

"Besides, Richard, she doesn't need anything to improve her ability. She's a fantastic artist, probably the best I've ever taught." Ms. Woods started stacking the dessert plates to take to the kitchen.

"Thanks Ms. Woods, I appreciate that." I smiled.

"That's true, she is very talented. I just needed an excuse to share a history lesson." Dad gave me a little wink.

It was unlike him to be so comical. Was it Ms. Woods' presence that was making him so light-hearted? If this was the side she brought out in him, then I supposed I could try to accept their dating as a good thing.

Shortly after the dishes were cleared, Dad and Ms. Woods' headed out for an evening stroll.

"I'm going to go too, mates." Simon grabbed a slice of pie from the plate on the kitchen island and squashed the whole thing into his mouth. "Some of us have to get up early and get to work," he mumbled around the food.

Ethan tossed the dish towel he'd been using to dry a pot at him. Simon swallowed and grinned good-naturedly as he tossed it back. He pointed a finger in Ethan's direction. "Don't stay out too late, *little brother*. You've got work to do yourself tomorrow."

Before Ethan could respond, Simon was gone and it was just the two of us alone in the house again.

Twenty-Two

The sun had set by the time the two of us settled across from each other at the kitchen table to work on our algebra homework, the overhead hanging light bathing us in a dim glow. I wanted to get the drawing I had seen at dinner down on paper as there was no way I wanted it floating around in my subconscious while I was trying to fall asleep, but this work was due in the morning, and I needed to get it out of the way before I could draw. We worked in silence for a while, until I glanced up to see Ethan staring off into space.

"Stuck on a tricky question?" I teased.

"Sorry, it's nothing." His expression relaxed, but the look in his eyes was still disconcerted.

I set down my pencil. "Okay, either you are the worst liar ever, or you really want to tell me something, but you aren't sure if you should." I stood up and came around to sit next to him at the table.

He studied me for a moment with those intense green eyes of his, then took my hand and started absent-mindedly playing with my fingers.

"Suspense built, just lay it on me. It can't be any weirder or worse than anything I already know." I tried not to be distracted by his fingers intertwined with mine.

"It's about that story your dad mentioned at dinner."

"About the Glain Neidr stone? What about it?" I sat up straighter, my curiosity piqued.

"Your dad wasn't completely correct." Ethan ran his free hand over his face. "It's real."

My eyes went wide. "But Dad said it wasn't supposed to exist."

"Neither am I."

I focused on our linked hands. "I guess that's true. So if this mysterious stone does exist, what does that mean? Do you think it could help me?"

"I'm not sure; I've never actually seen it in action before. Like your dad, I've only heard stories about it. The Glain Neidr used to be in the possession of the Hleo society. It's believed to be made of the same hard stone the circular rooms are made from, and it does have an unexplainable ability to bestow the wearer with certain powers. The stories your dad told probably contain more truth than he realizes. It might be able to give you more control over your visions, but the necklace was stolen from the Hleo by a faction group of the Bana just over four hundred years ago."

"The Bana." I scrunched up my nose. I was really starting to hate those guys.

Ethan squeezed my hand. "This group was known as the Geltisians. Some of the older members of the Bana didn't like the new regime after Isaac's son Eric took over for his father. Eric was similar to Isaac in many ways, as far as his thirst for power and desire for control went, but he had a few quirks. Eric was obsessed with security and was a deeply paranoid person. Because of this, members of the Bana felt he put too much emphasis on fortifying and protecting the Bana's position around the globe and, as a result, their society was moving too far away from luxurious enjoyment and pleasure."

"We wouldn't want that, would we?" I pursed my lips. *Power, wealth, and pleasure at any cost, what do these lowlifes want with me?*

Ethan gave me a wry grin "In any case, this group of frivolous partiers broke off from the main Bana and Eric's rule. The Geltisians were only focused on amassing wealth. Somehow they found out about the Hleo's collection of priceless artifacts. They planned a heist and made off with over half of the objects in the collection, including the Glain Neidr. The Geltisians weren't an incredibly organized or motivated group, and eventually they fizzled out, but by the time they did the necklace had been sold off. I don't know where it ended up after that." Ethan tapped his finger on the table as he spoke.

"So it's missing." My shoulders slumped.

Ethan contemplated me, his eyebrows furrowed.

What aren't you telling me? "Ethan?"

"It is missing, but there is one place we could go where we might be able to dig up some information on it."

"Where?" I held my breath, hoping he would say what I wanted to hear.

"The Hleo have much more extensive records on hard-to-find historical artifacts than the average library."

"So what are you saying?" I was practically falling out of my chair I was so excited.

Ethan sighed. "I think we need to take a look at their library. We need to go to Veridan."

I wanted to do a cartwheel. Ethan was giving in on going to the stomping grounds of the Hleo leaders. The words he'd spoken earlier flashed across my mind and my face fell a little. "Do you think they'll agree to see me?"

"I'll contact The Three and tell them you've requested to speak with them. I'm hoping Alexander's sudden interest in you, as well as your connection to the Hleo world through Elizabeth, will be enough to convince them. But if they refuse, there is still a way for us to get there." Ethan flipped the cover of his textbook closed.

"How?" I leaned in closer and my knee grazed against his.

"The Hleo learned a long time ago that the mysterious draws far more suspicion than the ordinary. To blend in effectively they founded the Memores Foveat Historical Society, a legitimate organization working to preserve pieces of history across the globe that are in danger of being destroyed . Veridan is the American headquarters for the society, and for the most part the grounds are open to the public."

Ethan ran a hand over his forehead. "It's not ideal, but if The Three refused to meet with you, we could visit the grounds on our own. The only trick would be trying to access the closed-off part of the library where the rare and classified manuscripts are kept."

I took in the strain around his eyes, the tight line of his lips. Clearly this would not be his first choice of action. *Is he breaking the rules for my sake?* Our relationship had already put him in jeopardy.

I had a feeling that if we showed up unannounced at Veridan, The Three wouldn't be too pleased with Ethan, and the last thing I wanted was to get him in more trouble.

"Would The Three be okay with that?"

He slid one arm around the back of my chair and rested the other arm on the table so I was inside his arm span. "It doesn't matter if they're not. You're right, Hannah, we have to do something, and we're just spinning our wheels looking at your pictures over and over again. I'm sure they're going to resist, and I doubt they'll actually give you any concrete answers, but if we can get to Veridan and get our hands on some information about the Glain Neidr, it might be able to help you. Then maybe you can be free from all this destiny stuff. That would be worth any risk we had to take."

"I just want to stop feeling like a freak show. I want to know what I'm supposed to do, so I can do it. But, there are certain parts of all this destiny stuff that I would be unable to live without." I slowly slid my arms around his neck. He was the one thing that I knew I couldn't live without, and the one reason I was so glad all of this had happened to me.

He slipped his arms around my waist and pulled me in until our lips met. As we kissed the world melted away. All I wanted was to hold on to this moment, to stay right here with him. This was the closest we had been since Katie's movie night. Ethan had been putting in extra effort to keep an eye on Dad since the kidnapping. Between that, work, school, hanging out with friends, and trying to figure out my drawing ability with Simon, there hadn't been much chance for us to be alone together. Part of me wondered if Ethan was using all of the distractions as an excuse to avoid being alone with me.

The intensity between us was rising; his kiss grew more urgent. I pressed against him, and was about to sit on his lap, when he jerked away.

"Sorry," he exclaimed breathlessly, sliding his chair back so we weren't touching.

"No problem," I replied, also breathing hard. I wasn't sure what else to say. He seemed so reluctant to take our relationship further physically, and I didn't want to push him. I still hadn't figured out a way to ask what Simon had meant when he'd said it would be bad for us to sleep together.

He cleared his throat. "I should contact Veridan. Now that we have a plan there's no sense putting it off." He got up from the table and went to make the call. Or was it to put more space between us?

I tried to go back to my homework, but now my mind was completely pre-occupied. What were The Three like? How much would they be able or willing to tell me? What did the place Ethan called home when he was off duty look like? A ripple of excitement worked its way through me. Was it possible I was about to find all of that out?

Ethan had mentioned once that the grounds we quite expansive and surrounded by dense forest. Would it be like a fortress, with typed passwords and retinal scans, and the sort of security seen in spy movies?

As I read and reread the math problem in front of me, giving it my divided attention, I hoped Ethan would be able to get us an audience with The Three sooner than later.

Twenty-Three

Ethan, Simon, and I drove in silence to the train station in New Haven. It was one in the morning, and we were due to board a train headed for Richmond, Virginia that would depart in less than an hour. Ethan had managed to arrange a meeting with The Three for five days after his phone call, so here we were in the middle of the night, on our way to see them.

Ever since Paige and Uri kidnapped my dad, Ethan had been worried we were under some sort of surveillance, so he came up with a covert strategy to get us to Veridan. The two of us had snuck out of my house in the middle of the night and cut through the path that led to the street behind, where Simon had been waiting with his car. Ethan's Jeep and my car remained parked conspicuously in my driveway.

Simon was behind the wheel as we closed in on the New Haven train station, a forty-five minute drive south of East Halton. Once Ethan and I were safely on the train, Simon would return to my house and keep watch over my dad while we were gone.

I sat in the backseat watching the occasional car's headlights pass by, always nervous that the driver would make a quick U-turn and come after us. The adrenaline generated by our clandestine mission was making it impossible to relax. I wouldn't be able to breathe easy until we were settled on the train, and Ethan was absolutely sure no one had followed us.

We drove into the train station's parking lot and Ethan and Simon surveyed the space. I didn't notice anything suspicious, only a handful of parked cars, and not a soul walking around. They seemed content with our surroundings and Ethan grabbed our bags from Simon's trunk. "Thanks for the ride. Let me know when you're back at Hannah's house."

"Will do." Simon kicked at an icicle hanging on the bottom of his car. "Say hi to everyone at Veridan for me."

"Sure, we can do that." I placed a hand on his forearm. "Thanks for watching my dad while we're gone."

"No problem, love. I'll attempt not to lose him this time." Simon's tone was jokey, but the regret in his voice undermined the humor.

"He's in excellent hands." I gave him a reassuring smile.

"We'll see you in a few days. Let me know if there's any trouble on your end." Ethan slung the strap of my bag across his chest.

"You too," Simon said.

Ethan nodded and stepped up onto the curb. I gave Simon a wave, then followed Ethan into the station. He paid for the two tickets with cash and we walked out to the platform to wait. There wasn't anyone else around besides the guy at the ticket kiosk, but Ethan was on edge. His shoulder muscles were tensed, and his eyes subtly inspected the exposed space every so often. He hadn't said anything, but I knew it was only a matter of time before Paige struck again, and since Uri had been confirmed alive, or at least not killed in the cottage fire, the Russian assassin would no doubt be looking to exact revenge against Ethan.

We sat quietly on a bench waiting for the train. I absentmindedly scrolled through my phone, glancing over at Ethan once in a while. He was best left alone when he was in this frame of mind. He would be trying to stay completely focused on the task at hand, and I didn't want to be the one to break that concentration. It was hard, but I kept reminding myself that even though we were together, his first job was to keep me alive; trying to convince him otherwise was fruitless.

We both stood as the rumble of the approaching train grew louder. As planned, we'd only had to wait about ten minutes for it. Ethan was doing all he could to minimize the risks. The station's overhead PA crackled out the announcement that we could board. We handed our tickets to the conductor and made our way into the first passenger car. A man in a rumpled business suit slept in the back corner, a college-aged couple were passed out a few rows up from him, their oversized camping backpacks spread out on the seats across from them, and an elderly man sat at the front of the car, engrossed in a novel. We kept moving and found that the next car was empty. Ethan motioned to the rear and we settled in—me on the inside seat, Ethan in the aisle seat—with our backs to a wall.

The train shuddered and jerked and slowly began moving just after we were seated. The lingering heaviness of needing to sleep crept over me and I stifled a yawn. I gave my head a little shake, trying to wake myself up.

"You should try to get some sleep. We aren't going to arrive until morning, so there's no sense staying up for the whole trip." Ethan fiddled with our bags, making sure they were secure in the seat across from him.

"Yeah, maybe I'll do that. I want to be rested for our time at Veridan." I let my head fall back against the headrest, which was surprisingly soft. I was trying not to freak out about meeting with The Three. Ethan had told me a little bit about them, but I had no clue what they were going to say to me. I figured that, even if they were cryptic and refused to divulge anything helpful, at least we had the backup plan of tracking down the Glain Neidr. I only hoped we would be able to find some useful information in Veridan's library. I closed my eyes and my mind started to paint a picture of what Veridan could look like. Would it be a castle? A barracks? I couldn't wait to get there. Excitement churned in the pit of my stomach.

I tried to doze. The gentle swaying of the train almost lulled me to sleep a few times, but I could feel Ethan's tension. Every once in a while I would open my eyes to peer over at him, and every time he was staring off with a concerned frown on his face. We had been traveling for over an hour when I finally couldn't take it anymore.

"Hey, is everything okay?" I gently placed a hand on his. He took it for a second, giving it a light squeeze before releasing it again. We had both agreed that once we were on the train we needed to act as though we were simply friends. We couldn't afford to have anyone notice anything romantic between us while we were on our way to The Three, even a normal civilian who could be questioned about us for some reason.

"You should be sleeping." Ethan turned to look at me.

"I'll sleep in a bit. You seem worried, is there something you haven't told me?" I raised an eyebrow. *Why is he avoiding my question?*

Ethan ran his hand across his forehead. "The Three are worried about you. They think the attacks on you have been more aggressive than on the usual protected and, given your unique ability, they're wrestling with the best way to proceed. I haven't even told them about the latest incident involving your father. From the reports I've given, I've painted the picture that your biggest threat was Adam, that all the attempts back in the fall were part of a larger plan he was orchestrating to keep me distracted. Because things died down after that, The Three relaxed a little, but now, with what just happened, I'm not sure what they will think." Ethan drew in a slow breath. Now that he'd told me what was on his mind, the muscles across his shoulders seemed to have relaxed a little.

"Do they think you're not doing a good job of looking out for me? Because I don't see what else you could possibly do." I shrugged. *What is he so worried about?*

Ethan looked at me for a second, an unreadable expression on his face, then he smiled. "I'm sure I'm just worrying for no reason. Forget I said anything, I just haven't been back to the grounds in a long time." His tone was casual, but his eyes remained veiled. Was he keeping something from me? I let it go since there was something else I wanted to ask him.

"What about Adam?" In the weeks following Adam's attempt on my life, Ethan had scoured the area for any clues that would lead him to Adam's trail, but Ethan's old enemy had vanished. I knew Ethan was frustrated. He had been pressing all of his connections tirelessly, trying to track down Adam's location, but so far his efforts had been futile.

We hadn't really talked about Adam since the fall, not even about what it meant to Ethan that his sworn enemy was up and walking around again, and not six feet underground in a coffin, where Ethan had left him decades ago.

Ethan's jaw tightened. "There haven't been any signs of him. I don't know if he's working with Paige this time. It feels different somehow. If I were to guess, I would say he's still hiding out, probably trying to come up with a new plan of attack, and that she's working without him."

"I'm sure you're right. He took a long time to prepare his plan at the library, so he'll probably take a while to come up with something else. I'm not worried though; I know you and Simon can handle it. I just wondered how you are with the whole situation." I bit my lip and watched his face for a reaction. He looked conflicted, as though it was an issue he didn't want to think about.

"I'm mad at myself that he managed to get as close to you as he did." Ethan tapped the armrest of his seat. I winced at the double meaning of his words. Adam had wreaked both physical and emotional havoc in my world, and I mentally kicked myself once again for being taken in by his charm.

I twisted the silver ring on my index finger. "He was very cunning, and he had the advantage because you believed he was still buried."

"He always was crafty. It's hard because I thought I was done with him. I guess I always knew there was the possibility he would escape, but I didn't want to believe it. I should have killed him when I had the chance, but…" Ethan's gaze shifted towards the window and he stared out into the passing blackness.

"But you were friends."

He contemplated my words for a moment. "I guess that's it. I always believed that, no matter how angry and bitter he was, eventually he would be able to work through it, but he's not the same person he once was. I suppose I'm to blame for that." Ethan's green eyes seemed darker than normal.

I shook my head. "How can you be to blame for that guy's actions?"

"When I turned him in, he went off the deep end. I don't know if I made the right decision. It was a complicated situation and maybe if I hadn't given up on him a lot of people would still be alive, including Lucien." Ethan's voice was barely above a whisper as he mentioned his mentor, a man Adam had killed many years ago.

I crossed my arms over my chest. "He let a protected die. You were only doing your job. And just because the Hleo kicked him out, or whatever, doesn't mean he needed to immediately go revenge crazy. He could have tried to lead a normal life. He's just a terrible human being, and he deserves whatever punishment he gets."

“You’re right, of course. Still, I let him hang around too long, and it almost cost me you. As soon as I get the chance, Adam’s life will come to an end, and you will never have to worry about him again.” Ethan’s voice was thick with anger as his brow crinkled in a deep frown.

My heart skipped a beat. I was about to wrap my arms around his neck, not caring about the promise we had made to keep our distance, and pull his mouth to mine, when the conductor opened the door to our train car. We both froze and I quickly shrank back, incredibly annoyed at the man’s bad timing.

Once the conductor had passed through our car and we were alone again, Ethan gently slipped his fingers between mine and brought my hand to his lips. “Thank you for being you,” he whispered as he released my hand. Happiness washed over me as I rested my head on his shoulder.

We drifted into silence, each lost in our own thoughts. Why didn’t Ethan want to tell The Three what had happened to my dad? What did he think they would do? A knot formed in my stomach. They wouldn’t tell him he couldn’t be my Hleo anymore, would they?

Twenty-Four

I wasn't sure what time it was when I awoke, but my head was no longer on Ethan's shoulder. I was leaning towards the window of the train, and Ethan had moved to take the seat facing mine. At some point Ethan had covered me with one of the train's travel blankets, and I was glad for its cozy warmth.

The sun was up and filtering warmly through the glass as we glided along the tracks. Scenic rolling hills of lush fields and forests stretched as far as the eye could see. Because we were traveling south the trees were already starting to bud, and the landscape was greener, less bleak than the scenery near East Halton.

I reluctantly slipped my arm out from under the cover to check my watch. It was already after eight. It had been nearly three in the morning by the time I had fallen asleep. *Ah, a nice five hours of rest.*

Ethan's eyes were shut. As I watched him, I realized this was the first time I'd ever seen him sleep. Did he somehow feel safer as we got close to the place he called home when he was off duty? The train was set to arrive just before nine. Should I wake him? I straightened in my seat and his eyes opened. His gaze met mine and a warm smile spread across his lips.

"Good morning." He sounded rested and somewhat relaxed compared to the night before.

"Morning. Thank you for the blanket." I rubbed my hand across the fuzzy blue covering.

"You looked cold." Ethan checked his watch before glancing out at the passing scenery, a large apple orchard that covered hundreds of acres. The trees were just beginning to bud; they would be gorgeous in about a month when they were in full blossom.

"The train looks to be on schedule, we should be arriving shortly." He stepped into the aisle and stretched his arms above his head.

I followed him and we made our way to the dining car to get a cup of coffee and something to eat before the train reached Richmond. A driver would meet us at the train station and we would head straight to Veridan, which was located in the countryside of Virginia.

We each got a coffee and I chose a blueberry muffin, while Ethan grabbed a bagel. We slid into one of the green vinyl booths that lined both sides of the dining car. Just as we finished our meals the train started to slow down, and an announcement overhead informed us that we had arrived at our stop.

Once we had exited the train, we wove our way through the station until we came out the other side to a large parking lot. Ethan scanned the lot, slowly and deliberately. I joined him, although I wasn't sure who we were looking for. After about thirty seconds I spotted a guy a little older than Ethan, probably close to thirty, dressed in a chauffeur's uniform complete with hat, waiting patiently off to the side of the exit doors. I had expected him to be holding a sign with our names on it, I guess because they always are in the movies, but he wasn't. It didn't matter though, Ethan seemed to recognize the guy, and gave him a nod of acknowledgement as we approached.

"Michael." Ethan stuck out his hand.

Michael shook it enthusiastically. "Ethan, good to see you again buddy. Let me grab those for you." The chauffeur reached for my overnight bag. I handed it off, but Ethan kept his bag with him.

He turned and touched my upper arm. "Michael Katz, this is Hannah Reed."

"Hi." I shook his left hand awkwardly since he was holding my bag in his right hand.

"Nice to meet you, Hannah." Michael gave me a friendly smile as we headed towards a sleek black town car.

"You too."

Michael kept pace beside Ethan. "So what have you been up to since Buenos Aires? I heard about you taking out Martinez. Man, I hated that guy."

"It was unavoidable. He had me cornered in a back alley." Ethan's eyes locked with mine, pleading for understanding as he held the car door for me. I gave him a slight nod as I shuffled past him into the backseat. For better or worse, that was what Ethan did.

"Hey man, no explanation needed, the more Bana scum cut down the better." Michael climbed behind the wheel and soon we were on our way. The chauffeur was chatty and kept the conversation going for the duration of our drive. He had a similar build to Ethan's, but was a little taller and lankier. His short dark hair curled a little, and complemented his dark eyes and infectious smile.

He wanted to know all about where Ethan had been and what he'd been up to the last few years. As they talked, I noticed that Michael answered all of Ethan's questions, giving far more information than Ethan had asked for, while Ethan skillfully avoided answering Michael's questions directly, keeping his responses vague with answers like "overseas," or "in Eastern Europe for a few months."

We drove for over an hour. The wilderness grew thicker as we traveled, until it had been a good twenty minutes since we had passed by any sort of building. My curiosity about the Hleo's headquarters kicked into high gear as we drew closer. I peered out the window at the tree-lined highway as Michael started slowing down. He pulled off the road and turned in at a security gatehouse, a red-and-gray-bricked building with a steep clay-shingled roof. He drove under a wide stone arch and stopped to talk to the guard posted at the station. A moment later the steel bar rose and we continued on our way.

Copper peaks of rooftop began appearing through the trees. We wound our way up a narrow paved road, through a dense forest, until the trees thinned out and I could see all of the estate. My breath caught in my throat as I took it in.

We were coming up to a massive front lawn, a long, perfectly manicured rectangle with laneways bordering either side that curved around and met at the front of the house. In the middle of the flat grassy space was a wide, round fountain, shooting a cascade of water straight up into the air. Even though it was the tail end of winter, the grass was lush and green. Beyond the yard was the estate, a sprawling manor pulled straight from the pages of a fairytale. The sand-colored, Chateauesque building consisted of four distinct sections of ornamented and elaborately carved stone. Columns, archways, and a mixture of rectangle and rounded windows adorned the façade of the manor, while a gray-shingled roof, trimmed out in green copper, rose high into the sky, flanked by several chimneys. It was hard not to gasp at the sheer grandeur and awesomeness of the building.

"Ethan, this place is magnificent," I whispered. My shoulder brushed against his. Ethan nodded, but he went stiff at my close proximity and I immediately backed away. I was really going to have to watch my behavior, or we would be caught for sure.

Michael drove up the laneway to the right of the rambling lawn and stopped the car in front of the main entrance, two impressive wrought iron doors. He climbed out and walked around to open the door for Ethan and me. I shimmied out of the seat, keeping my eyes on the impressive structure as I waited for Ethan to join me. A few people strolled around the immaculate grounds, but no one seemed interested in us.

We were standing on the expansive walkway when a woman holding a clipboard came out a side door from the left wing, made her way across a walkway partly covered by rounded archways, and walked over to us. "Ethan, how good to see you again."

She had the look of an administrative assistant, with her blonde hair tied back in a sleek ponytail at the nape of her neck, dark mini skirt and white button-up blouse, fashionable glasses, and sensible flats.

"Bridget, it's good to see you too." Ethan gave her a warm smile. "I'd like to introduce you to Hannah Reed." Ethan rested a gentle hand on my back.

"Hannah, we've all been very excited for your arrival." Bridget's lips curved up but her blue eyes remained reserved. *Does she not mean that*?

"I'm excited to be here."

"You're free to wander the grounds. I'll have Michael take your stuff up to your rooms. The Three are unfortunately tied up in foundation meetings all day, and won't actually have a chance to make your acquaintance until this evening. The festivities begin around seven, so—"

"Festivities?" Ethan's eyebrows shot up.

Bridget's eyes narrowed. "You do remember protocol, don't you, Ethan?" She sounded annoyed by his interruption, but kept the professional smile on her face.

"Of course." Ethan fists tightened.

"Right. As I was saying, the festivities—an awards ceremony for the foundation—will begin around seven, in the main ballroom." Bridget spoke slowly, and Ethan caught my attention and discretely rolled his eyes. "Party guests will likely start arriving sometime this afternoon since the grounds have been opened to the public for the day. If you could try to keep to yourselves as much as possible, I know it would be greatly appreciated."

Translation: stay away from regular foundation members. The woman was starting to get to me too. Who did she think she was?

Ethan sighed. "I know, Bridget. So, are we staying on Waverly floor?" He inclined his head in the direction of the left tower, where Bridget had come from.

"Actually, we have you on Ashby. Quite a few foundation members have chosen to take advantage of staying overnight, since opening up the house to guests isn't something we normally do. Waverly is almost completely booked, so we had to move you elsewhere." Bridget consulted her clipboard. "There are only three other Hleo on your floor, so you shouldn't be disturbed."

"Which rooms are we in? I can take our stuff; Michael doesn't need to do that." Ethan nodded to our driver, who was now leaning against the town car looking bored. Michael gave him an appreciative grin.

"Hannah is in the Heathwood Suite, and you will be in the adjoining Heathwood servant's room, since you are her Hleo, after all. It's on the third floor." Bridget looked up from her paperwork, and handed Ethan two brass room keys.

"I remember where it is." Ethan's voice was flat.

"Okay, well, I have other things to attend to so I'll leave you to it." Bridget didn't react to Ethan's tone. "Michael, if you want to report back to the garage, I'm sure they will have more people for you to pick up from the airport. Hannah, I will see you around." She spun on her heel and headed back the way she had come.

"I guess I need to get back to the garage." Michael made a face and climbed back into the car and drove off, leaving Ethan and I standing on the front terrace.

Ethan picked up my bag. I followed him to the main doors. When he reached them, he transferred both bags to one hand and opened the wrought iron door, holding it for me as I approached. He shot me a wry grin as I passed by him. "Welcome to Veridan."

Twenty-Five

My eyes went wide as I meandered into the front foyer and took in the grand entrance hall, a long room with ornately carved arched doorways leading off in all directions. Vaulted dark cherry wood ceilings rose above us as we stood on the polished, taupe-colored marble floor. An opening in the wall to our right led into a beautiful solarium. Lush green plants filled the space, and sunlight poured in through the transparent ceiling. The room beckoned me with its warmth and glow, but Ethan walked in the opposite direction, towards a massive, spiraling staircase.

"We can drop our bags off and then I'll give you a proper tour." Ethan glanced back over his shoulder, following my gaze to the sunlit room.

I fell in step behind him. "Sounds good to me."

Our footsteps echoed on the marble as we circled our way up three stories. An intricate banister ran along the inside, and a rounded wall curved along the outside. Slanted windows afforded a great view of the front lawn and the surrounding forest as we made our way to the upper levels of the house.

Ethan stopped on the third level and headed to the right. "This is the floor active Hleo usually stay on. I had thought because you're not a Hleo they would have given you accommodations on the second floor where the general public stays, but this area is just as nice." Ethan led me through a wooden door into a beautiful parlor.

"This is amazing," I breathed as I ran a hand gently along the billiard table in the center of the room.

"It is pretty spectacular." Ethan nodded, but didn't stop. We crossed through the wood paneled space, exiting through a door disguised as part of the wall. *How crafty*. Ethan pulled the door shut behind us, and we stood in a long hallway containing a number of closed doors. Ethan trotted about halfway down, clearly knowing exactly where we were headed, and stopped at a door with a brass nameplate that read *Heathwood Suite*.

I held my breath. What could my room look like, when everything else had been so grand? Ethan inserted one of the keys into the lock and pushed the thick oak door open. I'd been expecting incredible, and I was still impressed. The ceiling towered above us; coffee-colored paneling with ornate crown molding covered the top half of the walls, while the bottom was painted a buttery yellow. A picture window ran from the crown molding to the floor, luxurious curtains framing it on either side. A massive canopy bed took up one side of the room, and a sitting area with a chaise lounge and two chairs built with the same wood as the bed stretched across the other. A collection of other furniture—an armoire, more chairs, a dressing table beside the bed—was scattered throughout the room.

"Ethan, I can't sleep here. This room looks like it's been perfectly preserved for at least a hundred years." I wandered gingerly into the space, avoiding a Persian rug lying on the beautiful wooden parquet floor. The last thing I needed was to destroy a priceless antique as my first interaction with Veridan.

"It's okay. Most of this furniture is reproduction; the originals are kept in secured storage." He sounded amused by my reverence. "Hleo use all the rooms on this floor when they come in from the field. The society only leaves it looking this way in case nosy museum guests make their way up here to see if the entire house is historically accurate."

"If you're sure." I gently set my overnight bag on the deep crimson bedspread, the same color as the curtains and the fabric on the furniture. Strolling through the room, I caught a glimpse through an open door to my left of an equally elegant bathroom.

When I reached the floor-to-ceiling window, I realized that the bottom half of the glass was actually an exit leading out to a rounded stone balcony. I grasped the handle, about to open the door, when I remembered something Bridget had said. My hand still on the knob, I looked back at Ethan. "What did Bridget mean when she said you'd be staying in the adjoining servant's room?" He crossed through the sitting area over to a narrow door on the far right wall, and pushed it open to reveal a significantly smaller and more modestly decorated space, although it still had a pair of cozy reading chairs pulled up to a stone fireplace.

I swallowed hard as I walked over to stand in the doorway. "We have connecting rooms?" I tried to sound completely un-phased by the idea of Ethan sleeping in practically the same room as me.

"I am your Hleo after all." Ethan parroted Bridget's earlier comment as he set his bag down on the bed. "The idea is that I need to be able to get to you always, and as unlikely as a threat here would be, I still need access to you on the remote chance a member of the Bana showed up and blocked your bedroom door." Ethan sounded indifferent towards the idea, although he did avoid my gaze as he spoke.

What do you really think of adjoining rooms, Ethan? "That makes sense." I backed into my room, tripping over an end table as I went. "I'm okay." I popped back up to my feet as Ethan hurried over to me. I had never been in Ethan's bedroom in all the time since he had come into my life. Occasionally I had gone over to the little bungalow he and Simon were staying in, but Simon had always been there, and I'd stayed in the living room.

I cleared my throat. "So, protocol?"

"Protocol." Ethan closed the door to his room, and we both moved into the plush sitting area of my bedroom. "The Hleo society has a protocol for everything it does. On the rare circumstance a protected is brought to Veridan, or any of our headquarters across the globe, the rule exists that it can only be during a time when Memores Foveat has some sort of public event going on. That way their presence blends in with the arrival of other guests. Bridget neglected to mention the event when she set up our visit, but I'm guessing it will be a black-tie affair with all the usual foundation members."

"A black-tie event?" I bit my lip as I mentally ran through the contents of my overnight bag.

"The foundation loves formality and elegance, but don't worry, it will be fine." Ethan gave me a reassuring smile.

I flopped down on the chaise. "I don't have anything even remotely close to appropriate for something like that. I thought we were just coming to see The Three."

"I had thought with the special circumstances surrounding you that they would forgo that specific protocol. I should have known better, since Bridget runs the administrative duties around here." Ethan sank down onto one of the armchairs.

"It doesn't seem like you two get along all that well."

"She's sort of like an annoying big sister who gets a kick from being able to boss everyone around. I can appreciate she has quite the job to do running the admin around here, but I think she enjoys harassing anyone she feels isn't falling in line a little too much. She can be a lot to take sometimes."

I straightened a cushion resting on the soft red velvet chaise. "Why don't you show me around?"

"Sure." Ethan stood and the two of us headed out again. He locked the door behind us, and slipped the keys into his pocket. I couldn't wait to get a look at the luxurious and mysterious manor Ethan had spent so much time in. The headquarters of a society no one knew existed had to be full of secrets. Maybe we'd stumble across at least one of them while we were here.

Twenty-Six

Ethan led the way back to the billiard room. "Active Hleo have downtime between assignments and they usually stay at one of the six stations around the globe. This lounge is for them and for new recruits that are still in training and Hleo that are here on extended work assignments, like Michael."

"Do you get a lot of downtime?" I walked around the large room, trying to picture the different Hleo I'd met playing pool, or chitchatting in front of the large fireplace on the comfortable-looking brown leather couches. Somehow I couldn't quite imagine any of them just relaxing, except maybe Simon.

"Every time we complete an assignment and Victor calls us back in, we're expected to stay for at least a month to decompress. It gives us a chance to unwind, relax, and get ready to take on the next persona." Ethan leaned against the doorway that led back out to the stairs, watching me. I was in no hurry to go. I plunked a few random keys of the piano sitting in the far corner, and scanned the titles of the books on a wall of shelves behind the piano.

"Is it hard to move from one identity to another?" I asked as I joined him.

"It can be, especially if you're stationed somewhere for a long time. The time off is a good way to reground yourself." Ethan held the door open for me and we continued our tour. As we reached the top of the staircase, Ethan explained that the sleeping quarters for new Hleo recruits—dormitory-style rooms that weren't overly exciting—were on the opposite side of the stairs.

We reached the second level but Ethan stayed on the stairs. "This is Waverley floor, designated accommodations for members of Memores Foveat." Ethan motioned to the hallway directly under the one we were staying on. "I'd show them to you but…"

"They're completely booked." I scrunched up my nose.

"Exactly." Ethan trekked down towards the main floor. As we explored, the enormity of Veridan kept hitting me. "It's strange that the Hleo would have a place like this."

"Why is that?" Ethan raised an eyebrow.

"The Hleo are all about secrecy and anonymity. It's odd to me that they would have this big ornate museum that's open to the public. It seems like it would be really hard to guard."

"I thought that too when I first came here, but I've learned that their strategy is to hide in plain sight. No one really questions the presence of the Hleo around here because a logical explanation exists. They work as interns and employees of Memores Foveat. That way they can be out in the open without looking suspicious." Ethan's hand rested on the banister.

"I get that the historical foundation is a great cover, but what if a member of the Bana showed up? Isn't it dangerous for The Three to just let people wander around here freely?" As if to prove my point, a young couple walked past us on the stairs. Ethan nodded to them politely, and they smiled in return. I wasn't sure, but I thought they stared at me a second longer than normal. They were gone before I could be certain, but I squared my shoulders, trying to appear poised just in case.

"It's sort of like The White House, or Buckingham Palace. The people who live in those buildings are considered some of the most important people on the planet to protect, but the grounds are still open to the public, or at least parts of them are. Even though thousands of people are in and out of those landmarks in a day, they are probably some of the most secure places on earth. And it's the same here. The amount of surveillance, check points, and hidden escape routes is incredible." He stopped and I realized we were standing in the main foyer where we had first come in.

"Surveillance everywhere. Are there cameras in the bedrooms?" I examined the upper corners of the large room, trying to spy a hidden camera. I was definitely not comfortable with the idea that someone would be watching me while I slept.

Ethan followed my gaze and smiled. "There are cameras in the bedrooms, but they've been designed not to record unless a forced entry alarm is triggered from the doors, or one of the panic buttons is activated by the individual in the room."

"So, tonight when I'm asleep…?"

"There will be cameras in your room, *not* recording you, unless someone tries to break into your room from the outside." Ethan's grin suggested he found my paranoia humorous.

I let out a sigh of relief. "Good, because I was not down with that whole private eyes are watching you, big brother thing."

Ethan stared at me for a second, then laughed. "Come on. I'll show you the solarium."

I followed right on his heels, excited to get a look at the glowing room. We stepped down into the sunken space as sunlight poured in from the beautifully crafted wood and glass ceiling.

The light felt warm and the greenery infused the space with a sense of calm. I took a slow breath. "This room is fantastic, it's so peaceful."

"It was originally used as a greenhouse so Hleo would have access to fresh vegetables year round. They grew all kinds of medicinal plants as well, but with the advancements in both medicine and technology, the botanical work of the Hleo sort of faded away. Now they just grow plants and flowers in here for decoration." Ethan let a large green leaf slip between his fingertips.

"Well, it's still beautiful, even if it's not useful anymore." I sat down on the marble ledge of the fountain in the center of the room and closed my eyes.

I could have stayed in the sun-filled room for a very long time, but now that we were down on the main floor, we were running into more guests. Couples and small groups walked around, taking in the history and architectural detail. We had only been in the solarium a minute or so when a plump elderly couple entered from an archway opposite where we had come from, so we moved on to another room before they could approach us and start up a conversation.

From the solarium we walked down a hall that led to a formal ballroom, a magnificent banquet hall with towering ceilings. The carved wood walls were covered with detailed tapestries. A large chandelier hung in the center of the room, and a gigantic triple-hearth stone fireplace graced the end wall. The showstopper though, had to be the full-sized pipe organ that sat in its own gallery on a second-level balcony, looking impressively gothic and enchanting. This was clearly where the evening festivities would take place. People were milling around everywhere, setting up tables, adding floral arrangements, doing last minute polishing.

"Wow." I breathed quietly, so as not to attract attention. "I can't believe how incredible this room is," I whispered to Ethan.

"It's been used for basically every major social gathering Memores Foveat has hosted through the years, from banquets to concerts." Ethan inclined his head towards the organ.

As we talked, I noticed more than one of the workers in the room peering over at us every now and then. They were trying to be casual, but I got the distinct impression they were very curious about the two of us. A young, dark-haired woman holding a box of tablecloths turned from what she was doing. As soon as she saw Ethan she dropped the box on the table and strode over to him, arms open wide.

"Ethan è così bello vederti, is so good to see you." She wrapped her arms around him.

Was that Italian? That did make sense, given her olive complexion and deep brown eyes.

Jealousy knotted in my stomach as he stepped back. *Come on Hannah, get it together, it's just a hug.*

She kept going before he had a chance to respond. "E 'passato troppo tempo. Stai benissimo, come sempre. Così come sei stato?"

"It has been awhile. It's nice to see you again too, Allegra."

My eyebrows shot up. I didn't realize Ethan understood Italian. He motioned to me. "Allow me to introduce you two. Allerga Fiore, this is Hannah Reed."

"Yes, of course. Hannah, it's so nice to meet you." Allegra's accent was thick as she took my hands in hers and gave them a squeeze.

"You too." I smiled but glanced over at Ethan. *How do you know each other?*

"Is Ethan being a good host, showing you everything?" Allegra gave him a grin.

"Yes, we've been making our way around. He knows a lot about this place." I nodded.

"Ah yes, Ethan is the best, so skilled." Allegra set an affable hand on Ethan's upper arm and it was all I could do not to bristle.

"He's very good at his job. I discover a new ability of his all the time. For example, I didn't realize he knows Italian." I forced my eyes off of her grip before my jealousy became painfully obvious.

"Ethan? He's a master linguist. What is it that you speak, ten different languages?" Allegra's laugh tinkled like an annoying little bell.

"Something like that." Ethan looked from Allegra to me, an uncomfortable tightness in his expression.

"I guess you wouldn't know those details about him though, would you?" Allegra beamed innocently at me.

"Right. Because he isn't supposed to share personal information with his protected." I picked at a loose thread on my sweater, trying to show off my knowledge of the inner workings of the Hleo.

Allegra shook her head. "No, because Ethan is a very private person. He always keeps everything to himself."

"Oh." I blinked. I thought of everything I knew about Ethan, all the memories and personal details he'd shared with me, and swallowed back a satisfied grin.

"We should really let you get back to work. I'm sure there's a lot to do. And I still have the back half of the manor to show Hannah." Ethan took a step towards the exit of the ballroom.

"Of course. Well I'm sure I'll see you tonight at the do, Hannah. Ethan, stare attenti con questa ragazza. Ritengo che ella abbia una sbandata per voi." Allegra had a mischievous gleam in her eye.

"Thanks for the heads up, Allegra. I think I can handle it, though," Ethan said.

"Ciao." She called over her shoulder as she strode back to the table she'd been working at.

I waited until we were out of the ballroom and standing in a long gallery that had massive tapestries running across its walls before I spoke. "I understood ciao, but what else did she say?"

Ethan cleared his throat. "She wanted to warn me. She thought you might have a crush on me."

"She what?" I clenched my jaw.

"She was trying to be playful."

"I'm sure she was." My hands balled tightly into fists.

"Hannah, if you're feeling intimidated, or jealous maybe, you should know—"

I shook my head. "It's all right. I mean, I don't exactly love that the girls around here are all gorgeous, but I get it. You have a very long past contained in these walls." I took a deep breath.

"That is true, but Hannah, I've never had a romantic relationship with any of them. I promise you." Ethan leaned in slightly closer to me.

I couldn't help but smile. "I'm fine. Allegra actually said something that sort of eased my jealousy, oddly enough."

"Really?" Ethan cocked his head to the side.

"She said I wouldn't know things about you because you're such a private person, but…" I lifted my shoulders slightly.

"Oh. Well, you can feel pretty confident in the fact that you know more about me than probably any other person on earth," Ethan said. His tone was casual, but my heart swelled. Did he have any idea how much those words meant to me?

"So, where are we now?" I forced my attention to the intricate depictions of different mythological and historical stories of legend woven into the wall art.

"We're in Veridan's tapestry gallery. It's pretty easy to guess why it's called that." Ethan motioned to the wall-hangings. "The society uses it as an overflow area when they have a large guest list, or, if they are having a formal sit-down dinner in the ballroom, they'll have the festivities move this way when the meal is done."

I followed him as he led me out of the tapestry room into a beautiful music room, and a proper salon. Then we made our way onto a magnificent stone terrace at the back of the property. A leafy canopy acted as a shelter on the patio, which had been built right around thick, twisting tree trunks.

"The grounds are beautiful." I walked over to stand beside one of the trees, looking out at the blossoming gardens stretching in every direction. The trees and plants were just beginning to display color and life again. They would be spectacular in the summer.

"They are even more amazing when the flowers are in bloom." Ethan took a deep breath of the fresh March air.

"I can imagine."

"I've always found wandering around them a good way to clear my head. There are so many paths leading off in different directions it's easy to keep from bumping into anyone as you walk."

My heart warmed. I was so glad that I had a chance to see this place that meant so much to him.

After a few minutes I turned away from the gardens to study the back of Veridan and noticed an entire wing of the building that we seemed to have neglected on our tour. "What's over there?" I pointed to the far left side of the manor.

Ethan followed my gesture. "That's the training facility of the Hleo, classrooms, meeting rooms, practice areas, that sort of thing. I asked about taking you there, but I was denied. It really isn't all that exciting, so you aren't missing much."

"What sort of training?" I was a little disappointed I wouldn't get to see the area where Ethan had spent so much time, being molded into the person that he was now.

"When a recruit first comes here, they begin with lessons on the history and purpose of the Hleo, coupled with secrecy and shadowing instruction. It sounds strange, but it's a skill to blend into the background of someone's life, especially when you're getting used to the extra strength and speed that comes from being branded. Then there's physical training, martial arts, fencing, and other weaponry. Basically, they equip us to go up against any sort of threat and eliminate it swiftly and effectively.

"We also go through survival exercises—starvation, sleep deprivation, and suffocation—to prepare for what it feels like to be without the necessities of life while continuing to live. They're only short-term exercises, but they do help, especially with learning how to stay in control mentally during those situations." Ethan swept a scattering of dead leaves off the railing of the terrace.

I watched as they danced through the air and landed on the lawn below. "That sounds intense."

Ethan nodded. "It is, but totally necessary."

"So, what specifically have you been trained for? I mean, besides *tons* of languages."

Ethan rolled his eyes. "I completed basic training, so the fighting and elusive behavior skills–"

“I think you might need a brush up on being elusive, I saw right through you from the beginning.” I grinned.

Ethan narrowed his eyes playfully at me. “Hmmm.” I could tell he wanted to say more, but held his tongue as two men in business suits came out the back door and strolled by us.

I made sure I maintained a platonic distance between the two of us as we walked across the terrace. Clouds had drifted over the sun, causing the temperature to drop significantly as we made our way back inside. “Okay, what else?”

“I don’t know. I’ve simply learned whatever I need to in order to help me blend in with the people I’ve protected. It’s amazing to see all the different ways people live their lives, and I like the challenge of trying to figure out the best way to fit into their world.” Ethan ran a hand through his hair. *He really cares about the people he protects.*

I followed Ethan back inside, down the hallway towards a pair of massive wooden doors. “Where are you taking me now?”

He pulled one of the doors open and swept his arm in front of himself in an ‘after you’ gesture. “To my favorite room.”

Twenty-Seven

The vast library was comprised of two levels of shelves filled with scores and scores of books. Lofty windows spanned the height of the wall across from the entrance where we stood; flooding the room with light. A large black marble fireplace against one of the walls filled the library with a cozy warmth, while a Baroque-style mural of angelic figures frolicking among the clouds adorned the ceiling above us.

"This is breathtaking." I did a slow turn trying to take it all in.

"I've always found it very peaceful." Ethan straightened a high-back chair that sat on one side of a large reading table in the middle of the room. I almost laced my fingers through his as he stepped away from the table—he was sharing a piece of himself I had a feeling few people knew about—but I thought better of it and kept my hands pinned to my sides.

We explored the bottom floor for a little while, before making our way up a spiral staircase, a beautifully sculpted wood and wrought iron structure that was a piece of art on its own. Once we were on the balcony level, I could see that a wall partitioned part of it off from the public.

"What's on the other side of here?" I touched the closed door with the tip of my finger.

"Those are the books that the Hleo would prefer the public not to have access to. They claim they are first editions of rare manuscripts, and some of the volumes kept back there are, but that section also houses more, out of the ordinary, books as well. That's where we'll have to look for information on the Glain Neidr." Ethan glanced around the space, but we were alone on the balcony.

"Are we allowed to go back there?" I arched an eyebrow, wondering if Ethan had mentioned to any of his superiors our chief reason for coming to Veridan.

"I still have to get it okayed by The Three. I'm going to talk to them tonight and try to arrange something for tomorrow." Ethan offered me a mysterious smile. "There was actually something else I wanted to show you."

"What?" My pulse sped up.

Ethan didn't answer. He simply strode across the balcony to the side opposite the Hleo-only area until we came to a dead end. I stared at the plain paneled wall, and then at Ethan, but he wasn't paying attention to me. He was studying the books on the end shelf. After a minute or so he pulled out a green book from the far end of the middle shelf, opened it and extracted a small metal key. He slipped it into his pocket and replaced the green book before reaching for a red one from a shelf just above his head and sliding it about a third of the way out. He did the same thing with a brown book on the bottom shelf. I held my breath, almost positive I knew what was about to happen. There was a soft *click* and the wall popped open to reveal a set of metal stairs that spiraled down right behind what would have been the fireplace's chimney.

"Come on." Ethan grabbed my hand and tugged me into the shadowy space.

"Where are we going?" I shot one last glance over my shoulder into the library.

Ethan flicked on a switch and the narrow stairwell was filled with dim light coming from wall sconces. "It's a surprise."

We reached the bottom of the stairs and continued down a long stone tunnel. *Where are you taking me, Ethan*? We had to be somewhere under the library. Closed doors dotted the tunnel, and for a brief second I thought he might be taking me to the circular room. Before I could open my mouth to ask, we stopped in front of a very ordinary looking, unmarked door. This couldn't be what Ethan had once described as the special Metadas room, could it?

Ethan withdrew the key from his pocket, inserted it into the lock, and pushed the door open to reveal a small room filled with filing cabinets. A dull fluorescent light buzzed overhead, and a table sat in the middle of the room with four metal folding chairs tucked in at it. Why would Ethan bring me down to a strange, slightly depressing little storage area?

"So…" I took a step further into the room.

Ethan shut the door behind me and crossed over to slide a chair out for me. "There's something here I want to show you. Something I think you have a right to see." He walked over to one of the khaki-colored filing cabinets, and punched in a four-digit code on a number pad. Grasping the handle on the middle drawer, he opened it and leafed through it. When he found a green file folder, he tugged it out and shut the drawer, then crossed over to a filing cabinet on the other side of the room and did the same thing, extracting a blue folder from its top drawer. Then he closed that drawer and walked back to me.

"What are these?" I frowned as Ethan set both files on the table in front of me. Before he could answer, the lettering on each folder grabbed my attention. The green file said *Noah Carter* along the filing tab, and the blue one *Elizabeth Seaton.*

I drew in a sharp breath. "Ethan." I glanced up at him, my eyes wide.

"I just thought maybe you'd want a chance to learn a little more about your parents." Ethan sank onto the seat beside me.

My heart raced. Information on my parents—the people who had given me life and yet whom I knew so little about—right at my fingertips. How had Ethan managed to pull this off?

"Does anyone know we're doing this?" I slid my hand slowly towards the folders.

"Miriam knows."

I hesitated. For some reason the thought of learning about Elizabeth Seaton and Noah Carter caused nervous butterflies to dance in my stomach. The blue file, Elizabeth's, was quite a bit thicker than Noah's, presumably because she had been a Hleo. I decided to start with Noah's.

I carefully opened the aged file folder and looked at the first page. It was a typed report about a new and potentially dangerous member of the Bana, Noah Carter, who had been encountered twice by members of the Hleo. The report detailed each incident, the first occurring in the fall of 1902, and the second only months later, in the spring of 1903. He appeared to be new to the Bana ranks, and eager to prove his value within the organization. The report concluded with the recommendation that a secondary Hleo be called in if this person was seen in the area of any given protected.

The next section of Noah Carter's file contained reports that took place a few years later. Noah was listed as responsible for the deaths of five protecteds and the attempted murder of a sixth, as well as two attacks on Hleo between 1908 and 1911. His MO was always the same. He would sneak into a protected's room while they were sleeping and administer a drug that stopped their heart. Death was painless and swift, and the protected always appeared to have simply died in his or her sleep, making his getaway incredibly easy.

My stomach churned. I turned away from the file and closed my eyes. "I don't know if I want to do this."

"I'm sorry. I know it's not a great account. If you want to, you can put his file away." Ethan gave my shoulder a comforting squeeze.

My fingers played with the edge of the file folder. Did I really want to read more? Noah was a cold-blooded murderer. Who was Elizabeth that she would have been attracted to someone like that?

Curiosity won out. I flipped the reports over and gasped. There I was, face to face with Noah Carter. A black and white mug shot was attached to an interrogation report; Noah had been captured by the Hleo. The report was dated May 1943. I studied the picture, trying to get a feel for Noah. He was staring directly at the camera, but, unlike the glum-looking individuals I'd seen in mug shots on television shows, Noah had an amused expression on his face, as though he found his capture entertaining more than anything else.

Even in black and white I could tell that his hair was light and cut in a rumpled, disheveled way, in a fashion fitting of the 1940s. I couldn't tell what color his eyes were, but as I traced them with my finger I realized they were the same shape as mine. He had a strong jaw line and a ruggedly handsome look. I could see why Elizabeth would have been physically drawn to him.

I scanned the report under the photo. Name: Noah Jonathan Carter. Age of recurrence: thirty-two years old. His hair color: light brown, eyes: blue, like mine. His height had been 5'10", not incredibly tall, and his weight was 178 pounds. After the list of physical attributes, a date and place of origin were listed. The exact date of transformation was unknown, but occurred sometime in 1898. He had been recruited from Denver, Colorado.

I bit my lip as I did the math. "He's technically younger than you."

"I guess that's true." Ethan's eyebrows scrunched together, as though he wasn't sure how to take that idea.

Since they had both been frozen in time at different points, Ethan was forever twenty-one, and Noah thirty-two, but if they had never gone through the transformation, Ethan would actually have been two years older than Noah. I shook off the tingling sensation pricking the back of my neck. I couldn't think about that, it was just too weird.

A transcript of Noah's interrogation came next in the file. The interviewer had demanded information on Bana headquarters, the new leader of the Bana, Alexander Mathieus, and any information Noah might have on how exactly the Bana were getting knowledge of protecteds' locations.

Noah had been charming but evasive in his responses about the leadership of the Bana. But he had opened up about his recruitment, and I read the account with interest. His father had died during an influenza outbreak, and his mother had taken a job as a live-in maid for a powerful organized crime family in Denver, just before the turn of the century when Denver was becoming a full-fledged city. She had tried to shield her son from her employer's business, but Noah had grown up immersed in that lifestyle and, once he was old enough, he had started working for the family.

He joined the Bana when they approached him while he was on the run after pulling off a string of bank robberies. They had offered not only limitless money and riches, but limitless power. He had nothing to lose.

Noah had gone through the Bana's transformation process. The interrogator had asked to see the marking. Noah had joked that if they wanted him to undress for them, they could have just asked, but then he obliged. It was noted that his marking was almost an exact replica of the Hleo marking with one exception, its coloring was a little more purple then the usual rust color of the Hleo's.

"So the Bana are branded with the same mark as the Hleo?" I frowned.

"Yes. Isaac wasn't able to perfect the branding serum, but he did understand that the mark must remain the same in order to be effective. The only way to tell the two marks apart is the color variation mentioned in your father's report." Ethan traced the figure eight scored by a double line symbol I was familiar with on the table with his finger.

"Interesting." I turned back to the interview but it ended there with a comment that it would be resumed back at Hleo headquarters. I flipped over the page, expecting the interview to resume, but instead found a lengthy incident report about Noah's escape. He had managed to break away from the transport vehicle they were bringing him back to headquarters in, and disappear. *He escaped the Hleo? Who was this person*?

There were more incident reports, all dated between 1979 and 1990, accounting for six different deaths. I shuffled through them quickly.

I swallowed hard as I read the last page in the folder. It was dated from just after I had turned two. It stated that Noah Carter was no longer a Bana threat as it had been confirmed that he had been killed somewhere just outside of Berlin, along with his romantic partner, defected Hleo member Elizabeth Seaton. The file was light on details. Apparently they had been found by a Hleo stationed in a small neighboring town, cause of death had been single stab wound to each, and the identity of the killer was, at the time of the report, unknown. An investigation would ensue.

A wave of sadness washed over me. My parents had been murdered in such a brutal way. Noah sounded like an awful person, but Dad had said he walked away from his life as an assassin to be with Elizabeth, and there were no incidents after 1990 on record, almost ten years before I was born, so maybe he hadn't been all bad.

I turned over that page of the report. I didn't want to linger on the details of my parents' deaths. A handful of photos were clipped together in the back of the file. "What are these?"

"Surveillance photos from different opportunities the Hleo had to go after Noah." Ethan picked one of them up.

It was odd to watch Noah's clothing and hairstyles, along with the buildings and cars surrounding him, change through the decades, without him aging at all. The last photo was in color. Noah was sitting at an outdoor café, laughing at something his companion was saying. Her back was to the shot, but she had shoulder-length hair, and his eyes—the same blue as mine—looked at her with such affection, I knew it must be Elizabeth.

I stared at the photo for a while. "He was quite the character," I finally said as I tucked the photo into the back and closed the file folder.

"That's one way of putting it." Ethan gave me a knowing look.

"Did you know him?" I bit my thumbnail.

"Only by reputation. I was in Africa when he was captured and brought in, and after his escape, my troubles with Adam started. I was focusing so much energy on getting a handle on Adam's destructive influence in my life, I was never assigned to try to go after Noah. By the time Adam was underground, Elizabeth had already been assigned to bring Noah in, so I never had the chance."

My forehead creased. "I can read all the bad things he did here on paper, but I wonder what he was really like."

"From my understanding, he was daring, and apparently very charming, especially with women. It's rumored that he was able to escape from the Hleo because he called two women over to the car he was being held in while the Hleo went in to make a quick phone call at a gas station. I guess he talked them into believing he was a detective and his partner had dared him to try and escape out of handcuffs, Houdini style, but now he was stuck, and not wanting to appear like an idiot he asked if they would be kind enough to give him the extra key that was kept in the glove box. He had to be charming to get away with a stunt like that.

"I know the reports don't exactly paint him in a favorable light, and he was very good at taking protecteds out, but I knew your mother. If she fell in love with him, then he must have had some redeeming qualities." At the mention of Elizabeth, Ethan rested his fingertips on the blue file I had yet to open.

"I guess so." I paused. I was scared I wouldn't feel any sort of connection to my biological mother, and that would be incredibly disappointing.

I took a deep breath, flipped open the folder, and was met with a picture of a young woman who looked remarkably like me. We had the same small nose and full lips, the same soft features, even the arch of our eyebrows was the same. The big difference was her eyes; they were dark like her hair and smaller than mine. The photo was only from her shoulders up, but she looked as though she'd had a lean build. The picture was attached to an official Hleo recruitment report, and I pored over its details. Elizabeth Mae Seaton, hair color: brown, eye color: brown, height: 5'7". She had been fairly tall for a woman. Her birth date was January 27, 1918 and under that date was a line that read *age upon first observation*: twenty-nine in 1947. Her town of origin was Worthing, Kansas. She had worked on her family's farm, and I smiled at the thought of my mom being a Midwest girl.

Her family information listed both parents, James and Amelia Seaton, living, and two brothers. Both of them had a date of birth and a date of death recorded after their names. I did the math and realized they had been young when they died. Her brother Mitchell had died in 1942 at the age of twenty-one, and George in 1943 when he was twenty-three. Looking at the dates I realized it was likely that they had been causalities of the Second World War, but the report didn't specify that.

Elizabeth's personality traits were detailed next, her reactions to situations, and her day-to-day behavior as observed by her recruiter, all positive for becoming a Hleo. She was considerate, initiative, adept at problem-solving, and held high regard for her fellow human beings. The second report concluded with approval granted to approach Elizabeth with the offer of a new life.

My eyes were glued to the page as I followed the transcription of her official acceptance. "I am honored to accept such an esteemed position. I have always felt as though a higher calling for my life was lurking just beyond my grasp. An invisible force has persuaded me away from the safe and established life I know as mine, and towards an exciting and challenging adventure that will test me to my very core."

Shivers ran up my spine. These were my mother's own words.

An induction report on her arrival and branding on April 6, 1949, came next, including her training record, which was exemplary, with exceptionally high marks in language aptitude and creative thinking.

"Creative thinking. Was she artistic?" I pointed to the words on the page.

Ethan tapped his chin with his knuckle. "I can't really remember if she was. I wasn't around Elizabeth very often, sorry."

"That's okay." I waved a dismissive hand. With the information I had in front of me, he had nothing to be sorry for.

Following the training record were case reports, tons of them, some written by hand, most typed. Information about the people she had protected, her run-ins with members of the Bana, and the places she had been. All her successes and failures were in this file, neatly laid out for me to read. She had killed a Bana to save a protected's life more than once, and put her life on the line numerous times in the name of duty. She had survived fires, collapsed buildings, impossible falls, starvation, hypothermia, and being stabbed and shot, all just to protect someone else's existence.

"Fearless," I breathed. How did she have the courage to take such incredible risks over and over again? A pang of regret knotted in my stomach. I would never meet her.

"That's the perfect word for her. She did what it took to do the job, regardless of the consequences." Ethan leaned back in his chair.

I was nearing the end of her case file, and flipped a page over to reveal a different type of report, a Special Training Evaluation. Most of the document had been blacked out with permanent marker. I handed it to Ethan. "What's this?"

Ethan took the report from me and skimmed through it. "I don't know." A frown formed as he read. He held it so we could both read the parts that weren't blacked out, but that didn't really help. Very few details were visible. I gathered that the report discussed a series of training sessions Elizabeth had completed, one every few months for about three years, and that the training had been done on site at Veridan.

"I've never heard of any specific special training that would be considered top secret. I'll look into it." Ethan set the report back down on the table.

I read it again and noticed on the last page that someone had only blacked out half of a word. The part visible read *riam*.

"riam." I put a finger on the paper. "As in Miriam?"

"That could be. I know Miriam was a big fan of your mother's; the two of them were very close. It's possible that Miriam had been conducting some sort of special training with Elizabeth. I'll see what I can find out." Ethan sounded nonchalant, but his gaze lingered on the page. He was definitely intrigued.

I set the report aside for the time being, uncovering one last document in Elizabeth's file, a Defect Report. It gave a brief overview of her betrayal of the Hleo organization by entering into a romantic relationship with a known Bana assassin. Her official date of removal from duty was August 16, 1995. Not terribly long before she'd had me. Had I been part of the plan, or just an accident?

The report listed her as a fugitive, and directed that, if seen, she should be apprehended alive and brought in for official removal of service. Stamped across the page in big red letters was the word DECEASED, and stapled to the report was the official confirmation of death, with details very similar to those in Noah's file. Another wave of sadness washed over me. I closed the file, trying to process everything I had just read.

"I hope you found that helpful." Ethan searched my gaze.

"It was. It's more information about them than I ever hoped to know. It's just sort of hard to realize how little I'm like them, especially Elizabeth. I wanted to feel as though I emulated her qualities, and instead I kind of feel that I'd be a disappointment to her." I drummed the table.

"In what way are you so different than she was?"

"Elizabeth was brave, and spontaneous, she just wouldn't quit." I shrugged.

Ethan's eyes darted up to the discreet camera tucked into the corner of the room before he gently cupped my face in his hand. "Two weeks ago you were single-handedly making your way through the woods to a Bana hideout to get your father back from a murderous assassin. If that isn't fearless risk-taking, I don't know what is. As for being spontaneous, you just dropped everything and jumped on a train on the off chance you'd get to talk to some of the most elusive people on the planet. Hannah, you are far more like her than you realize. It would be a shame if you didn't understand how amazing you truly are." Ethan's eyes were blazing as he studied me

"I never really thought of it that way." I bit my lip.

"You are incredible, please just accept that." He pushed away from the table and gathered up the folders.

I rolled my eyes, downplaying the praise, but my cheeks warmed. "I'll try." I stood to go, but turned back. "Could I have a picture of them? Would that be okay?"

Ethan hesitated. Then he bent forward so that his back blocked the files from the camera and pulled the surveillance photo of Noah at the café out of his file and a work photo of Elizabeth out of hers and pressed them into my palm. "Here you go." He held my fingers slightly longer than he needed to, and tingles of electricity flowed up my arm.

"We should probably head back to our rooms to get ready for tonight." Ethan released my hand. I nodded. Even if meeting The Three this evening didn't go the way I hoped, at least Ethan had just made this trip completely worth it.

Twenty-Eight

We made our way back upstairs and stepped into the billiard room just as a red-haired girl in a black sweater and tights came in through the door that led to our rooms. When she saw us, a huge smile spread across her face. She hurried across the room towards us to give Ethan a hug.

"Ethan, hey!" The girl threw her arms around him in a friendly manner.

"Lou, how are you?" Ethan returned the hug politely.

"I'm doing well. It's really good to see you; I heard you were coming in." Lou stepped away from his embrace.

"I guess word got around quickly." Ethan inclined his head. "This is—"

"You don't need to say it. I know who this is. Hannah, right?" Her copper hair swished as she talked. "You look just like your mom, well, except for the eyes; those are definitely Noah's." Lou took my hands in hers, studying me thoroughly.

"You knew my mom and dad?" My grip on her fingers tightened.

"Yeah, Liz and I were good friends, probably the closest thing to a best friend I had around this place. I was sort of her mentor, I guess you'd say. Until she got better than me, that is." Lou laughed as she released me. "As for your dad, I chased him over some rooftops in Spain once."

"What was Elizabeth like?" My heart rate sped up. I could barely contain my excitement. I had been worried people around

Veridan wouldn't have anything positive to say about Elizabeth because of Noah.

"She was amazing. Always up for an adventure, but at the same time always striving to do the absolute best job she could. She challenged me to be a better Hleo. Oh, and she was an awesome listener. We would stay up late talking, at least, I would be talking, and she would listen to whatever I had to say. She gave such great advice. She could always make me see a situation in a new light and inevitably I would end up taking her suggestion, even when I didn't want to." Lou gestured wildly as she talked. I listened intently, soaking in every word.

"I remember this one time I was protecting a somewhat removed royal. Not in line to the throne or anything, but you know, still noble blood. I was posing as a maid in his holiday château and there was a threat on his life that his guards ended up dealing with instead of me. The whole place went into lockdown and I knew they would string up anybody caught where they shouldn't be. Wouldn't you know it, I was in my protected's bedroom closet because I had been trying to track down the Bana, but he gave me the slip. For some reason Liz was with me…" Lou scrunched up her face. "I can't remember why, but it's not really important. Anyway, so there we were trapped in this closet while his guards are going mental ransacking every room to make sure the guy they caught didn't have an accomplice. We ended up shimmying into this oversized steamer trunk—Liz's idea of course—and holding our breath, hoping they wouldn't open it and find us." Lou shook her head.

I tried to picture it. "Were you scared of getting caught?"

"I was, but not Liz. That was her though." Lou pushed the sleeves of her sweater up. "So how have you been?" She shifted gears, turning her attention to Ethan. "I heard you and Ev were on the outs. You guys have been working together forever, what happened?"

I tensed at the mention of Ethan's former partner.

"We had a bit of a falling out." Ethan avoided my gaze.

Yeah, she withheld that your archenemy Adam was on the loose and almost got me killed, no biggie.

He drew in a deep breath. "I heard that she's been reassigned to active shadowing instead of background duty, so hopefully she's enjoying the change."

I swallowed hard. *Ethan knows what happened to Evelyn*? He hadn't mentioned her after the night of the Gala. I had assumed he'd let her go and not thought about her again. I tried to read his expression, but he remained stoic.

Lou poked Ethan in the arm. "That's too bad. I always thought the two of you would end up together, you both take the job so seriously." Ethan frowned and slid away from Lou's finger. She glanced over at me and winked, obviously pleased at being able to bug Ethan.

"Yeah, we were never really like that." Ethan shook his head. "I'm surprised to see you; I heard you were in France."

"I know. Three years later the old lady *finally* decides to sell her antique jewelry collection, and just like that I'm free. She hemmed and hawed over it forever. If I'd known that was going to be the choice, I would have talked her into it years ago." Lou rolled her eyes, but her smile continued to beam. "I just got back last week."

I wanted to keep talking to Lou, but she checked her watch. "I would love to stay and chat, but Bridget's got me on server duty for this evening and I'm already late."

Ethan stepped aside. "We'll let you go then."

Lou placed a hand on my arm. "I definitely want to talk more. Come find me later tonight or tomorrow and we can talk about Lizzy."

"That would be great, thanks."

She waved when she got to the doorway and then she was gone.

"That was Lou." Ethan motioned to the empty space where the whirlwind of a person we had just met had disappeared.

We started walking back to our bedrooms. "She was Elizabeth's best friend?"

"Lou, or Louise Riley officially, and Elizabeth were very close. Lou was one of the few people around here who managed to accept your mom's decision to leave and be with Noah." Ethan reached into his pocket for the room keys and opened my door.

"She seems amazing." I stepped into the room, then turned and gripped Ethan's arm to stop him. "Thank you so much for today."

"You are more than welcome." Ethan's gaze dropped to my hand. I reluctantly let him go. His fists were balled and held firmly at his sides. *This friends-only thing is just as hard for him.*

"I can't believe everything I've seen, and everything I've learned. It's only made me that much more excited to talk to The Three. I guess we just have to get through the party tonight." I glanced down at my blatantly casual outfit.

"It will be fine." Ethan fiddled with the key in his hand. "You look good in anything." His voice was barely a whisper.

I scrunched up my nose. "Thanks. Somehow I don't have your confidence in my ability to pull off the sweater and jeans combo at a black tie event though." I struck a model pose.

Ethan grinned. "You'll make it work, I'm sure. I'll give you some time to get ready. Is forty-five minutes good?" He took a step towards his room.

"That sounds fine." I nodded and shut my door. Butterflies fluttered in my stomach. Maybe I wouldn't look the greatest, but I couldn't shake the feeling that this evening would be significant, no matter what I was wearing.

Twenty-Nine

I bit my thumb as I wandered through the bedroom. *What am I going to wear?* Before I could give it much thought, something on the bed caught my eye. A beautiful midnight-blue evening gown and matching wrap. A pair of strappy heels had been tucked under the side of the bed, and an assortment of hair clips, makeup and other beauty products were displayed on the dressing table. I picked up a beautiful set of teardrop earrings and matching necklace. *Are these diamonds real?*

Excitement coursed through me as I held up the dress and examined myself in the floor-length mirror. It was a beautiful 1920s design, with a v-neck collar, drop waist and gauzy pleated gathers that hung unevenly to my calf. Was Ethan responsible for this incredible gift? He had been full of surprises since we arrived at Veridan.

I jumped into the shower, reflecting on everything I had discovered about my parents as I bathed. Elizabeth had been fierce, there was no doubt about that. I wanted to be more like her, and hoped that if the time came I would have the capacity to be as brave.

I shampooed my hair and Lou popped into my mind. A smile crept across my face. She reminded me of Katie with her bubbly enthusiasm, although there was a wisdom about her too, the kind that comes with life experience that Katie didn't possess yet. I liked the idea that Elizabeth would have been attracted to the same sort of person as I was for a best friend. Maybe I was more like her than I felt.

After slipping into the dress, I quickly did my hair in an up-do inspired by the same time period, and secured it with a sapphire-and-diamond-encrusted headband that had been left with the other hair accessories. I bent forward to examine my face in the mirror. I'd applied a more dramatic amount of makeup than I would normally wear, trying to go for sophisticated and elegant.

There was a gentle knock on the door. I stepped into the shoes, grabbed the wrap off the bed and strode across the room. I straightened my shoulders and opened the door. Ethan stood on the other side looking gorgeous in a full, one-button black tuxedo, cut and styled for the same era as my dress. His hair was swept back with gel, but retained a bit of the unkempt look I appreciated.

"Good evening, Hannah, you look absolutely lovely." Ethan's tone was formal, but there was electricity in his gaze.

"And you look very handsome." I smoothed down my dress, trying to sound nonchalant. Inwardly the butterflies were fluttering madly.

"May I escort you downstairs?" He held out his arm.

"Of course." I slipped my hand through the crook of his elbow and we strolled down the hall.

We made our way towards the sound of jazzy orchestra music. My breath caught as we reached the doors of the beautiful ballroom and walked into the grand space. The room had been transformed into a perfect replica of twenties art deco splendor. Ribbons of white and silver were draped from the chandelier, creating a canopy above, while bobbles of white lights were suspended in the open space between the ribbons, filling the room with a magical glow. The tables had been adorned with gold and crystal flatware and centerpieces of tall vases filled with pearls and diamonds and topped with white roses and feathers.

"Ethan, this is incredible." Everywhere I looked objects glittered and sparkled, from the champagne flute fountain just inside the entrance to the tinseled stage the orchestra was set up on clear across the ballroom.

"The foundation always goes all out for their events." Ethan spoke close to my ear so I could hear him over the din of the crowd and I caught a hint of shaving cream and woodsy aftershave. His breath was warm on my neck, and I swallowed hard. *Keep your head, Hannah.*

The majority of the crowd appeared to be middle-aged or better, and they had all gotten into the spirit of the evening. The women were decked out in flapper dresses, or drop-waist dresses like mine, and feathered and jeweled headbands or hats. The men wore suits similarly cut to Ethan's in an array of colors, many complemented by fedoras or spats. As I took it all in, I felt a little out of place. I had to be the youngest person in attendance by at least ten years, and I couldn't be sure, but some of the other party-goers seemed to glance in our direction every once in a while.

Servers, also dressed in era appropriate costumes, made the rounds with trays of champagne and hors d'oeuvres. Bridget was off in a corner giving instructions to a group of waiters, and Michael passed me holding a tray of appetizers. He gave a small wave as he went by, but kept moving.

"Don't you guys look beautiful." I turned to see Lou holding a silver serving tray with little, intricately-made appetizers resting on it. She looked elegant with her red hair styled in waves and pinned back into a bun, and a black sequined headband with a feather sticking out.

"Thanks." I rocked back and forth on my heels self-consciously.

Ethan subtly slid his arm out of mine. I knew it was a necessary move, but I fought the urge to sigh.

"Isn't this place an absolute riot? I love when they do theme evenings, much better than the average black tie shindig." Lou swished the skirt of her sleek black-sequined flapper dress for emphasis.

"I can't believe the transformation. The ballroom was amazing before, but now I feel like I've stepped right into the 1920s." My eyes scanned the room. Once again I felt awed by the decor.

"The foundation members eat this kind of thing right up. And who better to put on a past-era themed party than the group who's lived through it already, right?" Lou laughed. "I love your dress, by the way."

"Thanks, it just appeared in my room this afternoon. It's absolutely perfect." I glanced at Ethan to see whether he'd admit to being the one who gave it to me, but his expression remained neutral.

"It is perfect. If I were to guess, I'd say you have Miriam to thank for that one. She has a keen eye for fashion. I guess after four hundred years she's had lots of practice at putting together an outfit or two. I'd better keep circulating though. I'll catch up with you later." She winked and disappeared into the crowd again.

I whirled towards Ethan. "Four hundred years? Miriam is four hundred years old?"

"Four hundred and thirty-two." Ethan adjusted his crisp white pocket square. "She's the oldest of The Three. Gabriel's next at two hundred and eighty-five, and Victor is two hundred and four."

"That is crazy." I shook my head, trying to get my mind around it. What would the three of them look like?

"A little, but you can't tell that they're that old." Ethan grinned. "Are you hungry?"

"I should be I guess, but not really. I'm a little nervous about being here, and about meeting The Three." I scrutinized the crowd. *Are they here somewhere?*

"You don't need to worry. As standoffish as they've been, they're excited to meet you. They're torn because they don't want to taint your calling as a protected, but you're a source of a lot of curiosity."

"I guess I can see why they would want to meet me because of Elizabeth being my mom, but it still feels very strange that I would be of interest to anyone." I watched the cascade of champagne flow from the top flute of the makeshift fountain. It was mesmerizing and oddly calming.

Ethan opened his mouth to speak, but before he could, a blond guy in a black tux strode over and clapped a hand on his shoulder. "Flynn, good to see you, old buddy." The guy stuck out his hand.

Ethan gripped it. "You too, Kai. How have you been?"

"Still alive, so that's something right? You heard about Nick? I've offered to pitch in as acting head of security until they find a more permanent replacement." Kai shrugged. "And who do we have here?" He took my hand in his and bowed to give it a light kiss. My eyebrows shot up as I looked from him to Ethan.

"This is Hannah Reed." Ethan sounded casual, but his eyes stayed on Kai's grasp.

"Hannah, it's very nice to make your acquaintance. And may I just say, you are a vision of your mother's beauty." Kai finally let go of me and shot Ethan a look.

"Thank you." My cheeks warmed.

"The Three are well off. There's no one more qualified for lead guard." Ethan squared his shoulders subtly.

I studied him. *That was a quick shift of topics. Ethan, are you a little jealous*?

"Except for you. I tell you guy, I could have used your engineering skills back in Romania last fall. I ended up having to throw the bomb into the Danube. Just try keeping a fifty-foot water explosion right by a crowded open-air market out of the press," Kai exclaimed.

I narrowed my eyes. "Ethan's engineering skills?"

"Yeah, he's probably the best bomb de-fuser the society has. But I guess that's what an engineering degree from Cornell will get you." Kai lightly punched Ethan's upper arm.

"You have an engineering degree from Cornell?" I crossed my arms as I stared at Ethan. I knew that I shouldn't act so shocked or interested by Kai's information, but I couldn't help it.

"I was protecting a student at Cornell. I was his roommate and it was just easier to take the same courses he was taking." Ethan ran a hand over his face.

"He's so modest. As if just anyone could study engineering and pass with flying colors. This guy's a legend, Hannah; you're in good hands with him." Kai flashed me a set of perfect white teeth.

You have no idea. "I think so too."

"I have to keep moving, but hey, if you're around later a group of us are meeting up to play a little poker in the Keith Reading room. You know, once Hannah's all tucked into bed and you're off duty for the evening." Kai stepped away from us, glancing at Bridget who was gesturing him to come over.

"Thanks, Kai. I'll see," Ethan replied.

My jaw tightened. Why did he have to imply that I'm just a job? I turned to Ethan, wanting to ask him a series of follow-up questions to the exchange that had just occurred. *Who was Nick? How did Kai know Elizabeth? Why didn't he tell me about having an Ivy League university degree? And was he going to go play poker later?* I opened my mouth but the uncomfortable frown on Ethan's face stopped me. He was on edge. There would be time for me to grill him later.

"So point out The Three to me." I scrutinized the crowd. "I don't want it to be 'oh, hello, Hannah, how good of you to come.'" I put on my best over-the-top British accent and waved my hand regally. "And then I clumsily knock over this champagne fountain trying to curtsy." I swung my hand dramatically towards it, pretending to knock it down. Ethan looked past me, and his back straightened. My heart sank. "Which one is it?" I mouthed.

Ethan kept his gaze on whoever was behind me. "Good evening, Gabriel."

I sheepishly turned to meet Gabriel, a gentleman with snowy white hair and thick moustache. They stood out against his tanned complexion, as did his piercing blue eyes. There was a confidence and composure in the way he walked, but a kindness in his expression.

"Ethan, good evening, it's good to see you again. And this lovely young woman must be Miss Reed." Gabriel took both my hands in his.

"Allow me to introduce you properly. Hannah Reed, this is Gabriel Doukas, one of the three chairmen of the Memores Foveat Historical Society."

"Hannah, it is truly an honor to make your acquaintance." Gabriel gave my hands a light squeeze before releasing them.

"Thank you. The pleasure is all mine, though. I really appreciate being able to be here. There are so many things I can't wait to discuss with you."

"Of course, my dear. There will be time for any and all questions in the morning. For now, simply enjoy the evening and the festivities." Gabriel grabbed a champagne flute from a passing server and handed it to me. We wouldn't be discussing anything of importance that night.

"Thank you, I will." I took the bubbly drink from him and glanced at Ethan. *He knows how old I am, doesn't he?*

I hadn't admitted it to Ethan, but I had been hoping that The Three would answer the questions I had about myself and my ability and that we wouldn't need to look for the mysterious, long-lost Glain Neidr. Of course during a formal themed party probably wasn't the best time to try to get those answers.

Gabriel cleared his throat. "Hannah, I hope you don't mind, but I would like to borrow Ethan for a little while. I know he is your escort for the evening, but I need to speak with him privately." His tone was courteous, but suggested it wouldn't matter if I did mind.

Everything in me longed to refuse anyway. I didn't want to have to wander among a pack of strangers. I held out my hand in a 'go ahead' motion. "Of course."

"I'll meet up with you later." Ethan touched my elbow lightly before he followed Gabriel to a small room just off the entrance of the ballroom. As they made their way through the door, another man, about forty years old, with brown hair and a confident stride, joined them. I frowned. The second man looked familiar, as if I had encountered him in the distant past, but I couldn't place how I knew him.

I wrung my hands together. What could they want to talk to Ethan about? No doubt they were talking about me, but was he in trouble? Did they know about us? Blood rushed to my cheeks, making me lightheaded. *I need air*. I threaded my way across the crowded floor towards the balcony. Massive French doors led out to a long, covered balcony. A blast of cold air hit me and I curled the wrap tightly around my arms as I made my way outside.

There were only a few couples out on the balcony, and I kept to myself as I rested my elbows on the railing and faced the crowd inside. I kept my eyes locked on the room Ethan was in so I would be able to join him the moment he came out again. After a few minutes of staring at the closed door, I sighed and turned to look out over the expansive landscape. Apparently their discussion was going to be a long one.

Even in the dark the grounds of Veridan were stunning. Lampposts and solar lights dotted the manicured gardens and along the paths that seemed to lead in all directions.

"It's very peaceful out here." A quiet female voice behind me pulled me from my thoughts. I spun around to see an elegantly put-together woman, probably in her mid-sixties. Her straight, silvery hair fell to her shoulders and shimmered in the moonlight, as did the sage-colored evening gown she wore.

"It is." I slid down the railing a little so she could join me.

"A welcome change from all the peering eyes inside, isn't it, Hannah?" The woman moved to close the gap between us.

My back went rigid. “I’m sorry, have we met?”

“No, not officially. My name is Miriam Ellsworth. It is a pleasure to make your acquaintance.” She spoke with a sophisticated English accent, evenly toned, with years of wisdom layered through it.

I pressed a hand to my chest. “Miriam, of course; I’ve wanted to meet you for a long time. I hear I have you to thank for this dress. It’s amazing.” I motioned to the midnight blue garment.

“I thought you would be in need of something fitting for the theme of the evening. I’m glad you like it. You remind me so much of your mother and I remember she always looked beautiful in blue, although you do have your father’s eyes, don’t you?” Her violet gaze locked with mine.

“So, you knew both Elizabeth and Noah?” I tucked a loose strand of hair behind my ear, willing my nerves to calm. Miriam was the member of The Three I was most interested in talking to.

Miriam shifted to stare out at the gardens. “Yes. I was especially fond of your mother. She was an exceptional individual.” Her voice carried a wave of sadness.

“I’m starting to think so too. Ethan showed me information on both she and Noah this afternoon. I wish I could have known them.” I tapped a finger on the cool stone of the balcony railing.

“And they would have loved to have known you.” Miriam’s gaze was understanding. *How do you know that, Miriam*? I opened my mouth to speak, but she cut me off. “Are you enjoying your time here?”

“Yes. Veridan is truly incredible. I could spend days here, just taking in all of the detail, and Ethan knows so much about it.” I shot a sideways glance towards the room Gabriel had taken Ethan into. The door was still closed.

“I suppose spending such a great deal of time here, he has picked up a personal appreciation for Veridan.” Miriam’s features softened at the mention of Ethan’s name.

“He’s around here a lot then?” I fumbled with my wrap, trying to settle it around my shoulders.

Miriam studied me, her face unreadable. *I need to act more disinterested.* When her eyes searched mine, I felt as though she was capable of perceiving my every inner thought, and I pasted on as casual a smile as I could muster.

"He's in and out as much as most of the Hleo." She indicated to the crowd of people inside with a slender hand. "Has everyone been kind and welcoming to you?"

"They have, very much so. Although, I'm not sure if I've been imagining things, but it seems people have been watching me." I smoothed down my dress as a gentle breeze caught the skirt and caused it to flutter in the wind.

"Yes, for that I must apologize. It's rare that a protected has come to see us. It has only occurred a handful of times since I have been involved with the Hleo, and that has been a very long time. Add to that the fact that you are Elizabeth's child, and the members of the society that live around here are very curious to catch a glimpse of you," Miriam said.

"I'm really not that exciting."

"You are more exciting than you realize." Clouds drifted across the sky, blocking the moon and hiding Miriam's expression in shadow.

"Am I?" *Please let her tell me something meaningful.*

"Hannah, I know you've come seeking an explanation for your uniqueness, but you must appreciate the complexity of your request."

"I do, but I need to know if there have been others."

"Others like you?" She tapped her lips with her finger. "I cannot answer that definitively, but in my time, I have never seen another with the ability to see other protecteds as you do."

"Besides you, that is."

"I suppose. Although, I think you'll find your ability differs from mine in some ways." Miriam clasped her hands behind her.

"In what ways?"

"Your ability appears to exist on its own; it needs no secondary outside source to trigger it, as mine does."

I frowned, more confused than ever. She appeared to be admitting she only saw protecteds in the mysterious circular room. *Should I mention that I already know about the Metadas room? Maybe not.* I wasn't sure if Ethan had been at liberty to tell me about it and I didn't want to get him into any more trouble than he may already be in.

"So, the images don't just pop into your head at random the way they do for me?"

"No, that seems to be something completely unique to you,"

A couple passed by us and gave Miriam a warm nod before continuing back inside.

"What about my drawing ability, how does that fit into the picture?" I lowered my voice.

"It seems to be the outlet your body had chosen for you to translate the images from your mind to something tangible that can be shared with others."

"How do you translate the images you see for others?" I cocked my head to the side.

"When a protected's image materializes in my mind, it carries with it information about that individual. I am able to comprehend the person's identity, not only what they look like. Within the image, I gain their name, age, and an understanding of who they are." Miriam's gaze shifted subtly to the ballroom. Was she sharing information that perhaps the other two wouldn't want her to?

"I wish my visions were as complete as that. What else do you see?"

"The visions play like video recordings, as though someone has captured a short period of time in a protected's life and I am watching that footage from my mind's eye. These visions give us a timeline as to when a Hleo should enter a protected's life. They act simply as a guideline, however." Miriam took a step towards a topiary and plucked a wilted flower from it.

"That is incredible. Do you know why I've been given such a strange ability? Is it the reason I'm a protected? I assume it must be, but how can I be sure, and what does that mean for my future?"

She set the flower delicately on the railing. "In this life we are all given different abilities and talents, Hannah. They are tools that can help to guide us, but it is still our decisions, how we choose to use our gifts, that dictate the course our life will run."

"So you're saying that I'm a protected because of some decision I'm going to make? It's not about what I'm supposed to do with this ability?" I scrunched up my nose. Miriam was being too cryptic for my taste.

"I can't tell you how to use your ability. I know you want me to, but that is not information for you to have right now. It would affect the calling the Metadas has placed on your life. What I can tell you is that every decision you make takes you further along your journey to understanding yourself, and eventually to the moment fate has in store for you. We are all led by our decisions and the consequences of those decisions, every one of us." Miriam's violet eyes glowed as she spoke.

"Even you?" I crossed my arms.

"Even me." Miriam looked out over the grounds. A thin mist of cool evening fog had rolled in, shrouding the gardens with a certain mystique.

"So you chose to be one of The Three? It was a decision you made, not what destiny programmed you to do?"

"It was."

"And you knew it was the right decision?" I watched her face closely. This was what it all boiled down to. If Ethan was protecting me for a decision I would make, how would I know the right choice?

"There are limitless paths we may take in our lives, limitless choices we can make, and yet people can be drawn to a certain path; it is that inclination that helps us with our choices." Miriam's eyes were soft with empathy, as though she comprehended my struggle.

I bit my lip and shot another look at the door that Ethan was behind. It remained closed. "Is Ethan in trouble?" I asked quietly, trying to disguise my concern as passing interest.

"Ethan has broken many of the regulations the Hleo live by. The others are discussing his actions with him. They want to understand his reasoning better, and go over the possible ramifications of his decisions." Miriam sounded kind and reassuring, as though I really had nothing to worry about.

"Are they going to punish him? Because, it's not really his fault he told me about all of this. He was forced to when a member of the Bana tried to kill me. And I talked him into bringing me here. He didn't want to, but I pushed until he gave in."

"Ethan is not going to be punished, that is not the intent of the discussion. Although the rules are in place for the safety of both the protected and the Hleo, there are always exceptions to those rules. We understand that, and truthfully, we were all very curious to see you; a child of a Hleo is an extraordinary thing indeed. We were willing to make an exception in order meet you." Miriam smiled.

The tension left my shoulders. "I'm just glad Ethan will be all right. And I am grateful that you were willing to make an exception, for whatever reason." *If he's not in trouble, why hasn't he come out yet?* A breeze rose and a chill coursed up and down my spine. I tucked the wrap tightly around me and moved in the direction of the doors, hoping Miriam would follow my lead.

She stepped into my path. "It is a dangerous thing to love a Hleo."

I stared at her. Ethan had made it very clear a relationship between a protected and a Hleo was the ultimate treachery, and I didn't want to think about how they punished someone for breaking that rule. "What do you mean?"

Miriam's shoulders drooped slightly. "A Hleo is called to a different life than normal human beings. They are asked to always be at the ready to fight, to serve no matter what the cost, for the greater purpose we are all here to serve. The risk in loving one of these is great, both to a person's body and to their heart." The wisdom and knowing in Miriam's tone was unmistakable. She had obviously seen a relationship like ours before and there would be no denying it to her now.

"How could love be dangerous?"

"Although love is one of the strongest forces in this world, it can also serve as a weakness when it causes one to lose his or her focus, to become distracted. It can also be used as a weapon if the wrong person finds out about it."

An image of Uri at the cottage flashed through my mind. Once he had sensed Ethan's feelings for me, he had immediately tried to use them against Ethan. I shuddered at the memory of his hands on me, but pushed the thought out of my mind. I was more interested in knowing what Miriam meant about the danger to my heart. "I understand the physical danger—as a protected I'm already in danger—but how can loving a Hleo affect my heart?"

"A Hleo has been separated from the natural order of life to serve a very important purpose. That separation forces them to give up certain luxuries that normal humans can partake in. One of these is love. A Hleo stays only temporarily in one place; it is the nature of what they do. When they become too attached to a protected, the hole they leave when it is their time to go can be a huge void to try to fill. That is the primary reason they stay in the shadows of another's life." Miriam's face was soft with compassion. Was she telling me to get out before it was too late? *If she only knew.* I had passed the point of no return with Ethan; from my very core I knew that. He was as much a part of me as I was, and I was convinced he felt the same.

"Are you going to say anything to anyone?" I pressed my hands to the balcony railing, staring at my fingers. Her gaze was too knowing, and I wasn't sure how I would react to her response.

"No. It is not my information to share." Miriam rested a hand on mine. "But I hope you will seriously consider my words, and think through the decision you need to make."

Before I could respond, Gabriel and Ethan walked out onto the balcony. I hadn't even noticed their return to the party.

"Thank you, I will." I bent my head close to Miriam's so only she would hear. She gave a small nod and then smiled at the two men.

"Ah, here are the two most beautiful women of the evening." Gabriel held out his hands as they approached.

"Hello." I glanced from Gabriel to Ethan, looking for any sign of worry, but Ethan appeared relaxed.

"Oh Gabriel, always the gentleman." Miriam straightened Gabriel's lapels, while he lightly wrapped his arms around her in a somewhat intimate gesture.

What's the relationship between these two?

"I've been having a lovely conversation with our dear Hannah here." Miriam stepped away from Gabriel. "And Ethan, it's always a pleasure to see you. Welcome back to the festivities." Miriam swept Ethan into a warm embrace.

"And you as well, Miriam. You look as elegant and graceful as ever," Ethan said, a sense of familiarity in his tone. This woman obviously meant a lot to him.

"Your kind words are always appreciated." Miriam moved beside Gabriel so that we created a closed circle on the balcony.

"Well, my dear, shall we move on to the more formal events of the evening?" Gabriel stuck out his arm to escort Miriam.

"Of course." Miriam rested her hand on the crook of his elbow and the two of them headed back inside.

Once we were alone, I leaned in closer to Ethan so we could talk privately. "So, are you in trouble?"

"No, I'm not in trouble. They wanted to talk to me about my decision to bring you here, and to understand better how you knew anything about them or this place. I've given them updates about everything that's happened, how I was forced to reveal the truth when I saved you, Adam getting people to come after you and his calculated attack at the library, but I think they needed to hear me explain it all again in person. They're uncertain about a protected having so much knowledge of what all of this is about. The incidences of that happening are so few they wanted to talk about how best to proceed from here. They are fascinated by you, that's for sure, and although they try to act indifferent, I think they're thrilled that they will get a chance to interact with you."

Was that pride in his voice? The weight of what I was about to do, meet with The Three, pressed down on me. *I don't want to let Ethan down.* I was starting to feel the cold and took a step towards the doors. Once we were inside, we would have to stop talking about all of this; since the members of the historical society didn't know anything about greater destinies and higher callings, we couldn't afford for one of them to overhear us. Before we went in, there was one more question I wanted to ask. "Did they mention anything about…" I pointed from him to me.

A hint of a smile crossed Ethan's lips. "No, they don't know that particular detail of my time in East Halton."

"I just wanted to make sure." I took Ethan's arm as we headed back into the ballroom. I couldn't tell him that Miriam had figured out something was going on with us. I was too scared of how he would react to that information, and I was still trying to process what Miriam had said about Ethan eventually leaving. I didn't want to believe that part; I couldn't accept it. I just wanted to be happy and believe that we would live in our own little fairytale world forever, although the longer I was at Veridan the more I started to question whether that was even possible.

Thirty

It wasn't long after the last of the awards were handed out for the evening that people began to drift and make their exits. It was almost midnight and soon there were only a handful of people left in the ballroom.

"I think I'm ready to call it a night." I lifted my napkin off my lap and placed it on the plate in front of me. I wanted to be rested for my talk with The Three in the morning.

"That makes sense, it's getting late. I'll escort you." Ethan pushed his chair back, then pulled mine out for me.

We maintained a polite distance as we exited the room and made our way upstairs.

"I had a very nice evening." I stopped outside of my door and let my hand linger on the knob.

"So did I. I'm glad you enjoyed yourself. These events can be a bit overwhelming at times." Ethan stuck the key in his door but didn't open it.

I cleared my throat. "You seemed pretty comfortable. I guess you've been to plenty of them, huh?"

Ethan shifted his weight from one foot to the other. "I've been to one or two, whenever they've thrown one while I'm here."

"You're really good at this, aren't you?" After a day of hearing endless accolades about Ethan's abilities and skills from everyone we ran into, I had to acknowledge what he would never admit to me.

"Good at what?" His forehead creased.

"Being a Hleo. I mean, I've always known you were capable or I wouldn't still be here. But multiple languages and bomb defusing? You're really good at this secret guardian stuff."

He blinked. "I just do what needs to be done."

"It's more than that. You fit in so well here at Veridan. And the people around here really love you."

"Hannah–"

"No. It's okay. I don't mean it as a bad thing. I just never realized how much this place is a part of you, that's all." I played with the ends of my wrap.

Ethan reached for me. "Hannah you don't need to worry that–" He fell silent and took a step back as a couple rounded the corner and started down the hallway towards us.

They looked to be in their mid-thirties and walked casually beside each other. They weren't touching, but there was a closeness that suggested they were romantically linked. They nodded politely to Ethan and me as they passed and kept going.

"Well, I'll let you get to bed. I'll see you in the morning?" Ethan's voice immediately became formal and I guessed that the couple was fellow Hleo.

"Yes, of course. Good night." I opened my door and walked inside my stately bedroom.

"Good night." Ethan's tone remained reserved as he entered his room.

I shut my door, then slipped out of the beautiful dress, careful to hang it up in the armoire in the corner of the room. I changed into my pajamas—a tank top and a pair of boxer shorts—and let my hair down. Once I was ready for bed, I climbed under the covers, relishing the feel of the luxurious sheets against my skin.

At some point during the evening someone had been in the room and drawn the curtains and lit a fire, and now flames cast a warm glow over the room. I watched the shadows dance across the walls and ceiling as the fire crackled, the day and the evening, and everything I had learned, playing over in my mind.

The information about my parents and the admissions Miriam had made were incredible. That my ability was different even than hers left me feeling more confused than ever. If only she had been willing to divulge what choice it was that I had to make. Since learning about my drawing ability, I had believed that was the reason Ethan was in my life, but now we were back to square one. It all came down to a simple choice, but what choice?

And then there was Ethan. Everyone here loved him, and from the light in his eyes, and the tone of his voice when talking to Miriam or Gabriel, he loved this world too. I thought back to his words at his parents' house, his declaration that I was his future. Had he really thought that through? Miriam had said it was only a matter of time before he would be required to leave me. He had, after all, been physically altered just to do this job and the expectations on him were not to be taken lightly. What would I do if Ethan did choose me over his calling, and ended up resenting me for it?

I tossed in the bed. If only there was some way I could be reassured, some way I could know for certain Ethan was truly convinced he wanted to pick me over the Hleo. I flopped onto my back. *Ethan.* I ached to see him and feel his arms securely around me. I bolted upright in bed. *I know how to confirm Ethan's feelings.* We needed to connect on a more intimate level. We were already so wrapped up in each other mentally and emotionally, it only made sense that the physical was the last step in making us inseparable. I had been longing to share that part of myself with Ethan for a while. I was pretty sure I was ready for it. At the very least, I didn't want to wait any longer.

My pulse sped up and I checked the time on the little antique clock sitting on the night table. It was after two in the morning. I quietly slipped out of bed and treaded over to the full-length standing mirror. My hair still had some lingering curls from being up all evening, and my tank top and shorts looked okay. They weren't ripped or stained, anyway. Some might consider it a seductive look.

I maneuvered carefully around the sitting area furniture, over to the adjoining door. The fire had died down and the only real light in the room was the moonlight streaming in from a crack between the curtains. I twisted the doorknob gingerly and took a deep breath. *It's now or never.* I eased the door open and peered into Ethan's room.

He sat up in bed, eyes wide in the dim moonlight. "Hannah, is everything okay?" he asked in a hushed voice as he jumped out of bed and crossed over to me. He was wearing a plain black T-shirt and grey shorts, and his hair was rumpled. He looked completely adorable.

His eyes, full of concern, searched mine, which only made me want to be with him more.

"I couldn't sleep." I matched his whisper as I glanced at the door. No one could hear us, could they? When I looked back at him, his expression had changed. The concern was gone, replaced with something quite a bit more intense. My breath caught.

His hand slowly slid across my waist. Electricity sparked between us. His fingers curled around the fabric of my shirt and he tugged me gently to him so our bodies grazed each other. Neither of us moved for a moment, and then, as though a switch had gone off, we consumed each other. Ethan's hand tightened around my waist and his other one came up around my back, drawing me into an intense, searching kiss.

I wrapped my arms around him, drawing him to me until we were firmly against each other. His lips moved from mine down to the curve of my neck, to my collarbone and then back to my mouth, all while his hands kept me locked against him. His grip was caressing and gentle, yet strong.

Suddenly he scooped me up in his arms and carried me to his bed. His lips stayed on mine the entire time. As he laid me down on the sheets, I pulled his shirt up over his back and shoulders until it slipped over his head. *This is it.* I drank in the sight of his strong arm and stomach muscles. This was the moment I had been thinking about for so long now, the moment Ethan and I would be united in the only way we hadn't been yet.

My hands clutched the hem of my tank top ready to slide it off, but Ethan jumped off the bed with such force and speed it was as if he'd been burned. He moved to the other side of the room, near the fireplace. A guilty look crept across his face. "Hannah, we can't do this." He sounded disappointed. Was that because of what we had been doing, or because we had stopped?

"Oh." I drew my knees up to my chin and wrapped my arms around them, fighting the sting of rejection as I sat alone on the bed.

Ethan took a few long, slow breaths, before pulling his shirt back on and walking slowly to the edge his bed, keeping a fair space between us. "It's not that I don't want to. I think by my reckless actions you can tell that I want to, more than you can possibly know, but this isn't the place. There are too many eyes watching every move." Ethan inched closer. I could tell he was wrestling with whether to pull me into his arms to reassure me I wasn't being rejected, or to keep his distance because he couldn't trust himself near me.

My gaze dropped to the rumpled covers. "I thought the cameras didn't watch bedrooms unless an alarm was triggered."

"They don't, but there are still many ways we could get caught. If they found out about us, it would be the last time I'd be allowed to see you, and I can't be separated from you, I won't be. I don't trust anyone else with your life." Ethan sank down beside me and took my hand in his, his fingers threading through mine.

A flicker of relief fought against the crushing hurt over him ending what was happening between us so abruptly.

"I just wanted…" I trailed off. It felt too vulnerable to say what I had been thinking.

Ethan stroked my cheek gently with his thumb. "Hannah, you are so special and you deserve this moment to happen when it's right, not for any other reason. I have a feeling you might be rushing into something you're not quite ready for because of being here in this place, listening to these people, and thinking that I could somehow ever choose being a Hleo over you. I want only you and I want to be with you, but not as a way for you to hold onto me, if that's what this was about." Ethan searched my face, his eyes blazing with concern.

I almost laughed. He knew me so well. *How can he possibly pinpoint my motives so accurately?*

I leaned into his palm. "I miss you."

Ethan sighed. "I miss you too. I'm used to existing with complete self-restraint. After letting that down a little when your dad was on his trip, well, once it's gone it's hard to reestablish. I think putting up boundaries between us again has been harder to do than I realized it would be." Ethan's hand slid back to his lap. "And I definitely underestimated how intense my desire for you would be."

I swallowed hard.

Ethan shifted on the bed. "I know I've been running sort of hot and cold on you the last little while where our physical relationship is concerned, and that's not fair. There is a reason for my behavior. You see, when—" A knock on the door cut Ethan off.

"Flynn, I know it's late, but I need to speak with you." The male voice was commanding.

Was that Kai? I gulped. Had security found out about us already?

My eyes went wide and my mouth dry as I stared at the door. "Do you think—" I hissed, but Ethan put a finger to his lips. My heart pounded in my chest as I scanned the room for hidden cameras. Were they recording us, after all? Heat flared in my cheeks at the thought of what they would have seen.

"I'll be right out." Ethan called out as he strode across the room to retrieve a pair of jeans he'd slung across the back of a chair. I eyed the adjoining door. *I need to get back to my room.*

Once Ethan was clothed, he strode back over to me. He pressed his forehead against mine, and cupped my face in his hands. "Wait in your room for me while I go talk to Kai. Remember that, no matter what, I love you." Ethan's voice was so low I had to strain to hear it, but I nodded.

"I love you too," I breathed. When he moved back, I slid off the bed and tiptoed over to my bedroom. I stepped through the doorway and started to close the adjoining door. Ethan shot me one last look before I shut it tightly. I chewed on my lip as I was left standing alone in my bedroom.

I walked back over to my bed and climbed under the covers. What were the two of them saying? Had we been caught? The thought screamed at me. What other reason could Kai possibly have for waking Ethan up in the middle of the night? I realized I was holding my breath. I exhaled slowly, willing Ethan to return with some sort of explanation. After five minutes I pushed the covers back and made my way over to the sitting area. My stomach churned. Was this it? Would my rash plan to bring Ethan and I together ultimately be the thing that ripped us apart?

I paced the length of the room for twenty minutes, praying we hadn't been caught. Finally I heard the sound of Ethan's door opening and closing. I clenched and unclenched my fists, waiting until there was a gentle rap on the adjoining door.

I flung it open. "Well?"

Ethan came into my room and closed the door behind him. He dropped down onto the little couch. "We're fine. Kai wanted to talk to me about something else."

"Something else." I exhaled, the gut-wrenching anxiety beginning to dissolve. "At this time of night?"

"Yes. Because Hleo don't technically need to sleep, the concept of *off the clock* gets disregarded a lot." Ethan rested his elbows on his knees and slid his palms back and forth against each other.

"So we're safe?" I sank down beside him, careful to leave a decent amount of space between us.

"Yes, we're safe." Ethan nodded, but didn't meet my eyes.

What aren't you saying, Ethan? I tucked my legs up underneath me. "I'm sorry. I wasn't thinking. I know I should never have done such a risky—"

"You don't need to apologize." He twisted to look at me, a reassuring smile crossing his lips.

My shoulders relaxed. "Okay. I have been freaking out since the second you walked out the door, but if you say we're good, then good. I'm so relieved." I pushed my hair off my face as the last of the nervous adrenaline wore off. "So what did he want to talk about?"

Ethan hesitated. "I had asked Kai to look into the Glain Neidr and he wanted to share what he'd found out." There was a strange tone in Ethan's voice, keeping me from getting too excited. "It doesn't look like that's going to pan out for us."

I slumped back against the couch. "Really?" I had been starting to get my hopes up about the mysterious necklace. Dad's stories had made it seem incredible.

"Really." Ethan stood and walked over to the fireplace, prodding at the burned down embers in the hearth with a poker.

Was he disappointed by the news or was there something he wasn't telling me? I wanted to ask, but something in the way he held himself, his intense concentration on the fire, suggested he wasn't ready to share any more with me. A sudden exhaustion struck me and I yawned.

"You should get to bed." Ethan replaced the poker in the metal holder and strode back over to me.

"Yeah, I guess so." *Why are you in such a rush to get away from me?* I sighed. I was too tired to think straight. We could talk about this tomorrow. He wandered back over to the adjoining door again, and I followed.

"Well, I guess this is good night." I stopped in the doorway and pressed one hand to the frame.

Ethan wrapped his hand around my waist and pulled me close; his lips brushed against my ear. "Good night. I'll see you in the morning."

I closed my eyes, reluctant to move.

He held me for a moment and then his grip slid away and he stepped back to shut the door. I climbed back into my bed and stared up at the canopy. My mind wouldn't shut off. *What a night.* It definitely hadn't ended the way I thought it would when I'd slipped into Ethan's room.

It was hard not to obsess. First his putting a quick stop to getting physical, and then Kai interrupting Ethan just as he had been about to explain his behavior when it came to that part of our relationship. *I really would have liked to have heard that*. It had to be connected to Simon's warning somehow, but what was the reason, exactly? And why had Kai felt the need to talk to Ethan at two in the morning? Seemed a strange time of day to relay the simple message that we weren't going to be able to find the Glain Neidr. Was there more to it than that?

I flipped my pillow over, punching at it in frustration. I only hoped my meeting with The Three would be more satisfying than tonight had been.

Thirty-One

I mentally rehearsed the points I wanted to make to the leaders of the Hleo as I got dressed the next morning. I was trying not to fixate on the events of the night before. I needed to focus my energy into what I was going to say to The Three.

A light knock sounded on the door just as I finished getting ready. I ran over and yanked it open. Ethan stood in the hallway, looking gorgeous in dark jeans and a forest green sweater that made his eyes even more vibrant than they normally were. His hair was still a little wet from the shower, and he smelled faintly of shaving cream and soap.

"Good morning, I hope you slept well." Ethan's eyes searched mine.

"I tossed and turned a bit, too much excitement last night, I guess." I shut my door and started down the corridor.

He grabbed my elbow, stopping me. "Are we okay?"

I smiled. "We're okay."

Relief flashed across his face. "Good."

We walked downstairs, bypassing the ballroom as the delicious scent of bacon beckoned us to a large dining room. A long table set up against one wall was covered in an assortment of breakfast foods. There were baked goods, fresh fruit, hot and cold cereal, eggs, pancakes, sausage, and bacon.

"Wow, everything looks so good." I eyed the spread and picked up an empty plate from the end of the table. I grabbed a croissant, a few pieces of bacon, and some fruit. So far I hadn't seen a single soul. It felt a little like we had the place to ourselves.

"Memores Foveat does know how to be good hosts to their guests." Ethan also reached for a plate.

I walked over to one of the round dining tables, gingerly setting my food down before sinking onto a chair. "So when are we meeting with Miriam, Gabriel, and Victor? After breakfast?"

"Actually they can't meet with for another hour or so." Ethan set down a plate loaded with scrambled eggs and sausages and took the chair beside me.

My shoulders slumped. "Oh. That's too bad. I was hoping to meet with them right away." The longer we waited to talk to The Three, the more likely I would lose my nerve and not say all the things I wanted to.

"I know. They have to wait until most of the foundation members are on their way again before they'll be free to talk to you." Ethan picked up his fork.

"I get it. I'm just anxious." I took a bite of a strawberry. "So I know Kai told you not to bother with the Glain Neidr, but I've been thinking about it. It couldn't hurt for us to do a little digging of our own, right? Just because he doesn't know where it is, doesn't mean we wouldn't be able to figure it out."

Ethan lifted his glass of orange juice and took a sip. "I don't think The Three want you in the secured area of the library."

"Oh." I blinked. I hadn't been expecting that. "You could go in and look around and grab whatever books might be helpful and bring them out for us to look over."

"No, Hannah, Kai said it's not worth it. The necklace is long gone." Ethan shook his head. His tone was level but I sensed a hint of frustration.

"But…" I bit my lip. "Isn't that the reason we came? You've already said I'm not likely to get much from The Three, and now you're saying we can't even try to find the Glain Neidr. Why are we here then, Ethan?" I fought to keep my voice down. I was sick of roadblocks and I couldn't believe Ethan appeared to be the one putting them up now.

He took a deep breath. "Veridan is a place of secrets, Hannah. I'm sorry that everyone here works so hard to keep those secrets buried. I wish I could give you all the answers you want, but it's just how it is. That's why I tried to tell you it probably wasn't a good idea to come here." We were still alone in the room, but Ethan kept his voice low.

"Fine." I ripped off a piece of croissant and shoved it into my mouth. I didn't want to fight with Ethan here of all places, but my frustration was mounting.

Ethan covered my hand with his. "I do have something else to show you though, to pass the time until your meeting."

He sounded apologetic and I softened. "What?"

"I'll take you when you're done." He motioned to my plate.

I set down the last bite of my pastry. "I'm done. What do you have to show me?"

"Come on." Ethan stood. I followed his lead and the two of us made our way back up to the third floor lounge. A fire was crackling nicely in the fireplace, and a steaming mug of coffee sat on one of the end tables beside the plush leather couch.

"I think someone will be back soon." I gestured to the drink.

"I'm counting on it." Ethan sank down on the couch across from the coffee drinker's seat. I crossed my arms, about to ask what was going on, just as Lou came through the door.

"Good morning, you two. I remembered I had some old photographs of Elizabeth in an album, so I went to grab it from my storage locker." Lou held up a brown, weathered-looking photo album that must have been at least fifty years old.

"Hi Lou, I didn't realize we would see you today." I gave her a friendly smile and glanced over at Ethan, who grinned knowingly. My heart melted. Here I was thinking he was hiding things from me, and all the while he'd been thoughtful enough to set up a meeting with Lou.

Ethan stood and wandered towards the billiard table, presumably to give us some privacy. Lou plopped down beside her coffee and patted the empty seat next to her. I settled in and she cracked the photo album open.

Lou pointed at the first picture. "This one was taken right after Elizabeth arrived at Veridan for training." She moved her finger to a shot of my mother standing by Veridan's gatehouse, a steamer trunk beside her and a truck full of sheep in the background. "I was supposed to go pick her up at the train station with this Hleo, Bruno. On our way we got a flat tire. When we finally arrived at the station, Elizabeth was nowhere. I was worried we'd lost her, so we headed back to Veridan to form a battle plan to track her down. As we were pulling up I could see a farmer's pickup truck at the gatehouse and there was Elizabeth, climbing out of the back of the truck. She'd caught a ride with a farmer transporting some sheep. She flung her trunk down and walked over to Bruno and me to introduce herself. I knew immediately that we were going to get along." Lou shook her head as she gently tapped the photo.

She showed me pictures of her and my mother posing together at different locations around Veridan. There was a shot of the two of them in 1960s bikinis swimming in a pond, and another of Elizabeth in bell bottoms, standing on a big rock and looking as though she was playing king of the castle. I studied them all with great interest.

Lou pointed to a shot of Elizabeth in a dorm room. "Liz was trying to learn Russian here, and wanted to be left alone." My mother was looking up from a desk with an annoyed expression on her face.

The first half of the book contained black and white pictures and the clothing and hairstyles made it fairly easy to tell that the images spanned the 1940s to the 1960s. Even as the styles changed Elizabeth remained the same, frozen and ageless just like Ethan and everyone else who were part of this world. A twinge of anxiety ran through me. As things stood presently, eventually I would bypass all of them all in age.

Lou tapped her chin. "You know, in the fiftyish years that we were friends, I can only remember two times when we had a huge argument. One about an assignment, I don't even remember what it was anymore, and the other was the time she told me she was going to leave with Noah."

"Really?" I stared at a picture of the two of them, dressed in formal gowns and standing on the same balcony I had been on with Miriam.

"Really. I tried to stop her. Told her it would be the worst mistake of her life. It took me awhile to come around, but eventually I realized I was wrong."

She flipped to the last page of the photo album and I gasped. "This is what I really wanted you to see." Lou pulled the snapshot out for me to get a better look. It was a photograph of Elizabeth and Noah sitting on a blanket spread out on the grass in a park on a beautiful summer day having a picnic. Elizabeth held a smiling baby girl in a pretty yellow sundress in her arms. The picture had become a little discolored from age but it still showed a loving family enjoying an afternoon together.

"That's me," I breathed, my hands shaking as I grasped the photo. I had only ever seen one baby picture of myself from before my parents adopted me. It had been taken right after I was born. I had been wrapped up in a baby blanket, sleeping, the only person in the shot.

I knew Elizabeth and Noah hadn't had the luxury of stopping for family portraits, but to see this, to know that there had been happy family moments together, meant so much. Ethan came over to stand behind the couch and look over my shoulder.

"Yeah, you were a cutie for sure," Lou said.

"How did you get this?" I glanced up at her, still in shock. I had been under the impression that once Elizabeth had run off with Noah, that had been the end of her contact with any members of the Hleo.

"She sent it to me. I was stationed in Vietnam. I hadn't heard from her in six years and then, out of the blue, I get this picture and a letter from her. She apologized for taking off without saying good-bye. She wanted me to know that our friendship had been very important to her, and that she was happy. She wrote that you, Hannah, her daughter, was her happiness, and that I should be happy for her if I could be." Lou rhymed off the contents of the letter with the familiarity of someone who must have read it and reread it many times.

I swallowed back tears that threatened to spill onto my cheeks. "Do you still have the letter?"

"No. Unfortunately I had to get rid of it. At the time there was still a mandate to track her and Noah down. I was worried that, if someone found the letter, they would think I knew how to find Elizabeth, which I didn't. I just wanted her to have the chance to live the life she wanted, so I got rid of the letter. But not without memorizing it first." Lou tapped the side of her head. "You can keep the picture, you really should have it."

"Thank you so much." The words didn't feel adequate to express how much having this photo meant to me.

Ever since learning I was adopted, I had wondered if my biological parents had wanted me in their lives. Even though both Ethan and my dad had reassured me Elizabeth and Noah had always planned to raise me, I still felt the same doubt. I questioned if giving me up had ultimately been the most convenient choice. Seeing this photo made me believe they had wanted a normal life away from the madness of the Hleo and Bana worlds.

"Hannah, I hate to interrupt, but it's almost time for your meeting," Ethan said gently.

I straightened on the couch. It was time. I needed to go have the conversation I hoped would answer my questions. "Of course. I should let you get on with your day anyway, Lou. Thank you so much for meeting with me." I stood, still clutching the photo tightly in my hand.

"My pleasure. It was really fun to go down memory lane. I hope we get a chance to connect again. In fact…" Lou grabbed her bag from the floor and dug through it until she produced a pen and a scrap of paper. She quickly jotted down a number on it and handed it to me. "It's my cell phone number." She shot a glance at Ethan. "I'm not really supposed to give it out, but if you ever get sick of this guy…" Lou cocked her finger at Ethan jokingly, "…or you need something, as long as I'm not in the jungles of Bolivia or something, I'll be there."

As if I could somehow get sick of Ethan. "Thanks." I slipped the paper into my pocket. "For everything." I waved and Ethan and I headed back out of the lounge, and downstairs towards the library, ready for the next step of our journey.

Thirty-Two

The library was every bit as magnificent as I'd remembered, and again I marveled at its size. We veered off to the left of the entrance where a wood-paneled door sat tucked away in the corner. It looked as though it had been designed to blend in as part of the wall. Ethan gave a quick knock.

I clenched and unclenched my fists as we waited for someone to let us in. I knew what I wanted to say to The Three, I just hoped they would listen.

Bridget answered the door and ushered us into a large meeting room. "They're already here."

"Great." Ethan's tone was innocent, ignoring the implication that we had kept everyone waiting.

The Three were sitting at a long, very official-looking table, and stood when we walked in. "Good morning Hannah, Ethan." Gabriel gestured for us to take the seats across from them. "I trust you slept well, Hannah."

"Yes, I've never slept in such an enchanting place. I can't believe this is your home, it's remarkable." I didn't like lying, but I couldn't tell them there hadn't been much sleeping going on.

"It is quite a place, isn't it? We're very glad you like it," Gabriel said. Miriam glanced over at him, but I couldn't read the look, exasperation maybe? Why? "I know you met Miriam and me last night, but allow me to introduce Victor Gunn." Gabriel motioned to the third member of The Three.

"It's nice to meet you, Hannah." Victor flashed me a charming smile and shook my hand.

"You too." I studied his refined, handsome face, trying to place how I knew him.

We settled into our seats and Victor leaned forward, clasping his hands together on the table. "I'll be the first to admit that we've all been pretty interested in meeting the offspring of one of our own. And from the reports Ethan's sent back, you seem to be one very unique and special individual. We know you find your ability frustrating, and we want to help if we can, so why don't you start by asking us the questions you have for us, and we'll see if we can provide any answers for you."

I opened my mouth to begin my rehearsed speech, but closed it again when I remembered something. A grainy memory from over five years ago. Dad and I had just arrived home from the cemetery after burying my mom. My house was full of people milling around during the reception that had followed the service. My grandmother told my father that a man wanted to speak with him on the porch. Dad went outside, while I spied on the two of them through the living room window. Dad had gotten very upset. He'd flailed his arms, disbelief and worry obvious in his body language. I hadn't been able to hear what they were saying, but I'd been startled by my dad's reaction. The man had held up his hands and spoken quietly. Whatever he had said to my dad had calmed him down. Dad had returned to the reception without a word to anyone. As I stared at Victor I could picture very clearly that he was the man from that memory. "You came to see my father." I cocked my head and squinted as I looked at him, wanting to be sure.

"Excuse me?" Victor eyebrows shot up.

"The day of my mother's funeral, you came to see my dad." I tapped the table nervously, trying to bring the memory in my mind into sharper focus. I kept my eyes on The Three, but felt Ethan look in my direction. He must not have been aware of that visit.

"I did come to see your father." Victor ran a hand through his dark hair.

I glanced at Gabriel and Miriam. There was no surprise in their expressions, so obviously they knew about the meeting.

"It was only two days after your mother's death that Miriam saw you as a protected. It came as quite a shock to all of us. We all knew that Elizabeth had a child, and we eventually tracked down where you ended up after your parents' deaths, but the Hleo society was content to leave you be. We did have someone check on you every once in a while during your childhood, to make sure there were no markers of your Hleo heritage that would keep you from leading a normal life, but from our limited observations everything seemed fine."

A shiver ran up my spine at the thought that someone had been watching me as a child.

"When your mother was killed, and then Miriam saw you, we all went on high alert. We were worried that the Bana had somehow learned of your calling before we had and were after you. It took a lot of scrambling, but we discovered that an old craving for revenge had motivated your mother's death. We tracked down her killer but he was completely unaware of what lay in your future."

"Your father, being the clever man that he is, was scared his wife's death had been a murder, and what that could mean for your wellbeing. We were concerned he would go into hiding with you, so we decided to tell your father that we had dealt with the Bana member to ease his mind. I made that journey myself under the guise of an ordinary Hleo." Victor's blue eyes, filled with empathy, stayed on mine as he spoke.

I frowned as I replayed the memory in my mind. "He was upset."

Victor rubbed a hand along the back of his neck "He was. To have it confirmed that his wife had been murdered was, understandably, overwhelming for him, but he seemed somewhat comforted when I told him that the threat against you was gone. We did not tell him of your calling, though. We were worried that, in an effort to protect you, he would be tempted to share the details of your unique destiny with you, and we didn't want you finding out about it." Victor gazed from Gabriel to Miriam and then back to me. "But here we are, I guess."

"This visit wasn't in the file on Hannah that I received when first assigned to her." Ethan's voice was respectful, but the slight quaver suggested that he was confused, and maybe a little annoyed.

"This visit was about addressing Hannah's father's concerns more than anything, so we felt it wasn't necessary for you to know." Victor's tone suggested that was all the explanation Ethan was going to receive.

"I see." Ethan shifted in his seat.

"I'm glad we've been able to clear up a confusing memory for you, Hannah, but perhaps we should move on to today's discussion. What would you like us to answer, exactly?" Gabriel leaned forward in his chair.

"First of all, I want to thank you for seeing me. Ethan told me that it's not a usual custom of yours, and I do appreciate it. I guess my first question for you would be, do any of you know if there have been others like me?" I avoided Miriam's gaze. I had her answer on the subject, but what would the other two have to say?

The Three looked at each other; it was as though they were communicating without speaking, able to understand each other from facial expressions alone. Or maybe they could read each other's thoughts. I really had no idea what the extent of their power was.

Gabriel smoothed down the sleeves of the navy sweater he wore. "I understand that Ethan has explained to you that each protected has a calling unique to them. The plans that have been destined for each are always different. So no, we have never seen a protected who receives visions of other protecteds."

The three people who knew the most about the Hleo and the Metadas had never seen anyone like me before. I ran a hand across my forehead, trying not to feel like a complete freak. "Do you know why I can see protecteds?"

This time it was Miriam who spoke, without the silent conversation. "We do not know why. It is not for us to understand why right now. Any reasons we could give you would be theoretical, nothing tangible or useful that you could cling to as a definitive answer."

She was holding back, they all were, I could sense it. I had a feeling they knew exactly why I could see protecteds. They clearly had no intention of sharing that information with me though, and I couldn't help but sigh in frustration.

"Okay." I exhaled slowly. "If you don't know why, do you at least know what I'm supposed to do with this ability? Gabriel, you see the big plan, right? Have you seen anything regarding me?" I clasped my hands together. *I'm practically pleading*. "If I could just know what's coming, I could prepare myself. I feel like I'm stumbling in the dark towards a big hole. I'm trying to avoid falling into it, but no matter what I do, I'm stumbling closer to the edge. If you could just shed some light on this situation, maybe I could avoid that hole."

Gabriel's eyes softened and I felt a shred of hope. "Hannah, we can appreciate how you feel, and our hesitation isn't meant to be uncaring. You are in somewhat of an unfortunate position. Being brought into a circle of understanding about the Hleo has affected your natural decision-making processes. The choices you will make now are not necessarily what they would have been if you had never been told of our existence. We have had lengthy discussions about the best way to proceed with you and we feel that it is imperative that we protect as much of your natural instincts as we can. To share with you the glimpses—and keep in mind they are simply that, glimpses—we have seen would ultimately change the outcomes. For you to learn what is to come would change how you use your ability. I'm sorry, but that isn't information we can share with you." Gabriel slid his hand across the table and placed it on mine gently. "I know that it isn't what you came to hear, and it does mean that for now you continue walking blindly towards your future, but it is the way it needs to be."

I felt like a deflated balloon as I stared at the grain lines on the table. Every bit of anticipation that had coursed through me when we'd first arrived at Veridan was gone. We couldn't look for the Glain Neidr, and so far this meeting with The Three was simply confirming what Ethan had warned me about.They had the answers, but they weren't going to share them with me.

What could be waiting in my future that learning about it would change how I would react? It had to be big, which only made not knowing that much scarier.

I raised my chin. It was a long shot, but I had one last-ditch suggestion. "I get what you're saying, I really do. I'm trying to respect the decision you've come to, but I wanted to propose one more idea. It is my understanding that the world is controlled by the Metadas, that everything you do is a result of the instructions it gives you in the circular room. Is there any way I could go in that room, and see if the Metadas would speak to me?"

Ethan stared at me, but I refused to meet his gaze. I hadn't told him what I was going to propose, because I knew he would have disapproved and tried to talk me out of it.

The Three looked at each other, obviously thrown by my suggestion. Victor cleared his throat. "Hannah, we're a little surprised you know about this room."

"I take responsibility for that, sir. I felt that it was useful for Hannah to understand as much as she could about the Hleo." Ethan's hands were clenched together so tightly on the table, his knuckles gleamed white.

Gabriel held up a calming hand. "It's all right, Ethan."

The Three conversed in their silent way. After a moment, Victor and Gabriel gave Miriam a slight nod, and she turned to me. "Hannah, we cannot grant that request. The room is designed for those who have been changed in the branding ceremony, and we could not guarantee that it would be either wise or safe to allow you to enter it."

"I thought you might say that, but I want you to know that I'm different. My dad told me that I'm not the same as other people. He and Mom noticed it while I was growing up. Somehow the altered physical state that Elizabeth and Noah had as Hleo and Bana got transferred to me, at least partly. I don't get sick; I've never had severe headaches, a significant cold, or even the flu. Dad told me of an instance when I was a toddler where he walked in on me drinking poisonous cleaner, and it didn't affect me. I guess I'm immune to poison, somehow." I pressed my lips together. I was trying to be concise but felt that I was rambling.

I shot a glance over to Ethan. His eyes had widened. I hadn't told him about my health. I was still processing it myself and hadn't known how to explain it to him. The Three also looked surprised, but quickly regained their composure. "We were not aware of this, and although it is intriguing, it does not change the fact that it is not meant for you to go in the room." Miriam's tone was warm but firm.

"We do not know what is in store for you in its entirety, but we are still confident that a moment will come that will give you the clarity you seek." Gabriel gave me a compassionate smile.

My shoulders slumped. *Why had they agreed to see me in the first place?*

"We know you're probably questioning why we asked you here when we were unable to give you much information, but it is with reason." Gabriel ran a finger along his eyebrow. "Ethan has kept us informed of the attacks involving you over the past months, and although he has assured us that Adam Chambers was the mastermind behind these attacks, we are concerned. There is always a threat level against protecteds that Bana are able to find, but this is different. The Bana appear to be targeting you relentlessly, and because of your unique gift, and from our glimpses of your future, we feel it is vital you are kept safe. We are at a crossroads of sorts. We try to allow protecteds to lead their lives as normally as possible, so their natural reflexes will guide them in their decisions, but we feel, with your extraordinary circumstances, it is necessary to alter our protection strategy. Hannah, we feel it would be in your best interest if you stayed here, with us, at Veridan," Gabriel finished.

My jaw dropped open. I twisted to stare at Ethan. His gaze was fixed on the table. *He knew they would do this.* That must have been why he had neglected to tell The Three about my Dad's kidnapping. He had been trying to downplay the threats so they wouldn't make me come live at Veridan.

"But, I…" I wasn't even sure how to respond. A wave of dizziness hit me. I couldn't just leave my entire life behind. I was in my last year of high school and hoping to go to university. I couldn't leave Dad and Katie and everyone, they would never understand.

"Your safety is our outmost concern. It's why we're making this unorthodox proposal, but we also think we might be able to help you figure out how to use your abilities if we were able to observe them." Victor's smile beckoned me to give in.

"Would Ethan still be assigned as my Hleo?" My heart was in my throat.

"Ethan would be reassigned. You would be protected by every Hleo stationed here." Victor motioned to the door, pride ringing in his voice as he mentioned the security force available on the grounds.

I nodded slowly. "I see." I was working hard to keep my breathing even. I had to say no, I just had to. *What if they don't accept that answer?* I gulped. "I'm grateful for your offer, and I do want to be able to control my ability and figure it all out, desperately, but I can't leave everything I know to hide out here. Ethan has been an amazing bodyguard. I'm confident he can continue to keep me safe where I am, at home."

Gabriel's attention turned to the tall window at the end of the room. I followed his gaze. A dove had landed on the windowsill and bobbed along it for a moment before soaring away into the open air again. Gabriel focused back on me. "We urge you to think this through. We aren't sure what your gift's potential is, but we feel it's great. With great potential comes great risk that someone with dark intentions will try to exploit it. I don't exaggerate when I say that Ethan is one of the best we have here, but even his abilities have a limit."

I studied them. Victor and Gabriel were deeply concerned, it was clear in their furrowed brows. Miriam's expression remained unreadable, though. *What are you thinking, Miriam*?

"I understand what you're saying, and it does make sense, but I can't leave my friends and family. There are relationships in East Halton I can't live without." *Like my relationship with a certain Hleo*. "I would really like to be able to go home again, if you don't mind." I held my breath, scared their suggestion was actually a command and they were only being polite to keep up the appearance of civility.

Gabriel sighed. "Hannah, your will is always your own. We would never force you to do something you feel you can't. You are free to come and go as you please, but if at any time you come to feel as we do, that this is the safest place for you, then please come back and we will make immediate arrangements for you here."

I nodded. "Thank you, I appreciate your kindness. I just know right now I need to be at home."

Gabriel stood. "We will respect your wishes. It has been a true pleasure to meet you, my dear. I'm sure we will see you again." Victor and Miriam followed Gabriel's lead, as did Ethan. I got up too, and we all moved away from the table, and started for the door.

The men paused in the meeting room, while Miriam and I ended up alone in the library. Miriam rested a slender hand on my arm. "It will all make sense soon." She spoke low and I stared into her deep violet eyes, trying to figure out the thoughts she wasn't verbalizing.

"Couldn't it make sense today?" I wrinkled my nose.

"It isn't time yet, but it is coming. I promise you, all will be clear very soon now."

I frowned at her cryptic message. "Okay." I nodded, trying to accept what she was saying, that I should be patient.

Just as Ethan, Victor, and Gabriel joined us in the library, Bridget made her way over to us, appearing from around a shelf of books.

"We should let you go. You still have your trip back to East Halton," Gabriel said.

"I'll page Michael to bring the town car up to take you to the train station." Bridget flashed us a professional smile.

"Thank you, Bridget." Victor placed a hand on her shoulder and her grin brightened.

"Until next time then." Gabriel grasped my hands in his and gave them a light squeeze.

"Next time." I waited for him to release me and then took a step back.

Victor shook my hand and Miriam gave me a hug, then they said good-bye to Ethan and they were gone. I was dying to talk to Ethan, to try to explain why I hadn't told him about my health anomalies, or my plan to ask about the circular room, but the firm set of his jaw kept me from speaking. How angry was he? I pushed back my shoulders. I wasn't overly pleased with him either. After all, he could have warned me about The Three's living arrangement suggestion for me. A frown creased my forehead. It was probably best to wait until we were alone before trying to hash everything out.

Thirty-Three

"Ethan, could I speak with you for a minute?" Bridget had led the way out of the library, typing on the phone in her hand as we went, but when we reached Veridan's grand staircase, she slipped the phone into her pocket.

"Of course." Ethan had a grip on the banister but released it when she spoke.

I glanced awkwardly from Bridget to Ethan. "I guess I'll just go pack."

"You know the way back?" Ethan asked.

"Yes." I stepped onto the first stair, but Bridget held up a hand to stop me. "Actually, Hannah, I already had someone from housekeeping pack your things. Your bags have been brought down to the front hall. If you want, you can wait out there for us. Michael should be here soon to take the two of you to the train station."

It took everything I had not to roll my eyes. "I'll just be out there then." I trudged towards the front entrance. Bridget was cutting into my explanation time with Ethan. I didn't want to wait to resolve our issues.

From the reflection in a long gilded mirror on the wall in front of me, I could see Bridget usher Ethan into a small room just off the foyer. She followed him in and shut the door behind them. I whirled around to stare at the closed door. *What does she want with Ethan?* I flopped down on one of the long wooden benches that bordered the room and sighed. For a moment there was only silence, then I heard voices. Bridget and Ethan's voices to be exact. They sounded tinny, and far away. *How can I hear them?* I stood up and moved around the area until I traced the sound to an old air vent in the wall above me. No one appeared to be around, so I stepped up onto the bench to hear better.

"Ethan, I wanted to ask if you might be interested in a reassignment. We need another well-trained teacher for the new Hleo recruits, specifically in martial arts and covert strategy. We could also use another person fluent in Mandarin and Russian," Bridget said, and a pit began to form in my stomach.

"I noticed there are a lot more new Hleo than normal," Ethan replied, and the uneasy feeling grew. Why hadn't he immediately declined the offer?

"Yes, they were all seen by Victor, I assure you." Bridget sounded anxious.

"Why so many?" Ethan asked.

"I'm not really—"

"Bridget, it's me."

I pressed my ear even closer to the vent.

"I don't know exactly what's going on, but a few months ago, Victor started having visions of more and more Hleo. At first it was five or six, instead of the usual two or three, but it's slowly been gaining until last month it was twelve. At first no one questioned it—Victor was envisioning these people so that was that—but now Gabriel has started coming away from his time in the room very agitated. No one except Victor and Miriam knows what he's seen, he won't tell anyone, but whatever's coming has him worried." Bridget's voice had lowered and I struggled to hear her. I rose up onto my tippy toes to get closer to the vent. What was happening here at Veridan?

There was silence for a moment. Ethan must be digesting what Bridget had divulged. "I want you to keep me informed on any new developments. I have to decline the teaching job; I don't trust anyone else with Hannah. What about Marco, isn't he usually up for a rotation of teaching duty?" Ethan asked. The ache in my stomach eased. My keeping things from him hadn't been enough to push him away.

"Marco was killed." Even through the vent I could hear the pain in Bridget's voice.

"Killed…" Ethan sounded shocked. "Bridget, I'm sorry. I know the two of you were—"

"Yes, well, the vile lowlife that killed him has already been dealt with, but thank you for your concern," Bridget replied.

"First Nick, now Marco. The Bana are getting more aggressive, aren't they?"

"It seems that way, yes. I think it has to do with whatever Gabriel is seeing, but for now we just have to wait it out."

"I suppose so."

"Ethan, the real reason I'm offering you the teaching job is that The Three really want Hannah to come in. They haven't said anything specific, but I'm pretty sure she has something to do with the visions and the new Hleo as well. She seems to trust you, maybe she'd come in if she knew you were going to be here at Veridan." Bridget's voice had softened, losing the usual efficient clip.

"It's Hannah's decision," Ethan said quietly, as though he wasn't convinced I had made the right one by turning down The Three's invitation to live with them.

My eyebrows furrowed. How could I possibly have anything to do with Victor and Gabriel's visions? It didn't make sense.

"Just think about it, and maybe try to talk to her," Bridget replied.

"Yeah, all right, I'll see," Ethan said.

"Okay then, you should get back to work." Bridget sounded formal again.

I gritted my teeth. *Again, I'm just work to these people.*

"Checking for dust bunnies?" A male voice asked from behind me.

Startled, I lost my balance and teetered backwards. Thankfully, the guy caught me before I landed in a heap on the floor. I looked up to see Michael. He gave me an amused grin, his dark eyes crinkling at the corners.

"Sorry." Warmth rushed into my cheeks as he set me down on the ground. Had anyone else witnessed my bizarre actions but just passed by?

"Don't even worry about it." He waved his hand. "So who are we listening to?" He leaned in conspiratorially, but before I could answer, Ethan and Bridget rounded the corner.

"Ah, I see. Well, your secret's safe with me," he whispered as they approached.

"Thanks," I shot back, utterly mortified.

"Are you ready to go?" Ethan's gaze shifted from Michael to me as he and Bridget reached us.

"If you are." I forced a smile, but on the inside my stomach was churning. It wouldn't settle until I had a chance to talk to Ethan.

The four of us headed outside. Ethan and I said good-bye to Bridget, then climbed back into the town car that had brought us here only a day before. It felt like a lifetime ago, with everything that had happened. Michael pulled the car down the driveway and we started to put distance between us and the beautiful and overwhelming grounds of Veridan.

Thirty-Four

By the time we reached the train station my stomach was twisted into a huge knot. Ethan had spent the entire drive chatting with Michael. Ethan was always considerate and polite, but I was pretty sure that engaging in conversation with Michael had more to do with avoiding me, than with actual interest in what was going on in our driver's life.

Michael stopped the car at the entrance to the train station, and jumped out to get our luggage from the trunk. "Until next time, Flynn. Stay safe."

"You too, Michael." Ethan took our bags from him.

"It was nice meeting you, Hannah. Hopefully we'll see you around here again soon." Michael stepped off the curb and headed for the driver's door.

"Yeah, maybe." I pulled my coat closed as an icy wind blew across the sidewalk.

It was already late afternoon, and the sun was hanging low in the sky. Ethan went and bought our tickets while I sat and waited in a row of hard plastic chairs. It felt like it had been hours since Ethan and I had exchanged a word, and it was driving me crazy.

"We have about fifteen minutes to wait for the train. It'll be on platform A." Ethan pointed to the farthest platform as he came back over to me with the tickets in hand.

"Okay." I hopped out of my seat.

We made our way in silence over to where our train would arrive. I sank down on one of the long metal benches.

"I think I'll get a drink from that vendor over there, can I get you anything?" Ethan set the bags down beside me, obviously expecting me to stay put.

"Oh, um sure, I'll take a bottle of water." *I guess he doesn't want to talk.* Did he expect me to keep my mouth shut the entire trip home?

There were four people in line in front of Ethan, and it took him a while to order. By the time he got back, there was only five minutes or so before our train was supposed to arrive.

"Here you go." He handed me the bottle of water and plunked down beside me.

"Thank you." I grabbed it and took a sip. *Where do I start?* The silence stretched between us as I focused on a flickering fluorescent light just down the platform from where we were sitting.

I twisted to face Ethan and opened my mouth but he spoke up. "So that was Veridan." He drummed his hands on his knees. He met my eye for a moment before fixing his gaze straight ahead towards the tracks.

"It really is extraordinary. I can't believe that's where you've spent so much of your time over the years." *I can keep things light too, if that's what you want Ethan.* Maybe I could steer the conversation the right way.

"I'm glad you got to see it. I know it didn't turn out as you hoped it would, but I was still happy to share it with you." Ethan's expression was unreadable. Was he disappointed in me, or concerned?

His statement was as good a jumping-off point as any. "Ethan—" The rumble of the train stopped me. I exhaled sharply, but it was probably for the best. Once we were on the train we would have ten hours to clear the air.

"This is us." Ethan stood.

The train stopped and a few passengers exited. We waited until the doorway was clear, then we handed the attendant our tickets and boarded. There were already six passengers in the car we entered, so Ethan led the way to the next car towards the back of the train. A group of nine guys sat in that one, laughing and joking around. We crossed through it and a dining car. Three people occupied the next car back, a couple cozied up together, sitting just to the left as we walked in, and a middle-aged businessman reading a newspaper at the other end. There was one more car after the one we were in, but I could see through the windows in the doors that even more people were in it. Ethan paused and chose a seat halfway between the couple and the man. He threw our bags down and held out a hand in an 'after you' motion. I settled into the window seat and draped my coat over our belongings. Ethan discarded his jacket and dropped down beside me. Moments later there was a jerking motion as the train rolled out of the station.

"I'm just going to message Simon, check in with him." Ethan started punching numbers into his phone before I could say anything.

"All right." I blew out a slow breath and turned to stare out the glass. I could text Katie, but I had told her I was spending the weekend taking a specialized fine arts course, and I didn't feel like coming up with more lies to feed her. I watched the scenery go by, every once in a while stealing a glance at Ethan. Apparently his conversation with Simon was completely engrossing because he never once met my eyes.

He was mad, and clearly freezing me out, but what could I do? It made sense that he would want to make sure that nothing had happened to Simon or my dad in the short time we had been away. I was still sorting out how I felt about The Three's suggestion, and Ethan keeping it from me, and now I had to process what I had overheard Bridget discussing with him. Would he admit to me that she was trying to use him to persuade me to come stay at Veridan? Or would he make it seem like it was his idea? I needed to know.

My eyes grew heavy as the sway of the train lulled me, pulling me towards sleep. I fought the urge. I wanted to talk to Ethan; I didn't want to drift off with unresolved issues between us. Still, before I knew it, my eyes slid closed. The stress of coming to Veridan mixed with the lack of sleep had left me more tired than I realized, and I gave up struggling to stay awake.

I only hoped there would be resolution when I woke up.

Thirty-Five

It was dark outside when I opened my eyes. The interior of the train was dim, but overhead pot lights illuminated the space above every seat. I was stiff from sleeping in an upright position, and rotated my head back and forth, trying to loosen my neck and shoulder muscles. Ethan was now sitting in the seat across from me, and gave me a reserved smile.

"What time is it?" I rubbed my eyes with my palms, trying to shake the groggy feeling that was holding me captive.

Ethan checked his watch. "Just after midnight."

Midnight. I straightened up in my seat quickly. "How are Simon and Dad?"

"They're fine. Your dad's wrist isn't giving him too much trouble. Apparently they've been bonding while we were gone. I think Simon likes having someone who isn't a Hleo that he can still talk to openly. It allows him to share war stories of his triumphs with a person who hasn't heard them a thousand times.

"He also mentioned he hasn't seen any sign of Uri or Paige. I don't know if that means they are still trying to strategize and regroup, or if they've been removed from this mission, or if they somehow found out we left town and are trying to track us down." Ethan's voice held a faint bit of worry.

"I'm sure they don't know where we are, we were so careful when we left." I reached over to give Ethan's hand a reassuring squeeze, but he shifted in his seat at the same time, pulling his hands out of range. I jerked back, as though I'd been slapped. "Ethan I don't know what to say…"

He studied me for a moment. "You don't get sick?"

I bit the inside of my cheek. "I don't." His eyes were swimming with a mixture of confusion and hurt, and I hated that I was the cause.

"That was never indicated in any of the information the Hleo have on you." His forehead creased.

"No one knew, except for Dad. He only told me when we had that talk the night he came home from the hospital. I'd never noticed anything extraordinary about my health, but when he pointed it out to me I could see that he was right." Was this really the issue he was more concerned about? I was sure he was going to be furious with me for asking to go into the circular room. "I didn't know how to tell you, I'm sorry. I was still trying to figure out what being abnormally healthy says about me. I needed some time to process." I tucked my hair behind my ears.

"I didn't realize there would be physical repercussions of you being the child of a Hleo and a Bana. I thought the serum only affected the person being branded and that it wasn't genetically transferable. Although, I've never heard of a Hleo or Bana having a child before, besides Alexander's family that is, so no one really knows what to expect."

I leaned forward. "I'm still me. The same as you are still you even though you don't age. Please don't change how you feel about me just because you found out I'm not exactly what you thought."

"I could never change how I feel about you, it's just surprising." Ethan frowned. "Why didn't you tell me you were going to ask to go inside the room? You blindsided me."

"I don't know." I swallowed hard. Except I did know. *Because you would have tried to talk me out of it.*

Ethan ran a hand along his forehead. "It was hard enough to convince them to let you come since that goes against everything they believe about how to handle a protected. They don't want to taint critical decisions; they've seen that happen too many times before. Going into that room is dangerous. People occasionally break in and think they can handle what's inside, but it ends badly every time. They don't even let Hleo go into the room under normal circumstances. I don't care if you do have some of Elizabeth and Noah's altered genes, I would never consider letting you go inside.

What if something happened to you?" Ethan voice had risen and his jaw was tight.

"It's not your choice whether I go in or not." I crossed my arms. *As if he has any authority over me.*

"Hannah, I am always going to try to protect you, even if that means protecting you from yourself," Ethan shot back, eyes blazing. "I wish you had told me what you were thinking."

"It's not like you tell me everything you're thinking." I gritted my teeth. I had planned to apologize for catching him off guard like that, but he was being difficult. "You didn't exactly warn me that The Three were busy getting a guest room ready for me at Veridan, did you?" It was on the tip of my tongue to mention Bridget, but I didn't want to admit I'd been eavesdropping. Ethan opened his mouth to reply, but I held up a hand. "I need to know, Ethan. I need to know how my ability to see protecteds works, and what I'm meant to do with it. I'm willing to do anything to figure this out because I need to know how much time we have left. I mean, when my big moment comes, that's it, your mission with me is over and you're going to be expected to leave.

"I know you don't want to talk about it, but there are a lot of pretty big issues for us to overcome. These past few months have been the absolute best of my life, but we've been dancing around all the important topics, ignoring them, and we can't keep doing that. You are assigned to be in my life until I make this big decision, so what happens after I do?

"You're forbidden to be in this relationship, there's something holding you back in the physical stuff between us, and, oh yeah, I'm aging and you're not, which ultimately is going to drive us apart somewhere down the road. You can see it too, right? At some point I'm going to have to go back to life the way I knew it before you came. I need to know when that time will be so I can try to prepare myself for how I am ever going to exist without you." I dropped my head into my hands.

"Hannah." Ethan's voice was soft and persuaded me to look at him. When I did, I saw that the anger was gone. I wanted him to say that I was worrying for nothing, that I would be the last person he ever protected and that, until the day I died, he would be by my side and in my life as a constant. He didn't say any of that.

Instead, his gaze lifted over my shoulder and his expression grew tense. "Hannah, they found us. Uri is in the lounge car headed in our direction. He must have gotten on at the last stop. We need to start moving towards the back of the train as quickly and discreetly as possible, and find somewhere to hide until we can get off." Ethan took my hand in his and pulled me up into the aisle.

I glanced over my shoulder, trying to catch a glimpse of Uri, but there were too many people standing in line waiting for drinks.

We headed down the aisle in the opposite direction, leaving our coats and bags behind. We moved as fast as we could while not attracting attention. Ethan walked behind me, blocking me from Uri.

Of all the times for there to be a threat on my life. I clenched the fist of my free hand. All of those admissions for Ethan to deal with, and now they were just floating there until we dealt with the Bana.

We passed through the doors and into the next car. How could that guy possibly have lived? Ethan had pounded him to within an inch of his life, and it had been nearly impossible to breathe or see with all the smoke that had been in that living room.

"It's going to be okay, Hannah." Ethan squeezed my hand. I had been so lost in thought I didn't even realize we had reached the end of the passenger cars and were now standing at the entrance to the baggage car.

"What now?" I grabbed the closest seat as the train lurched around a bend.

"Sit here. Keep your head down. I'm going to see if I can get into the baggage car." Ethan was gone before I could respond. I sank down in a seat, trying to make myself as small as possible. After about ten seconds, Ethan yanked the door open and pulled me through the connecting platform into the baggage car. He shoved the door closed behind us and locked it.

The baggage car had nets running along either side, stacked with all shapes and sizes of luggage and other oversized parcels and boxes that people didn't want to carry with them. The train rocked hard again and this time I lost my balance. I fell forward into a wall of luggage and hit my head on the corner of a large metal case that was sticking out from one of the nets.

I cried out in pain and put my hand to my hairline where I had been struck. I drew my fingers back to see they were stained crimson.

"Are you hurt?" Ethan took my face in his hands to investigate the damage.

"I don't think so, not seriously. Just clumsy as always."

Ethan scanned the racks of luggage, and grabbed a beach towel that was sticking out of an overstuffed bag that had come unzipped. He joined me in the center of the car again and gently applied pressure to my forehead. His eyes kept darting from me to the door.

"I can't believe I hurt myself while you're busy trying to keep us from getting killed."

"Accidents happen, and I don't think it's too bad." Ethan pulled the cloth away and examined the cut. He seemed content and threw the towel to the ground.

"I really do hold you back, don't I?" It wasn't the time for a self-deprecating comment, but the words were out before I could stop them.

Ethan cupped my face in his hands. "Never."

A clanging sound at the door caused both of our heads to snap in that direction. Uri's face filled the small window in the door. A wicked grin spread across his lips, and he winked at me.

"Ethan." I grasped for him as we scrambled to the other side of the luggage car.

"Come on." Ethan ripped the door open, and pulled me through to a small balcony at the back of the train. The wind whipped past me, flinging my hair across my face, and I brushed it back impatiently.

I twisted around to check Uri's location. He was reefing on the door, presumably trying to break the lock. Ethan slammed the door we had just come through, blocking my view of the big Russian.

"We have to get off this train." Ethan was scanning the passing forest, a mix of evergreens and bare spindly trees still waiting for warmer weather to convince them to blossom. A full moon in the clear starry sky made it possible to see quite a distance but there didn't appear to be anything but wilderness stretching around us.

"You mean jump?" I surveyed the deep, snow-laden ditches on either side of the tracks as they whirred by in a blur. *I can't do that.*

"There's no other way." Ethan gripped my upper arms, forcing me to face him. "As you jump, let your body roll against the ground. I know it's tough, but try to stay as loose as possible."

I was breathing fast but nodded.

"Okay. On the count of three, you jump. I'm right behind you," Ethan shouted over the roar of the train before letting me go. I grasped the railing, trying to psych myself up to fling my body off the moving vehicle.

"One, two—"

A crashing sound in the luggage car let me know that Uri had made his way inside. Without thinking, before Ethan could get to three, I leapt from the train.

Even with the snow to soften the blow it felt as though every bone in my body was jarred out of place as I landed. The air bolted from my lungs as I tumbled and rolled against the hard, unforgiving ground.

As soon as I had regained my breath, I struggled to my feet. Ethan was about twenty feet away from me in the ditch, but running towards me to close the gap.

When he reached me, his hands grasped the sides of my neck. "You're okay?"

"I'm okay." *My body will definitely be feeling it later though.*

"Come on. We need to get into the shelter of the trees." Ethan grabbed my hand and guided me into the forest. We wove our way through the overgrown brush, pushing farther and farther away from the train tracks. Even though it was night and there was a tangle of shrubbery at ground level, the forest wasn't overly dense with trees and moonlight filtered through the branches. Our movements would be fairly easy to spot. Putting distance between us and the Russian was our best hope and I tried to force my legs to keep up to the pace Ethan was moving at.

Ethan released my hand and pushed through a particularly gnarled bit of brush, holding it back for me. "We need to find a different mode of transportation. I didn't see Paige on the train so I don't know if she's around too, but we should assume that she is. If we can shake this guy until we get back to East Halton, then Simon and I can come up with a strategy to deal with both of them."

The hem of my pants caught on a thorny vine and I angrily ripped it free. "Sounds good to me." *I'm so sick of this. Is it too much to ask for a normal relationship where we can have important discussions without having to dodge assassination attempts at the same time?*

We had been scrambling through the woods for almost ten minutes. I didn't hear anyone behind us, but I was sure jumping off a train wouldn't be a big deal to someone like Uri. Lights glowed in front of us, off in the distance. Was that some sort of building?

"Do you think we got away from him?" My foot slipped on a rock, but I managed to right myself before falling. *Come on, Hannah.*

Ethan tossed another look back over his shoulder and stopped so abruptly I almost banged into the back of him.

I followed his gaze. "What's wr—?" A movement in the shadows a hundred feet away stopped me. A figure stepped into a clear patch in the woods and the moonlight hit his face. Fear pulsed through my veins.

Uri had found us.

Thirty-Six

"Come on." Ethan broke into a full-on run in the direction of the lights. I pushed against the burning in my lungs. *Really wish I'd agreed to jog with Katie when she was in her fitness-crazy phase.* We finally made it out of the forest and came to a highway. The glow belonged to a three-story brick building that had an industrial look to it. A small town lay half-hidden in the darkness down the road to our left, but Ethan jogged across the highway, heading for the building with me in tow.

"We need to get inside. We'll find you somewhere secure to hide and I'll deal with Uri."

We raced along the side of the structure where a ramp led to a concrete platform and a heavy metal entrance door. When we got to the top of the ramp, Ethan smashed a large window beside the door with his elbow. The sound seemed to reverberate with extra force, shattering the peace and quiet of our surroundings. He reached through the broken glass to turn the lock, then flung open the door.

The inside of the building was dimly lit. Fear mingling with adrenaline pushed me forward as I squinted to scan the large space for a good place to hide. The open factory floor was filled with intimidating-looking machinery. Chains hung down from a wood and metal catwalk that ran around three walls of the massive room. Stacks of wood in various stages of processing were piled everywhere, but I gasped at the most prominent object in the room, a giant wheel, similar to the kind found on the outside of old-fashioned lumber mills.

I pointed to the wheel, which sat in a deep channel of water. "What the—?"

"Come on." Ethan didn't take time to look. Skid pallets were leaning against the wall beside several large metal cupboards. He crossed over to them and I followed close at his heels. There was a gap between the pallets and the cupboards. Ethan motioned to the space and I ducked into it and crouched down.

"Do not come out until I tell you to, no matter what happens." Ethan dragged a skid over to close the opening. "I mean it Hannah, no matter what. Do you understand me?" He searched my eyes intently. My mouth had gone dry so I nodded my assent.

Ethan placed the skid in front of me and strode to the opposite side of the room. I watched through a crack between the skid slats as he took up a position behind one of the big machines. *Please be careful Ethan.*

I tried to make my breathing as shallow as possible so that nothing would give away my location, and listened for signs that Uri had reached the building. My heart pounded in my chest. I was about to peek my head out to see if anything was going on, when I heard the sound of boots crunching over broken glass by the entrance.

"Hello you two; I'll bet you are surprised to see me again." Uri's tone was smug.

Neither Ethan nor I made a noise as Uri came into my view.

"Ethan, I am not sure why you would come and hide in such a place. It seems you have made another mistake. Although I think your most important mistake was not making sure I died in that fire." Uri was slowly making his way across the floor towards the machine Ethan hid behind. I held my breath.

"Are you going to hide like a rat cowering in the corner or are we going to fight?" Uri shouted, his voice echoing in the rafters. He walked in a slow circle, searching the room.

When his back was turned, Ethan pounced, brandishing the biggest wrench I'd ever seen. It looked as though Ethan was aiming for Uri's head, but at the last second Uri moved and it slammed into the back of his shoulders instead. I winced at the cracking sound and the wail from Uri that followed. The blow didn't take him down though. He whirled around and caught the wrench as Ethan swung it again. Ethan used his momentum to pull himself into a kick, connecting with Uri's side. Uri stumbled but recovered quickly and threw the wrench aside, obviously interested in fighting with his bare hands.

I bit my lip to keep from crying out as Uri picked Ethan up and slammed him against a heavy-looking piece of machinery. Uri was almost twice the size of Ethan, and stronger, but Ethan was faster, and he managed to swing his legs around Uri's arm and free himself, flipping Uri down to the ground at the same time. He sprang back up and they kept fighting, going back and forth across the open factory floor space like partners in some violent, destructive dance. They were getting closer to the reservoir's edge, where the wheel sat ready to accept them if one was strong enough to push the other into its massive spokes.

Ethan appeared to be gaining the advantage, finally starting to break through Uri's seeming invincibility. The Russian charged at Ethan one more time and Ethan flipped him over his shoulder and pinned him, this time yanking a knife from the sheath at his ankle and holding it to Uri's neck.

"You must know that even if I am unsuccessful in retrieving dear sweet Hannah, someone else will only come to do the job," Uri sputtered while trying to get free from Ethan's hold. "Alexander will not rest until the Bana have her. It is only a matter of time now before she is his."

Ethan flinched. It was only the slightest of movements, but it was all Uri needed to break free of Ethan's hold. He took a huge gash from the knife as it grazed across his neck, but it didn't slow him down. He clamored to his feet and managed to reverse the hold and lock Ethan's head in the crook of his arm. With his free hand he snagged a thick metal chain that was dangling down from the ceiling in front of him.

Horror washed over me as Uri yanked and the chain dropped lower. He hoisted Ethan up and started to wrap the chain around his neck.

He's going to choke him to death. I shoved the skid out of my way and jumped out from my hiding place. "Stop! Please, stop. Don't do that, don't kill him. I'll go with you, wherever you want, just don't kill him." I sprinted over to them.

"Hannah, no." Ethan gasped, struggling to free himself.

"So the girl cares for you too, does she?" Uri rumbled in Ethan's ear.

Just as I got near them, something struck the back of my head. Everything went dark for a second, followed by excruciating pain as I fell to my knees. Someone grabbed my hair and yanked me back up to a standing position. I cried out in pain as I thrashed around, trying to free myself from my assailant's grip. The blade of a knife sliced my flailing arm, and I froze.

"Hello, Hannah." A woman's voice murmured in my ear, smooth as silk. The cold steel of the blade pressed against my throat. *Paige.*

"Let her go, Paige. I'm the one you want revenge on." Ethan managed to choke out as he fought to get a grip on Uri's arm, still wrapped around his neck.

"Here's the thing Ethan, I think messing your pretty little protected's face up a little would be the perfect revenge," Paige spat out. With a flick of her wrist, she slashed the knife across my cheek. Not too deep, but enough that I cried out and reached for my face.

"Or perhaps if I broke a rib or two." Paige flipped the knife in her hand and rammed the butt end of it into my torso like a hammer. The wind rushed out of my lungs, and I crumpled back down to my knees.

"Please," I whimpered as I tried to regain my breath. She still had one hand tangled in my hair and she gave it a hard yank, snapping my neck back and forcing me to look up at her. Uri's cold laugh rang in my ears. He obviously enjoyed the brutal display.

"You are nothing more than a pawn in this game, and the sooner you shut up and realize that the better," Paige sneered. The hatred in her mysterious silver eyes was terrifying. She clearly wanted me dead as retribution for her lost love. For the first time I was actually thankful there was a strict order to bring me in to the Bana's leader, Alexander. I was sure that was the only reason she hadn't already killed me.

Ethan yelled. I fought against Paige's grip on my hair until I could look at him. He finally managed to swing his leg around Uri's arm. Uri stumbled, enough for Ethan to wrench himself free from the iron grasp he had been caught in. He fell to the floor, but quickly spun around and kicked the big Russian's legs out from under him. Uri recovered, and they began to attack each other again.

Paige crouched down in front of me and held up a zip-tie. She had sheathed her knife, and for a second I debated trying to make a run for it. My eyes darted towards the exit but she followed my gaze. "Please make a move. I would love nothing more than to 'accidentally' kill you while trying to bring you in."

My shoulders slumped and I held my wrists up together, staying silent as she pulled the plastic cord tight enough to dig into my skin. She yanked me back to my feet, likely hoping for a reaction, but I kept my eyes on Ethan and didn't fight her.

Both guys looked battered and exhausted. How did they have the energy to keep this up? Ethan jumped up onto a machine, grabbed the chain dangling in front of him, and kicked off, straight into Uri. In one quick movement Ethan wrapped the chain around Uri's neck and shoved him closer to the edge of the platform. Tangled in the links, Uri toppled over the flimsy railing lining the reservoir. A sickening crack rang out, followed by complete silence. The chain, still attached to the catwalk, went taut.

For several seconds, Ethan just stood there, covered in sweat, dirt, and blood, breathing heavily. Then he locked eyes with my captor. "Let her go, Paige." His voice was hoarse and gravelly. He spit blood onto the ground before taking a step in our direction. Uri had done a number on him. His left eye was swollen, the cheek underneath beginning to go black, and a cut above his right eye trickled blood. A wave of sickness washed over me to see him so messed up.

"Cut the bravado, Ethan." Paige pulled the knife away from me to wave it at him before resting it back against my throat. "You're lucky she isn't already filleted."

"We both know you can't kill her. They want her too badly for you to do that." Ethan took another slow step closer to us.

"That's true. They do want her badly. And I hope the plans they have for her destroy her. Then you can stand by and watch helplessly as the person you care about it reduced to nothing." The knife's blade dug a fraction deeper into my neck.

"Where's Adam?" Ethan crossed his arms. *Why is he changing the subject?* I swallowed hard. *He has no idea how to get me away from Paige.*

"Adam? What has Adam got to do with this?" Paige's weight shifted from one foot to the other.

“Aren’t you working together? I heard the two of you do everything together now.” Ethan cocked his head to the side, studying her.

“You heard wrong then. What, you didn’t think I could handle an operation like this on my own? Because I think I’m handling it very well.” Paige scraped the knife along my collarbone to prove her point. I pressed my lips together tightly, determined not to give her the satisfaction of hearing me scream at the sting of the abrasion. Ethan took another step towards us. He kept his eyes on Paige. The controlled fury in them would have been frightening, if it had been directed at me instead of her.

Then his expression changed. A sneer crossed his lips and he appeared almost arrogant, a look I didn’t recognize on Ethan’s face. “Sort of like how I handled your boyfriend? What was his name again, Joseph, Johnny? He was so forgettable, it’s not coming to me.”

“Don’t you dare mention him.” Paige jabbed the knife in the air at him, but her other hand clenched my hair tighter.

“What, you mean how his eyes rolled into the back of his head before his face smashed onto the nice steak dinner the two of you were about to share?” Ethan scoffed.

“You didn’t even give him a chance to fight, just snuffed him out like a candle, you coward.” Paige’s voice had become shrill, betraying her rage. Ethan was clearly trying to push her buttons, but why? There was a good chance if he made her mad enough, she would snap, stab me to death and be done with me.

“It was all he deserved, just another piece of scum cut down.” Ethan repeated Michael’s assessment of the Bana when he’d first picked us up. That was all Paige could take. She screamed at Ethan, but rather than ramming the knife into me, she yanked me by my hair and shoved me as hard as she could at the metal railing. It happened so fast I couldn’t even get a sound out as I toppled over the barrier and plunged into the freezing water below, narrowly missing the wheel.

It was so cold it felt like a million needles stabbing me all at once. Lightning pain shot across the different wounds Paige had inflicted. I fought against the shock that coursed through my body as I kicked my way through the dark, desperate to get some air in my lungs. I managed to reach the surface, but my hands were tied tightly and I struggled to keep my head above water as I fought with the plastic tie. Uri's lifeless body, hanging just below the edge of the platform, the chain securely wrapped around his neck, came into view. Before I could absorb the horror of that, my head submerged again. I kicked hard, resurfacing just as Ethan scrambled over the railing and leapt into the water. He landed beside me, while Paige leaned over the metal barrier, watching us from above.

Ethan held a knife in his hand. We bobbed along as he worked at cutting my hands free. I kept my eyes riveted on Paige. What would she do now? She still gripped her knife. Would she throw it at me? I had no way of getting out of the path of the weapon if she did. Instead, she flung it down. The blade dug into the ground. Hope flickered. Was she giving up? Paige stopped in front of an electric panel on the wall. My forehead wrinkled as she slammed her palm against a big red button. *What does that*— The wailing of sirens yanked me from my thoughts.

The sound of gears and machinery filled the cavernous room. *No. She wouldn't.* The two large metal doors that closed off the reservoir Ethan and I were in rose slowly. *We'll be sucked in.* As the door on the other side of the massive wheel rose, water from the river rushed in, and the wheel began to turn.

"Ethan." The word came out in a croak and I cleared my throat, trying to push back the rising panic.

"I know." Ethan finally cut through the plastic tie, and I spread my arms apart and began treading water. "Come on." He jerked his head towards a ladder fastened to the wall about halfway between us and the wheel.

We began swimming that way but we didn't seem to be getting any closer; if anything, it looked as though it was slowly moving away from us. It took me a second to realize the ladder wasn't moving, we were. The force of the wheel was propelling us closer to the second metal door, and the unknown darkness that lay behind it. *I do not want to find out what is behind that door*. I drove my arms through the water and kicked frantically with my feet. No matter how hard Ethan and I swam, though, we weren't getting anywhere.

"We have to go under the door," Ethan called over to me.

My stomach clenched. "But what's on the other side?"

"I don't know, but we can't get to the ladder and we're only going to exhaust ourselves trying. I'll get you out of this Hannah. You have to trust me." Ethan took my hand firmly in his.

"I do." I looked at him and we both stopped fighting the current, allowing it to carry us towards the opening. I inhaled one last time, and glanced up to see Paige still watching from the platform, her arms folded across her chest and an evil grin on her lips. The water dragged me down under the door and through to the other side. It was pitch black and I tried to hold on to Ethan but the current ripped us apart. I fought my way to what I hoped was the surface, desperate to take a breath. I could feel myself being pulled downwards as I thrashed around. I managed to gulp a mouthful of air just as I made a sharp descent and landed in a square metal chamber. The water was about waist high but rising fast as I searched for Ethan. He was a few feet away, and waded over to me.

"I'm here," he struggled to say over the roar of water pouring down on us. When he reached me, he looked around. "I think this is some kind of holding tank before the water is deposited back outside into the river," he shouted. "It's filling up fast, so we need to get out of here quickly."

He was right. I could no longer touch bottom. Ethan kept diving below the surface. *What is he looking for?* The only slivers of light came from small cracks in the ductwork at the top of the tunnel, where it had been welded together. I didn't know how he would be able to see anything. When he resurfaced, I grabbed his arm. "If we don't get out of this, I want you to know that I love you." He must have seen the hopelessness in my eyes, because he gave me a reassuring kiss.

"I'm getting us out of here. The floor to this compartment works like a trap door. I just have to figure out how to open it from inside. Just hold on for a little while longer." Ethan dove down again. This time he was under for longer.

As I treaded water and waited for him to return, fatigue crept over me. I was freezing, my arms and legs felt like lead, the cuts I had suffered were burning against the cold water, and my ribs ached. It would have been so easy to just give in and let myself sink, but I resisted the urge. If Ethan was going to keep fighting, then I would too.

"I've almost got it." Ethan's head popped up again. We were only an inch or so from the top of the chute, and I had to tilt my head back to keep it from going under. Before I could respond, the water closed over my head, submerging me completely. I couldn't see anything. My lungs burned and my head started to spin. *We're not going to make it.* A fog drifted through my brain. Suddenly I was being sucked downward again. Within seconds, the chamber drained and Ethan and I were spat out into the icy cold river below.

I was exhausted; I could see the shore and I willed my arms and legs to move to get me over to it, but the water was so cold. My body felt as though it weighed a thousand pounds. I couldn't even call out to Ethan for help, I was so tired. The edges of my vision started to go dark as I fought to stay conscious. My eyes fluttered closed and I stopped resisting the urge to sink. Then a strong pair of arms wrapped around me and suddenly I was lying on the brown, winter-killed grass of the riverbank.

"Hannah, can you hear me?" Ethan was on his knees leaning over me, a desperate look in his eyes. Even though I was out of the water, unconsciousness was fighting hard to take over. The cold felt as though it had seeped right into my bones, and I struggled to stay awake. I managed a slight nod so he would at least know I had heard him.

"Hold on Hannah, just hold on." Ethan scooped me up in his arms and ran up the embankment, holding me tightly to him. We had floated quite a ways down from the mill, but at the top of the slope was a parking lot for another factory situated along the same highway. There were only a handful of cars in it, but Ethan made his way straight to an older model pickup truck. He repositioned me in his arms so he could try the door. It was locked and he looked around, presumably for something he could jimmy it open with.

"I have to set you down for a second while I get into this truck." Ethan gently lowered me onto the back tailgate of the truck and climbed up into the bed to look at the rear window. In one swift action he snapped the lock and forced the window open. He knelt down so his face was close to mine. "I know you're tired, but can you try and get through this window and unlock the door? I won't fit and we don't have time for me to try and break in. You're half frozen. If you can unlock the door, I will take you somewhere you can warm up."

I blinked, trying to bring his face into focus. Everything around me had the hazy feeling of a dream. It took me a second to process what he was asking of me. “I think I can.” My teeth were chattering; I hadn’t noticed that before.

Ethan put an arm around my waist and helped me up and over to the window. I managed to squeeze through the tight little space, bumping the spot on my side where Paige had hit me with the handle of her knife as I wriggled over the windowsill. Pain shot across my ribs and I cried out, but kept going. I fell onto the front bench seat of the truck and lay there for a minute, fighting with my muscles to do what my brain was asking of them.

Finally I summoned the strength to stretch out my arm and unlock the door. Ethan yanked it open and shifted me into a sitting position before climbing behind the wheel. He reached in front of me and dug around in the glove box until he produced a small screwdriver. He jammed the tool into the ignition switch and fiddled with it until the engine fired up and we were off. Ethan flipped the heat on full blast before pulling me close against him. “Stay with me, Hannah.”

I wanted to, more than anything. But the darkness hovering around the periphery of my vision threatened to tug me down into oblivion and I wasn’t sure I could fight it anymore.

Thirty-Seven

I faded in and out of consciousness as we drove. A sign for the highway that would take us back to East Halton caught my eye but Ethan breezed right by it. *Where are we going?* Fifteen minutes later, we pulled into Barnesville, a small town along the New York-Connecticut border.

Why would Ethan bring me here? Why wouldn't he just get on the highway? All I wanted was to go home and crawl into my own bed. We turned down a residential street and started slowing down. He pulled into the driveway of a small bungalow with blue siding that looked very similar to his house in East Halton, and got out of the truck.

He came around to my side, opened the door, and picked me up. I was thankful he was carrying me; I didn't think I could walk on my own. Ethan walked to the side entrance of the house. He shifted me in his arms so he could pound on the door. After thirty seconds, a light came on above us, and a guy a little shorter than Ethan, with the same athletic build, came to the door in boxers and a T-shirt. His ruffled light brown hair was disheveled in a way that suggested that we had interrupted his sleep.

"Ethan?" The guy sounded confused as he rubbed his eyes.

"Hey, Travis. I need your help. She's suffering from hypothermia and needs to be warmed up right away."

Travis immediately moved aside so Ethan and I could come in. As if he was familiar with the place, Ethan carried me into the sparsely-furnished living room of the house.

"The bathroom's over there through the bedroom. There's a tub you can use to get her temperature up." Travis pointed to a door to our left.

Ethan carried me through the bedroom—the rumpled sheets confirming that we had dragged Travis out of bed—and through to the bathroom. Travis followed closely behind us, but stopped in the doorway.

Ethan lowered me down to sit on the edge of the bathtub while he turned the water on and waited for it to warm up. "We've got to get your wet clothes off." Ethan rested his hands gently on my shoulders.

"Okay." I was surprised at how weak my voice sounded.

"I'll be out here if you need me," Travis said, and disappeared back into the bedroom.

"I'll help you get the heavy layers off." Ethan hesitated as though to make sure I was all right with that.

I nodded and managed to stand up so Ethan could tug my dripping sweater up over my head. He left my tank top on, and moved to my pants, quickly undoing them and sliding them off. Only a day ago Ethan undressing me would have been exactly what I wanted, but now the action wasn't anything close to romantic.

He checked the water temperature and then held my arm as I lowered myself into the tub. It was likely only lukewarm, but felt scalding against my frozen skin. Pins and needles tingled through my fingers and toes.

"I'll slowly make the water hotter so your body can handle the change." Ethan sat on the edge of the tub to operate the tap. I lay back and closed my eyes, submerging as much of my body as I could. Within minutes I started to drift off. I didn't fight the urge. Ethan might be a little worried that I wouldn't wake up, but at least he wouldn't let me drown.

I wasn't sure how long I was out, but a gentle hand brushed across my cheek to wake me up.

I forced my eyes open.

Ethan stood beside the tub, holding a fluffy white towel. "We've used up all the hot water. I think it's best you get out of the tub before you cool off too much. Travis has some clothes you can wear and we'll cover you with blankets in his bed to keep your body temperature up."

I still felt exhausted, but at least my arms and legs didn't feel like they were going to fall off anymore. The warm water had done its work and the chill was almost out of my bones.

"How do you know Travis? Where are we?" I sat up in the tub.

"He's a friend of mine, a fellow Hleo. We're at his house." Ethan held out the towel. I grabbed hold of a bar screwed into the wall and hauled myself to my feet. Ethan wrapped the towel around me and grasped my elbow to help me step out onto the bath mat. I rubbed myself down quickly, then followed him into the bedroom where a sweatshirt and pair of jogging pants had been laid out on the newly-made bed.

Ethan straightened a pile of books on Travis's bedside table. "I'll wait in the living room while you get changed, then I'll come and take a look at those injuries Paige gave you, and tuck you into bed."

"Okay." I sat down on the bed, still wrapped in the towel. Ethan left and I slipped out of my underthings, and pulled the sweater and pants on. The clothes were big, probably our host's, but they were good enough for the time being. I wrapped my wet clothes in the towel and carried the pile back to the bathroom. After leaving everything on the counter, I returned to the bedroom, slid back the covers, and sat on the edge of the bed to wait for Ethan.

After a minute or so there was a light knock, and he walked in holding gauze, surgical tape, disinfectant, and scissors. "I'm going to check your ribs, then I'll take care of those cuts." Ethan knelt down in front of me and set the first aid supplies on the bed. He placed his hand against my rib cage and carefully but firmly began pressing. It hurt, but I tried not to flinch or make a sound.

"I think they're just bruised. I can't feel anything specifically out of place, does it hurt to breathe?" Ethan removed his hand, and I felt myself relax, realizing that I had been tensed up during his exam.

"Not really. It only hurts if I bump it on something."

"Let me see your arm." Ethan held out his hand, and I did as he commanded, pushing the sleeve of the sweatshirt up to my elbow so he could look at the three-inch gash on my forearm. As Ethan gently rubbed disinfectant over the cut, I gave him a small smile. "This reminds me of the night with Adam."

"Because you almost lost your life then, too?" Ethan frowned as he took a piece of gauze and covered the wound, taping it in place.

"I was thinking more of afterwards, when you bandaged me up and told me how you felt about me."

He cupped my chin in his hand to check out the cut on my cheek. "I'm just glad you're okay and that all you need is a little bandaging up." He dabbed an alcohol wipe across the cut, but didn't bandage it. He did the same thing for the knife abrasions on my neck.

"Me too." I nodded as he helped me lie back against the pillows. As I drifted once again towards unconsciousness, I could feel him wrapping the sheet around me tightly. His breath was warm on my cheek as he pulled the covers up around my neck.

"Thank you for saving my life," I whispered, my eyes closed.

"My pleasure." For a moment he didn't move, just stood there, beside the bed. His slow, even breathing lulled me closer to sleep. Then his footsteps echoed across the floor and the door clicked shut behind him.

Thirty-Eight

I awoke some time later to the sound of male voices talking quietly in the other room. Sunlight filtered in through the cracks in the blinds, and I looked at the clock on the bedside table. Three in the afternoon. I had slept for over twelve hours. I stretched in the bed, taking stock of how my body felt. Every part of me was stiff, as though I had run a marathon with no training, but thankfully I didn't feel cold anymore.

I rolled onto my side, debating between getting out of bed and joining the guys, or staying put a little longer to relish the warmth of the covers.

"So how did you luck out and get her?"

My eyebrows rose. *Is Travis talking about me?* I strained to hear Ethan's reply.

"I was assigned her the same as any other protected." Ethan's tone was casual.

"You always get the hot ones. If I get stuck with one more balding, middle-aged inventor trying to come up with the next world-changing technology, I'm going to switch sides." Travis laughed.

Ethan didn't respond. I bit my lip. What did he think of Travis? He sounded like a nice enough guy, maybe a little cocky, but he had welcomed us into his home no questions asked.

"So what's your cover?" Travis asked.

"I'm enrolled as a high school student at her school."

I could tell from the reluctance in his voice that he didn't like divulging information to Travis.

"High school. How thrilling. And she obviously knows who you really are," Travis prodded.

"She found out when an attempt was made on her life a while back," Ethan replied.

Neither of them spoke for a moment. *I really should get up.* I started to throw back the covers, but froze when Travis spoke again.

"So have there been any… benefits to this situation?"

Heat crept up my neck. Was he asking what I thought he was?

All that followed was dead silence, and I could only imagine what sort of look Ethan must be giving him.

"Sorry man, always the professional, how could I forget?" Travis sounded sheepish.

"It's fine," Ethan replied.

I shoved back the covers and stood up. Maybe my presence out there would keep Travis from asking any more intrusive questions.

"I think I'll check on Hannah."

Ethan's footsteps approached the bedroom door. I quickly smoothed down the front of my hoodie and ran my fingers through my hair. I dropped my hands when he entered the room, leaving the door open a few inches behind him so I could see into the living room.

"You're awake." Ethan crossed over to me and grasped hold of my arms lightly. I felt a little weak, but much better than I had. Not that I minded the contact.

"The bath and sleep did wonders. I feel better, how are you doing?" I reached a hand towards a faded gash across Ethan's eyebrow, shock rippling through me. *He went through a lot more than I did yesterday.* He must have suffered from hypothermia as well, but he had concentrated on taking care of me. My chest tightened.

"I'm fine. Uri didn't do nearly as much damage as it must have looked like he did at the mill. I had a long hot shower while you were resting, and I'm good to go. Super healing genes, remember?" His grip on my arms tightened slightly as he searched my face. "Are you really okay?"

"I'm good, really, I promise." I gave him what I hoped was a convincing smile.

The tightness in his muscles eased. Ethan let go of me and wrapped his arms around my waist. He pulled me close and kissed me lightly on the forehead. When a shadow moved across the bedroom floor, he stepped back quickly. I frowned. Travis must have walked by the door. Would Ethan and I never have an uninterrupted moment together?

"Your clothes are on the chair." Ethan pointed to the corner of the room. "I threw them in Travis's dryer so they should be dry."

"Thanks. I'll get changed and meet you out in the living room." I walked over to the chair and picked up my sweater.

"We should go as soon as you're ready. Your dad was expecting us back yesterday. I contacted Simon and told him about our delay, but I know your dad will be anxious to see you."

I nodded and Ethan left me to get dressed.

I quickly changed and straightened the blankets on Travis's bed. I folded up the clothes he'd loaned me and left them on top of the covers before I exited the room.

"Well, you're looking livelier today." Travis pushed himself away from the doorway between the living room and kitchen and strode over to me with his hand out. "I'm Travis. It's nice to meet you." He had a friendly, confident manner, as though he was used to every girl he met being instantly attracted to him.

"Hannah. It's nice to meet you too. And thank you so much for letting us stay at your house." I let go of his hand.

"No problem. We've got to have each other's backs, right?" He tilted his chin at Ethan.

"Thanks Travis, I owe you." Ethan's smile was a little tight.

"No worries."

"We should get going." Ethan held his hand out toward the door.

"Sure." I went out the door ahead of him and climbed back into the passenger side of the truck.

I studied Travis through the truck window as he and Ethan shook hands. How well did the two of them know each other? Travis was obviously another Hleo, so of course they had met, but were they close? How long had they known each other? What was their history?

I rested my head against the back of the seat with a sigh. Just another reminder that Ethan had lived an entire lifetime—more than one, actually—before me.

We drove back to the train station and left the truck sitting in the crowded parking lot. After purchasing two more tickets to New Haven, we settled in on benches at the indoor waiting area. I checked the clock every two minutes, hoping the train would arrive soon. After the events of the last twenty-four hours, I was more than ready to go home.

Thirty-Nine

Fields and forests slipped by the window as the train chugged along towards New Haven. We had been traveling for almost an hour before I noticed Ethan had been even quieter than normal. I turned away from the scenic view. He was staring down the aisle and appeared deep in thought.

"What are you thinking about?" I straightened in my seat.

"Nothing at all." The corners of his mouth curved up in a smile, but there was no conviction in his tone.

I took his hand in mine and squeezed it tightly. "I'm fine, Ethan. If you're sitting there blaming yourself for what happened, please don't. You saved my life; that's all that matters."

He studied our entwined fingers for a moment. "Maybe they're right."

"What do you mean?" My eyebrows furrowed. *Who are they?*

"Hannah, in the time that I've been in your life, you've almost suffocated, been run down by an SUV, burned, drowned, and lost your father." His voice was thick and he swallowed hard

I tightened my grip on his fingers. "But none of that was your fault. All those attempts happened because I'm a protected. They would have happened no matter who had been assigned to me, and if it had been anyone else, I might not have survived them."

"Maybe, but with Paige it was about more than carrying out a Bana order. She was seeking revenge against me, and hurting you to do it. I took a very dangerous gamble at the mill. Thankfully, we got lucky and she didn't stab you before throwing you in the water. With

Adam it was the same thing, more than just doing a job. I led him right to you. They are both still out there, Hannah, and maybe the best way to keep you safe is for you to go live at Veridan, just for a little while." Ethan's shoulders were stiff and he sounded resigned.

"I'm alive and well. You've done that, you've kept me that way in East Halton. Living at Veridan would mean giving up everything I know. I wouldn't get to see my friends or my father unless I came up with some elaborate story about why I've moved into a museum, and even then it would be difficult." I let go of his hand and gestured wildly as I laid out each point. "Plus Veridan would mean no Stanford, or university of any kind for that matter. I don't need some big beautiful cage to keep me safe. I trust you to protect me." I grasped his arm. "And what about you? What happens to you if I go there?"

"Bridget offered me a teaching position at Veridan. She thought if I was around, you might be more receptive to coming." Ethan rubbed a hand across his forehead.

"That's nice of her, but do you really think we'd be able to be together while I'm living under round the clock surveillance? Someone would always be watching us. We're already struggling to keep our relationship a secret from my father and friends, do you really think we could do it at Veridan, with security cameras and guards on duty all the time?"

He pursed his lips. "Probably not."

I took a slow breath. "Is that what you want?"

"No." Ethan sighed. "I've been so happy these past few months. They've been the best of my entire life, and I sincerely mean that. You were right when you called me out for not telling you what I'm thinking, and avoiding certain topics. And there are some conversations we need to have about how we can stay together, but no matter what the future holds, the one thing I'm completely certain about is you and me."

My heart warmed. "If that's how you feel, then the answer has to be no. I can't go stay at Veridan."

Ethan gripped the armrest. "I'm not sure I agree. I want to be with you, but I can't let my emotions dictate my actions here Hannah. How can I say I love you if I selfishly put my own desires ahead of your wellbeing?" His shoulders slumped. "Your stay at

Veridan would only be temporary and it would give us time to figure everything out."

"But how can I have my destiny moment if I'm kept away from society?" I shot back.

"How do we know it's a moment? You're so different from any other person I've ever protected. How can all of this be for one solitary second in time?" Frustration flared in his voice.

"It is, Ethan." I glanced around the car. Even though no one sat near us, I dropped my voice down to a whisper as the train slowed. "Miriam told me it is."

The loudspeaker crackled and a mechanical voice announced that we were only two stops from New Haven. We would probably get there within half an hour or so. A handful of passengers got up and shuffled by on their way to the exit. An elderly woman gave me a warm smile as she walked past, while a young-looking businesswoman gave Ethan an approving once-over. We waited for everyone to clear out and the train to begin moving again before resuming our conversation.

"When did she tell you that?" Ethan's eyebrows were furrowed.

"At the party, while you were talking to Gabriel and Victor." I bit my lip. "I was going to tell you, I just haven't really had the opportunity. I was asking her questions about destiny and the Hleo. I wanted her to explain my gift, since she's the only person we know who can sort of do what I can. She told me that we've all been given talents, but it is how we choose to use those talents that ultimately guide our course."

Ethan leaned back against his seat, silent as he digested what I was saying.

"I can't disappear, because I haven't made the all-important decision the Metadas wants me to make yet." I leaned in closer, hoping I was getting through to him. "I need more time. If the moment comes that you think things are getting too dangerous, then I will agree to go to Veridan and stay for as long as you want me to." I held my breath, waiting for Ethan's response.

He drummed his fingers on the arm of the seat. "As soon as I think it's necessary, you'll go?"

"As long as you promise you'll be there with me, I'll go anywhere you ask."

"I guess I can live with that." Ethan didn't sound entirely convinced, but he slid an arm around me and pulled me to him.

We rode quietly for the rest of the trip. As we arrived in New Haven, he let me go and I stood up. We made our way off the train and through the station. Simon had left Ethan's Jeep in the parking lot, keys hidden in the steering column, and in no time we were back in East Halton. We'd only been gone a few days, but it felt as though months had passed since I had gazed at the familiar front porch of my house.

As I pushed the door open, I heard voices coming from the living room. Ethan and I followed the sound to find Simon and my dad in the middle of a very intense-looking game of chess.

"Hi guys." I set my bag down in the hallway.

They both looked up from their game.

"Hannah." Dad stood and walked toward us, Simon right behind him. When my dad reached me he grabbed my chin in his hand and examined the cut on my cheek. "What did you do to yourself?"

I gently shook my head free and laughed. "Oh nothing. When we were on the train I stumbled and fell into a metal crate someone had sticking out in the aisle a little." I glanced at Ethan. *Close enough to the truth.*

Dad frowned. "That's a shame. You would think the train personnel would make sure passengers stow those sorts of items in a baggage area."

I shrugged. "You would think so."

"Other than that, your trip went well?"

I guess he hasn't heard all the details of our adventure. I was okay with his lack of knowledge, and glad that Ethan's altered genetics prevented any traces of the damage Uri had inflicted on him from being noticeable. No sense letting Dad in on things that would only upset him.

"It did go well. I really appreciated having the chance to talk to The Three. You would have loved it. The history and mystery of it all would have been right up your alley." I sank onto the couch, suddenly exhausted. "What have you been up to while we've been gone?"

Dad sat down on the armchair across from me. "It's been pretty quiet around here. Rose came over last evening and again this morning to play nursemaid, making me meals and tidying a bit. She had schoolwork to grade today, but said to say hello. Simon and I have been spending evenings talking history. It's been a pretty low-key couple of days. Nothing too exciting happened, except that some mail came for you on Friday." Dad gave me a cryptic smile.

Simon trotted off to the kitchen.

"Really?" My forehead wrinkled. What mail could I possibly… My breath caught. Could it be?

"Here you go." Simon returned and handed me a large white envelope. Ethan peered over my shoulder. The Stanford logo was inscribed on the top left corner of the package. I slowly turned it over in my hands before tearing open the top flap.

Fingers trembling, I slid the letter out of the envelope and scanned it quickly. I couldn't help but smile as I read the first line, congratulating me on my acceptance into Stanford University.

"I'm in." I looked from Dad to Ethan. All three guys cheered. Ethan came around the couch and pulled me to my feet, whirling me around in a hug. When he released me, Dad gave me another big hug, while Simon patted me on the back.

"I knew you'd get in." Dad voice's was bursting with pride.

"I can't believe it. I was so sure when Katie got her letter weeks ago and I didn't hear anything it meant I hadn't been accepted." I shook my head in disbelief. My thumb ran across the Stanford logo on the letterhead, joy swelling inside me. *Finally one question answered.* Even if I didn't end up attending Stanford, at least now I knew I could.

"I never doubted you'd be hearing from them. You are far too exceptional for them not to want you." Ethan's look was intense, and my cheeks warmed.

Dad squeezed my shoulder and then he and Simon resumed their game. I watched them for a moment before turning back to Ethan. I cared about these three men so much. Any one of them would give their life to protect me. *I really hope it doesn't come to that.* A shiver ran through me. Had I made the wrong decision when I turned down The Three's offer to stay at Veridan? It felt right, but if something happened to Ethan, Dad, or anyone else in my life because I wanted my freedom, how would I ever forgive myself?

"You okay?" Ethan touched my arm.

I met his eyes and forced a smile. "I'm fine. Happy to be home."

And I was. I needed to spend time with family and friends, and go to school, and do everything I could to make my life as normal as possible.

I had to trust Ethan. And hope that he could keep me safe long enough for me to make the decision that would put an end to this madness, once and for all.

Aliege

The third book in the Hleo series

by

Rebecca Weller

Check Out the Exclusive Sneak Peek

I held up my hands as I crossed the dimly-lit parking lot. "Look–"

"Are you crazy? Do you know how dangerous what you're doing is?" Ethan's usual calm demeanor was gone. He drove his fingers through his dark hair in frustration.

I shrugged. "He's harmless."

"How do you know that Hannah?" Ethan's green eyes flashed fire. "How do you know he isn't a member of the Bana stringing you along, trying to lure you into a trap?"

"I just do." I squared my jaw defiantly. The truth was, I didn't know for sure, but Milton definitely didn't look like a member of the Bana.

Ethan threw his hands up in the air. "You told me you were going to stay away from all of this, that you were going to drop it. Then you sneak off in the middle of the night to meet up with some stranger at a random coffee shop along the highway after an attempt is made on your life. Of all the—"

"Tell me Ethan, right now, what happened?" I stared him down.

He hesitated, dropping his chin and squeezing his eyes shut. "The brakes on your car were cut in a way that would look like mechanical failure, and the sensors tampered with so there would be no warning that the car was slowly leaking brake fluid."

Even though deep down I'd known he was going to tell me something along those lines, it still felt as though I'd been punched. I wrapped my arms around myself, trying to stop my stomach from lurching.

"Hannah–" Ethan reached towards me, but I backed away. I didn't want to hear that I wasn't responsible for this, or that there was no way I could have known.

"Don't say it." I shook my head and turned from him to stare at the restaurant.

"This isn't your fault." Ethan slid a gentle hand onto my shoulder.

I bristled and whirled back around to meet his gaze. "How can you say that? Of course this is my fault, it's always my fault. Every time a person ends up directly in the line of fire and suffers because of me and my stupid visions, it's my fault. We don't even know if the Bana want to kidnap me or kill me, and I'm sick of it, Ethan. Can't you see how sick of it I am?" I waved my arms wildly. The group of guys from school had exited the coffee shop and were looking over at our heated exchange with curious stares. I ignored them. "I'm walking around like some sort of sideshow at a carnival and I don't know how to fix it. I need something to change."

"I get it, I do, but what you're doing isn't safe." Ethan's voice was soothing as he held out his arms to me.

I crossed mine. "Milton isn't Bana. He's an eccentric little man who has devoted himself to finding the Glain Neidr." I watched his face closely. *This is your chance Ethan; come clean and admit you know the Hleo have the Glain Neidr.*

Ethan dropped his arms to his sides, his fists clenching. "You're right, Hannah, Milton Cambry's not Bana, but the people who are into these mystical artifacts are fanatical, they'll stop at nothing to get their hands on one, even if that means hurting someone in the process." Ethan's shoulders had tensed. I knew the sign; his composure was wavering.

"Just stop with all this dangerous talk, I know the stone is with the Hleo." I gave him a steely glare, hurt that he kept lying to me.

Ethan's eyes widened. "What are you talking about?"

"You don't have to keep it from me anymore. Milton told me. He told me that the necklace is with a secret organization that controls destiny. All this time you just kept saying you didn't know where it was, or that it was too dangerous to go after. How exactly are the Hleo dangerous, Ethan?" I leaned right into his personal space, not at all concerned that my voice was coming out in a full on yell. *Let people overhear me, I don't care anymore.*

"It's not with the Hleo, it's with the Bana," Ethan shot back, his voice as forceful as mine.

"The Bana." I blinked and took a step back. I don't know why, but the Bana had never entered my thoughts as Milton had been talking. Now, belatedly, I realized that made perfect sense.

"Yes, the Bana; the other organization that plays with destiny." Ethan glanced around, then lowered his voice. "And it's not with just any Bana member. It's with Alexander. He wears it as a source of power so he can see into the future the way Gabriel does. Not only that, but there's a duplicate, a fake that the Bana have fabricated. That way if someone does want to try to steal the stone, chances are good they aren't even grabbing the real one. Whichever necklace isn't around his neck is kept in one of the many secret Bana storage facilities around the globe."

"Is that what Kai told you at Veridan? That the Glain Neidr was with the Bana?" I shifted my weight from one foot to the other.

Ethan pressed his fingers to the bridge of his nose, as though trying to stave off a headache. "Yes." The word came out in a sigh.

"Why didn't you just tell me?" My forehead creased. "Maybe I would've been more understanding if you'd explained that to me right from the beginning." His lack of trust in me caused a lump to form in my throat. I swallowed it away.

"I'm not used to sharing sensitive information, especially with my protecteds." Ethan lifted his shoulders lightly.

I drew in a sharp breath. "I'm more than that." Calling me a protected felt like a slap in the face. I strode over to my dad's car, jabbing at the unlock button on the keys.

Ethan caught up to me and grasped my elbow to stop me. "I know. I'm sorry." He turned me to face him. "Alexander's ruthless, and he has every synthetic Bana protecting him as though it were their lives at stake, because it is. He guards the Glain Neidr with all the fervor he guards himself with, so whether it is with him or in storage, we'd be going up against the full arsenal of the Bana to get it. I was hoping that I'd be able to figure out something else. I know you want answers, but I have to keep you safe." Ethan eyes searched mine.

He wanted me to cave, and there was a big part of me that wanted to sag against his chest, feel the strong muscles in his arms surround me, and forget this terrible fight, but the anger and hurt won out. "Well, we haven't figured anything else out. Maybe it would be hard, but I know you could get past Alexander and his army, I just know it. I need to believe the Glain Neidr will work, Ethan, it's the only shred of hope I have that my life will go back to the way it was before all of this. It's become too much; I need things to be back to normal again. To go back to the way it was before I found out about the Hleo and Bana." The words tumbled out, clearly cutting through him. His eyes were dark with pain, but I couldn't stop myself, not after everything that had happened.

"Hannah–" Ethan breathed out, stumbling backward as though I'd pushed him.

"I need a night to myself, okay?" I climbed into Dad's car before he could say anything more and drove away, refusing to look back and see him standing alone in the empty parking lot.

How could Ethan have shut me out like that about the Glain Neidr's location? How could we be a real couple if we kept things from each other? I gripped the steering wheel tightly with both hands. That was the one question in my life I did know the answer to.

We couldn't.

Aliege

A continuation of the Hleo series.

All is not right in paradise. Hannah is convinced that the mysterious Glain Neidr stone is the key to unlocking the purpose behind her ability to see and draw protecteds. Ethan doesn't agree, but his refusal to explain why he doesn't want to pursue finding the necklace as a possible means of helping Hannah pushes a wedge between the two.

When an accident drives that wedge deeper, and a truth comes to light that rips them apart, Hannah is left alone, overwhelmed and confused about the future of her status as a protected and, more importantly, her relationship with Ethan.

Fighting to regain control over her own destiny, Hannah is forced to place her trust in the last person on earth she ever expected she would turn to. All in the hopes of restoring her life to the way it was before everything got turned upside down.

Coming Soon

Acknowledgments

The overwhelming support from my friends and family and the online community has been so inspiring. It has spurred me on and convinced me to keep pressing forward with this whole trying to share my writing and imagination with the world.

First off, I want to thank those who took the time to pick up a book from a stranger and give it a go; the bloggers and Good Readers who were willing to take a chance on *Hleo* and Ethan and Hannah's story. Thank you; Rosie, Jordan, Madison, Annabelle, Emily, Sarah, Eunice, Abbie, Mercedes, Mel, Sam, Larissa, to name a few. I appreciate all your positivity and hope that you will enjoy *Veridan* as well.

Secondly I want to thank the lovers of *Hleo*. The ones who have let me know in a big way just how much they enjoyed the book. You make my heart swell. Rene, Heather, Greg, Pam, Kari, Deanna, Jill, Bill, Brenda, Stuart, Melanie, Ciara, Emma, Holly, Melissa, Shirley, Pat, Lisa, Gina, and the ladies at work, honestly and sincerely, thank you. And to my very best saleswoman, Mom, thank you for having so much faith in *Hleo* that you can talk anyone into buying a copy.

Veridan would not be possible without the posse of people I bounce ideas off of. David, you will always be my favorite sounding board. I love you so much for supporting me in this dream and believing in me even when I'm being silly and unconfident. And my amazing editor, Sara Davison. An editing ninja who will check out the dictionary meaning of *hemmed and hawed* to make sure I'm using it correctly, who will nitpick until 1:23 am trying to make *Veridan* the very best it can be, and to whom I can bring any idea and know I'll get an honest opinion. Thank you, beyond what words can express, thank you.

I'm sure I'm forgetting people. I'm sorry if you're one of these. But one last big thanks to you, the person holding this book, for giving it a chance. I appreciate it more than you will ever know. I hope you fall in love with this next chapter of Hannah and Ethan's story.

About the Author

Scribbling down whatever her imagination could conjure, Rebecca Weller has been writing stories most of her life. Her hope is to inspire, and to use writing as a way to help others beyond the Canadian borders she currently lives in with her husband and two children.

Check Out: **https://hleoweller.wordpress.com** for more.

68889538R00156

Manufactured by Amazon.com
Columbia, SC
11 April 2017